EMOJIS

Evan Clouse

This book is dedicated to every person who cares about our personal freedom. To every person who cares about our democracy. To every person who shuns the politics of hate and division. To every person who accepts and embraces others for who they are. Thank you for your voices. Thank you for your caring. Thank you for your kind hearts. I love you all.

Acknowledgments

I would like to thank every person who has supported me and understands just how important this work is to me. Thank you for reading. Thank you for your input. Thank you for caring. You know who you are.

Contents

CHAPTER 1

CHOKE

A brilliant flash of lightning illuminated the arrogant face of the local restaurant critic as he caringly placed his plate of lemon-braised chicken and dill encrusted roasted red potatoes upon his dining room table. He put his linen napkin upon his lap, placed a potato into his mouth and savored the blend of flavors. "Perfect," he said to himself out loud. "Absolute perfection. Why is it so difficult for these so-called chefs to get things right? Oh, I know. Because the culinary arts are indeed an artform. Not just anyone can do it. You must have the gift. The touch. The delicate sensibilities. Unlike that hash slinger in Plymouth, I reviewed a few days ago. Bland. Uninspired. Pedestrian. An abomination. Yes, those were the exact words that I used to describe what they called "food." And I stand by it. I can't believe that this disgusting little place has been in business for thirty years. Since 1993. And the garish, 50's inspired décor. Black and white tiles. Red, plexiglass tables and booths. The silly little light blue waitress outfits. And that music! That horrible rock and roll music pounding in my ears! How can anybody enjoy their meal with that racket going on? Why not a nice string quartet? Or soft jazz? Oh, the décor and atmosphere are as reprehensible as the food.

Perhaps my little review will make their thirtieth year be their last, heh, heh, heh."

The violent waves were crashing upon the harbor rocks outside of his provincial home on the North Shore of Boston. He placed a bite of perfectly prepared chicken into his anticipatory mouth. A droplet of ecstatic drool fell upon his napkin as he picked up the Boston newspaper that he wrote reviews for. He methodically turned the pages until he came to his section. He laughed out loud as he began reading the rebuttal for his review of the Plymouth Rocks! Diner.

Considering the pomposity of this so-called "reviewer," I am not surprised by his inability to home in on what we are trying to accomplish at our Plymouth Rocks! Diner. It is not okay to pillage our establishment when your idea of a fine meal costs hundreds of dollars. Know this, Mister Reviewer. We provide our clientele with good food in a safe atmosphere. Eat where you would like. But stay away from my diner. You are not welcome here.

The man had to clutch his ribs to contain the sharp pains that were being caused by his explosion of laughter. "Oh, my lord!" he yelled out. "Pompous? Oh ouch, Ms. Cabot. You write a rebuttal about as well as you cook! Yes, my dear. You go ahead and sling your slop to the local plebes and obese tourists with their college mascot T-shirts. I will be dining on delicacies that you could never even imagine. And I will be doing so with a much higher class of people. Do not fret, my dear. I will most certainly never step foot into your squalor again!"

The early September 2023 storm intensified as sheets of warm rain battered the panoramic windows. The man tossed the newspaper to the side, cut a thin strip of chicken, and placed it upon his eagerly awaiting tongue. A gust of wind blew open a side window. The man immediately jumped from his seat and began frantically trying to close the pane as his beloved dining room was being bombarded by sheets of rain. The vicious winds were whipping his chiffon curtains in a frenzy, knocking over and shattering antique porcelain statues, plates, and vases. He placed the entirety of his one-hundred-thirty-eight-pound frame against the window and pushed until the window was finally closed and able to be latched.

A small tear fell from his dismayed eye as he surveyed what was left of the most precious room in his home. The curtains were saturated and hanging mournfully from their brass rods. Fragmented porcelain littered the flooded hardwood floor. And his delicately prepared meal was drowning in a pool of rainfall. A sharp chill ran down his spine as his mind tried to process the mayhem that had intruded upon his carefully designed utopia. He righted himself and sorrowfully went over to retrieve his plate from the saturated table. As he began to lift the plate, he looked down upon the soggy newspaper. The harsh wind had blown it open to page twenty-three and he was once again staring at the rebuttal of his review.

He felt a slight tightness in his throat as the words on the page began glowing. He thought that he must be hallucinating as the words that were glowing were reduced to only those at the beginning of a line. *Considering. home. okay. Know. Eat.* "W-what is happening?" the man yelled out as his throat began to tighten further. He clutched his throat and began coughing as his eyes were fixed upon the page of the newspaper. His body unleashed a torrent of sweat as he watched the glowing words be reduced to just the first letters of the first words of each line. C-h-o-K-E.

He could feel his throat constricting and blood rush to his head. His terror intensified as he heard the thunderous cackling of a woman boom throughout the room. He gasped for air as his throat continued to tighten. He reached for his phone and dialed 9-1-1. All that could be heard by the dispatcher was the violent choking of the caller. And ominous laughter. The phone slipped from his hand, and he fell to his knees. His fiery lungs were begging for oxygen as he heard the male dispatcher say, "Hello? Is anyone there? What is that laughing? We have your location. I am dispatching a unit to your home. Try to remain calm. Hello? Can you hear me?"

The man frantically thrust his balled-up fists up against his diaphragm in a vain attempt to dislodge the item that was not there. He could feel the pressure mounting in his head as his throat squeezed ever tighter. He briefly saw his reflection in a silver spoon that had fallen to the soggy floor. He was horrified as he saw the reflection of a desperate man with a swollen, purple face. His violent gagging continued, and he collapsed onto the rain-soaked wood. His tortured body lay still as it consumed the final bit of oxygen. Just before his body succumbed, he heard the cackling woman's voice say, "Contra eos qui suis vocibus alios opprimunt, habebunt locutions, heh, heh, heh."

"Well, that was easy," the chuckling seventy-one-year-old Sophia Cabot said to herself from her modest cottage home in Plymouth, Massachusetts. She was sitting at her vanity, casually brushing her flowing silver hair as she stared at a portrait of her ancestor. It was the painting of a young woman who had been tied to a stake. Her youthful body was being consumed by flames. Sophia looked closely at the woman's face. It was a face that was filled with determination. And rage.

Sophia's gaze drifted downward until she was staring at her own gleeful reflection in the vanity's mirror. Her deep wrinkles seemed to be dancing in celebration upon her experienced face. "Yep, I haven't used that one for a while. So, what do you think, great, great, great, oh whatever…grandma? Kinda fun, don'tcha think? Oh, don't give me that! I did *not* use my power to harness the spiritual powers of the universe for my own gain! He was a vile, evil man! His pomposity and lack of regard have put many restaurants out of business! So many hard-working people have lost their livelihoods because of his arrogance and his cruelty. And now, he has come for *me*. No, I won't hear it from you, Great Grandmother. Self-care is *not* self-indulgence! Self-care is *survival*! This was an act of self-preservation. For me and my family.

"My daughter and granddaughter are going through too much

right now to have to also deal with this. Who knows what impact that jerk's article will have on my business. The business that I have built and nurtured and loved over the last thirty years. Oh, I'm not worried about the locals. My clientele love my diner. But we both know, Great Grandmother, that the only way that I am able to stay afloat is the seasonal business that I'm able to generate. Without that, I would go under like a small boat in a Nor'easter. And just how many tourists will read this garbage and avoid my diner? No, I needed to *do* something. I needed to *act*. Again, for my self-preservation. I really intended to just write a rebuttal. I just wanted to defend myself and minimize the damage that he may have done to me. But, well, I was a bit angry when I wrote that. And you know what happens when we Cabots lash out when we're angry. The most applicable incantation just pops into our heads, and it takes over. I truly don't even remember typing those words.

"But what I will *always* remember is the look on that bastard's face as he struggled to survive. I will *always* remember his look of confusion, then terror as he heard me laughing at him as he died. I really hope I never get dementia. This is a memory that I wish to savor for as long as I exist on this plane.

"So, please, Great Grandmother. Do not scold me. I did what needed to be done. Besides, it was fun now, wasn't it? Come on, now. I can feel you wanting to laugh. I can feel your little ghosty lips starting to turn upward. I know that you were watching along with me as he threw himself around the room gasping for air. He looked quite silly, didn't he? Quite...*comical*, wouldn't you say? Ah yes! There it is! Laugh along with me Great Grandmother! For tonight I have rid the world of a little piss-ant. And tonight, we shall celebrate! Not just for this, but for my daughter's homecoming tomorrow. Yes, tomorrow the entire Cabot family shall begin to heal. And may the great spirits have mercy on anyone that gets in the way of the ladies Cabot!"

Sophia left her modest home and began the ten-minute trek to her favorite bar. She watched the final trail of storm clouds disappear from the evening horizon as the brilliance of the universe sparkled down upon her. She checked her silver strands in the tavern's window, opened the door, and suggestively sauntered her bell-bottomed and Deep Purple shirted frame into her favorite watering hole.

"Well, look who has decided to go slumming at the Sand Dollar, tonight," the jovial bartender, Vince, said as their local provocateur strode up to the bar and rested her behind on her favorite stool. "What'll you have, Sophia?"

"What the hell do you *think* I'll have, Vince?" Sophia snidely replied. "The same thing that I have *every* night. Gimme my shot of whiskey and a beer chaser. And use *clean* glasses this time."

The gathered locals roared with laughter as the chuckling Vince put down the glass that he was holding and retrieved a clean one from the shelf. He placed the filled cleanish glasses in front of his old friend and said, "So, Sophia, what do ya say?"

"What do I say about *what?*" Sophia playfully responded.

"Come on now," Vince answered. "You *know* what. How about that date that I've been asking you for over the last twenty years? You know as well as I do that we'd make a great match. We've been friends forever. We both love the Bruins, Sox, and Celtics. Hell, we both hate the Patriots 'cause of their dickhead owner. We love the same music. The same food. You are quite the looker and I'm not exactly chopped liver. I run five miles every morning. Come on. Just one date where we can hang out together away from this bar. Just one dinner. One movie. One night. That's all I'm asking for."

"Vince," Sophia began to reply. "You are a wonderful man and I truly do enjoy our friendship, but I believe you are looking for something more than I am able to give. Ever since I lost my husband thirty years ago, I vowed to never be tied down again. I vowed to never let another man put me under his thumb and control me. And belittle me. I am a product of the seventies. The good, *free-spirited* seventies. Not the ultra-conservative, Nixon, Stepford wives, three-martini business lunch seventies. Loud music with screeching guitars, faded blue jeans, tank tops, and being free to bed anyone that I want whenever I want. That's me, Vince. That's who I am. And once my bastard husband…um…sort of burned up, I decided that I would *never* put myself *or* my daughter in that position again. Once I saw how he was looking at his own eleven-year-old daughter I knew that I had to get her away from him. And I did as soon as…um… circumstances allowed. The moment he went out to sea alone that final time, I had our bags packed and was ready to move from Boston to Plymouth. I had put money away and bought my home. I had secured a loan to start my diner. I was going to get my precious daughter away from him. And, as fate would have it, his boat just kinda blew up in the middle of the ocean. So, all's well that ends well!"

"But Sophia!" Vince argued, "I'm not that bastard! I *know* how he treated you and I *know* the fears you had about what he might do with your daughter! But that was *thirty years ago* and that's not *me!* When are you gonna open up, and let somebody in?"

"Never," came Sophia's blunt reply. "I will *never* allow that again, my friend. I get my male companionship when I want it. And besides, I've *already* let somebody in. I have allowed my daughter and granddaughter in. They are moving back home tomorrow. They're going through such a terrible time, and they need me right now. And I guess I need them too. It's not about you, Vince. I *know* that you are a wonderful man. It's just that at this stage of my life, I'm not looking for a wonderful man. I'm just looking to get laid once in a while. And I can't do that with you because you would take it the wrong way and then our friendship would be over. And I truly value your friendship, Vince. Besides, I've told you over and over. I don't date younger men."

"Oh, what a crock of shit!" Vince bellowed as Sophia took a sip of whiskey to hide her grin. "That's just ridiculous. Younger men? I'm nearly seventy years old, Sophia!"

"I know, Vince," Sophia calmly replied. "You are two years younger than me. Why, I'd feel like a *cradle robber* if I were to…hey turn the TV up, wouldja?"

Vince went over to the vintage television set and turned up the volume. Everybody in the bar listened to the bubbly newscaster say,

"...was found dead this evening in his home on the North Shore. He was one of Boston's finest food critics for over forty years. Police say that they do not believe that foul play was involved, although he appeared to be eating chicken at the time. Well, that certainly sounds like *fowl play* to me, what do you think, Brett Billingsly? And how about our local forecast? Are we done with the stormy skies?"

"Thanks Sandra. Well, one thing that *I* won't be choking up over is our forecast. Just look at these seasonal temps as we move through the workweek..."

"Hey," Vince said. "Isn't that the same reviewer who gave you a bullshit write-up about your joint?"

"Oh, is it?" Sophia demurely replied. "Well, now that you say that, yes, I believe that it just may be him. I guess that's too bad. Even though he gave me a poor review, I'm *sure* he wasn't a...um...*bad* man. Ah well. Que Cera Cera."

"Wow, Sophia, you must have a guardian angel or something," Vince stated.

"What do you mean by that, Vince?" Sophia inquired.

"Well," Vince began to reply, "It just seems like anybody that crosses you has a bit of an accident, that's all. I mean, your husband. This douche. That corrupt banker that tried to foreclose on you a few years ago. That peeping tom. Oh, and that distributor who kept jacking his prices up. The bagboy at the grocery store that called you an old hag. Your daughter's first boyfriend who was getting a little too handsy. Then her second boyfriend. And her fourth boyfriend. They all seem to be taken out, somehow."

"And just what are you saying, Vince?" Sophia inquired as her anxiety was beginning to elevate.

"Oh, nothin'," Vince answered. "Just that you're the luckiest damned broad I ever met!"

"Well, I suppose I am," Sophia answered with a relieved giggle. "Must be my clean living. Alright fellas, I need to hit the road. I need to grab a pack of smokes and get home and get my girls' rooms ready for their arrival."

Sophia planted her sandaled feet upon the sticky wood floor and began flirtatiously sauntering toward the door. Before she left, she shouted out, "And I guess I know of *one* dickhead who won't be choking his chicken any longer! See ya tomorrow night, fellas!"

And with that, Sophia Cabot exited the Sand Dollar the same way that she did every evening. To uproarious laughter.

Chapter 2

A Reluctant Homecoming

Lori Cabot's heart was numb as she completed the forty-mile drive from her former home in Quincy to her mother's house in Plymouth. Outwardly she had a false smile pasted upon her pretty, forty-one-year-old face. Inwardly, she could feel the scars of betrayal being etched into her soul. She peered over at her seventeen-year-old daughter Morgan and her heart sank further.

"I'm so sorry about this, dear," Lori said softly to her sullen daughter. Morgan lifted her jet-black-dyed head to look at her mother. Her ear, nose, and lip piercings glinted in the morning sunshine as she tried to give her beloved mother a conciliatory smile.

"It's alright, Mom," Morgan said as she fought to hide her tears. Morgan was experiencing the same level of angst as her mother. She was sad at having to leave her friends in her old high school. She was depressed at the thought of having to learn to fit in at her new school. And she was furious at her father for how he had made her, and her loving mother, feel for her entire life.

"It's not your fault, Mom," Morgan continued, displaying a maturity past her true age. "It's Dad's. You did nothing wrong. *He* did. *He's* the one that tried to make you into something that you weren't. *He's* the one that would always yell at me and call me a freak just because of how I want to look and be who I truly am. And *he's* the one that is screwing his twenty-year-old assistant…again.

"I know how much shit you took from him over the years. I know how you tried to keep this thing together. For me. I know all the compromises you tried to make and how often you looked the other way when he was out playing around. I know how he tried to control the money so that you would have no choice but to be beholden to him. Hell, he tried to control everything.

"But I don't know that this is a bad thing, Mom. You should have left him years ago. You knew what he was, but you kept hanging on. You thought that you could reason with him. You thought that you could change him. You buried your true feelings, pasted a smile on your face and tried to keep things normal for me. You fought to give me stability. But I knew that it wasn't normal and it sure as hell wasn't stable.

"Hell, I've barely said a word to him for the past three years. Once I started to become a young woman with my own preferences and ability to think for myself, he really had nothing to do with me. He saw that I wasn't going to bow down to him and believe all the Cro-Magnon shit that he believes. His racist views. His homophobic views. His misogynistic views. He's nothing more than a knuckle-dragger in an expensive suit. He wants it to be the 1950's again where Black people and Gay people and women all "knew their place", as he puts it. I'm ashamed to be his daughter. That's why I never told him about my school choir concerts. I didn't want him there. I didn't want him around my friends or my friends' parents. I didn't want to be embarrassed by him.

"I don't blame you, Mom. I know that you tried to do what was right. I'm glad that you're finally able to see what he is and how harmful he has been to both of us. I'm glad that you've finally taken a stand. I'm so proud of you right now. Especially for changing our last names back to 'Cabot.' In fact, I've never been prouder of you, Mom. It sucks that we have to start over, but we'll do it. Together and with Grandma. I'm going to make new friends. You can finally have a career by using the kitchen in the diner for the catering service that you've always wanted. *You* are free. *I* am free. *We* are free. Free to live our lives without having to be judged or ridiculed or beaten down. We, the ladies Cabot, are free to be who we are and live how we want to live. And may God have mercy on the souls of anyone who crosses us. Especially assholes like my father."

Lori sat at a stoplight and stared at her daughter with awe. She briefly wondered who was the parent and who was the child in this scenario. She allowed herself to smile as she said, "You know what? You are my goddam hero."

"Oh, shut up," a slightly embarrassed Morgan replied just before they heard a honking horn and a man's screaming voice behind them.

"Move your ass!" the impatient man yelled out. "The light's green! Where didja learn to drive? New Hampshire?"

Lori began to take her foot off the brake. Morgan pushed her mother's leg back down, shook her head at her and flashed a mischievous smile. Lori smiled back as they listened to the man's rage increase. He laid on his horn and screamed out derogatory names. Lori and Morgan began to giggle mischievously as they watched the light turn from green to yellow to red. The man exited his vehicle and began marching up to the driver's side door. Just as his beet-red face appeared in Lori's window, the light turned green once again. Lori and Morgan laughed uncontrollably, stuck out their tongues, and flipped the man off just as Lori tromped on the accelerator and sped through the intersection.

"Oh my God, that was sooooo much fun!" Morgan screamed out as she jumped out of the car and began leaping and clapping in her grandmother's driveway. She was giggling with glee as her baggy black T-shirt and black cargo shorts bounced in a frenzy. "Yep," Lori replied. "I guess that's *one* way to make new friends in my hometown. But maybe we shouldn't have done that. I mean, what did it prove? All we did was irritate a guy who we'll probably have to deal with later. No, Morgan, I don't think that we did the right thing. It may have felt good at the moment, but the best course is to always keep our emotions in check and act intellectually. What we did accomplished nothing."

"Oh yeah, it did," Morgan answered while still wearing an evil little grin. "It made a statement that the ladies Cabot are back in town, and *nobody* is going to screw with us! Hi Grandma!" Morgan ran up to her blue jeans and T-shirt adorned grandmother and squeezed her tightly.

"Um, hi Mom," Lori stated sheepishly. "Thanks for letting us crash here until we can get...um...until we can find our own...um..."

"Oh, my darling daughter!" Sophia yelled out. "You *are* home! Now get in here and let's have us a group hug!"

Tears flowed from six brilliant blue eyes as the trio were encased within the joyful reunion. For the first time in a long time, Lori felt at ease. The feeling quickly dissipated when Sophia pulled back from her cherished family and said, "But I *told* you that that man was an asshole! Now, *didn't* I? I *told* you to leave him years ago. That he was toxic. That you could never change him. But did you listen to me? Nooooooo. Of course not! What would your dear old mother know about it anyway? I swear, Lori, you are stubborn as a mule. Once you get some utopian vision in your head with all your rainbows and unicorns and butterflies fluttering around, then there is just no shaking you. At least you've finally come to your senses!"

Morgan looked into the eyes of her well-intentioned yet completely undiplomatic grandmother and said, "Grandma, I love you, but right now isn't the time. My Mom did what she could. And this is hard for her, so lay off, alright?"

Sophia stared into the glowing blue eyes of her granddaughter. She could feel the intensity of her caring for her mother and the anger that she was generating. And she became frightened.

"Of course, of course," Sophia immediately backpedaled. "What am I thinking? I'm so sorry, darling. I shouldn't have said all that. I know how hard you tried and how much you loved that man...um... for some reason. This isn't a time to look to the past. This is a time for the future. Our future! The future of the ladies Cabot! Now, come, come, let's get you both settled in!"

As the trio made their way up the stairs to the second-floor bedrooms, Sophia thought to herself, *Well, my Morgan certainly has the gift. If only I could get my daughter to unleash her emotions. Just once. Then, this little divorce wouldn't be so much of a problem. I could take care of it I suppose, but it's my Lori's time to handle these things on her own. In her own way. She is much too old now to need my protection. Her destiny is hers, and hers alone. And, if Lori doesn't take care of it...well...I get the feeling that my granddaughter will, heh, heh, heh.*

Several hours and one long, well-deserved nap later, Lori came trudging down the stairs of her childhood home. She went into the kitchen to find her mother pouring a dollop of honey into a teacup. "Hello, darling," Sophia greeted. "I hope you had a good nap. Here, have some tea. It's just how you like it. And my dearest, I'm so sorry for what I said outside. I just can't control myself sometimes. Please forgive me."

Lori rubbed the sleep from her eyes, took the cup from her mother's delicate hand and sat at the kitchen table. "It's okay Mom. I know what a blunt and cantankerous old bitch you can be sometimes." The pair exploded into laughter and another warm embrace before Lori said, "So, who's at the diner, Mom? You really didn't have to take the whole day off for this. We know our way around."

"I wouldn't hear of it," Sophia replied as she sat next to her daughter. "This is your homecoming and I wanted to be here. I *needed* to be here. Besides, I've got a new manager who is quite capable of filling in for me when I need some time off. He's such a nice boy. And smart. Taylor is his name. I would fix him and Morgan up, but he's a bit older and I don't think that either of them swing that way. But I think that they may hit it off as friends."

"Uh, huh, Morgan doesn't really like to talk about...um...that, so did that dick's review have any impact on the diner's business?" Lori asked to change the subject.

"No, not at all," a beaming Sophia replied. "In fact, if anything, our business has picked up! All my local customers have been coming in more frequently and all the local shop owners are talking up my joint to the tourists who come in, so perhaps his misguided critique has been a blessing."

"Plus, he can't write another one," Lori replied. "I saw your rebuttal in the paper. It was kinda...um...short and strange, but it looks like you may have given him a heart attack or something! I mean, he keeled over dead, and I heard that the paper was lying on his dining room table. Weird, huh?"

"Yes, yes," Sophia answered. "Quite the coincidink. So, I thought that tomorrow I could get you set up in a corner of the kitchen and you can start..."

Sophia was cut off by her daughter. "Yeah, but it's *really* weird, Mom. I mean, now that I think about it, there have been an *awful lot* of coincidinks in your life. I mean, my father exploding on his boat. The bank dude that was hassling you falling off that cliff. That distributor that was found buried under pounds of ground beef. That creepy guy that kept looking in my windows when I was fifteen. They found him with his spine snapped after he fell on the Rock. My first boyfriend, who impaled himself on a javelin at his track meet. I mean, how the hell could *that* happen? My second boyfriend found hanging from his bedroom door with his dick out. Well, that one makes sense...um...kinda. Then, my fourth boyfriend got into that car accident."

"And that little bastard bag boy at the grocery store," Sophia muttered under her breath before catching herself.

"What?" Lori asked. "Oh, nothing dear, nothing," Sophia quickly replied. "I just remembered that I needed to pick something up at the grocery store, that's all."

"Oh, alright," Lori stated before continuing. "And now this restaurant reviewer. It just seems like anybody that gets in your way gets handled somehow. Damn, I wish *I* had your luck. I could kinda use it right now. No! What am I saying? No, that's no way to think. My ex may be a huge dick, but nobody deserves to die. Well, at least *most* people don't. And not for that. Being an asshole husband shouldn't be a death sentence. Just forget that I said that. I'm just really emotional right now."

"Yes, you are," Sophia stated eerily as an intrigued Morgan entered the kitchen and sat at the table. Sophia then chuckled as she grasped the hands of her beloved family. "You know, I have always found it quite amusing how women's emotions have been used against us. For ages, we have been told by men that we are too emotional and prone to hysterics. As if men aren't emotional. Why, they are the most whiney little babies when they are sick and prone to bouts of rage when their silly sports team loses. They take things *just* as personally and to heart as we do, if not more so.

"That is why many more men than women actually support the overthrow of our democracy. Their tender little egos and sense of self-entitlement have been bruised, so they lash out in anger. They are unable to control *their* emotions. There *is* no difference between the sexes when it comes to experiencing emotion. There are only differences in the societal *expectations* as to what is an *appropriate* expression of our emotions. Men can punch holes in walls. Women cry or become sullen. Same emotions, different expression. That is it.

"And I've always found it quite sad that there are many women who play into this myth. I don't know how many times I have heard a fellow woman say something like, 'I hate working with a group of women. You know how catty they can be,' or some such nonsense. Our fellow women do us all a disservice by harboring such beliefs. They perpetuate the myth that women are too emotional to be trusted with positions of leadership or authority, so the societal patriarchy continues.

"We are to be nothing more than caregivers. You just leave the things that must be done out of brute strength or courage to us men, dear. You're too delicate. You're too soft. You're too *emotional*. And when a woman *does* display strength, then the men become threatened, and she is called a 'bitch' or something. Damned if you do, damned if you don't.

"And the really sad part is that the men actually know better. They *know* that we are just as capable as they are. They *know* that it is actually *their* emotional outbursts which present the true threat.

They know that. And yet, they persist in harboring and spreading this stigma. Why? To keep us down. For control over us. And why do they want that? Oh sure, to make them feel strong and powerful and manly. But really, it is because, deep down inside, they recognize our emotions are our *strength*. And it scares the *hell* out of them. And it *should*.

"So, getting back to your main point, dear. How is it that I have been so lucky as to have douchebag men eliminated from my life? Well, let me just tell you this..." Sophia's voice trailed off for a moment and her lips curled upward into an evil little grin before concluding with, "Never underestimate the raw power of a woman's emotions. *Never*, heh, heh, heh."

CHAPTER 3

AN ALL-AROUND EDUCATION

Morgan trudged her way down the stairs as the way-too-early morning sunshine beamed through the windows of the Cabot home. "Um, Mom, I was thinkin'," Morgan began to say to her mother who was sitting cross-legged on the living room couch looking through an old book. "Listen, everything's been so hectic what with the divorce and having to move yesterday and everything, so I was just thinkin' that maybe I could just take a day off. Y'know, just kinda catch up on my sleep. Just for today, okay? I promise I'll start my new school tomorrow. Okay?"

Lori's eyes remained fixed on the words in the book as she let out a slight sigh and inquired with a soft forcefulness, "Are you dressed?"

"Well, yeah, I am, but..." Morgan answered before being cut off by her mother.

"Good. Then I see no reason for you to not go to school today. It is the first day. That is why we moved here yesterday so that you could start on the very first day of the new school year. So please grab some breakfast and we'll leave shortly."

"But Mom!" Morgan yelled back. "You don't understand! I've been through a lot! This is *really hard* for me! I just need *one day* to collect myself!"

"Yes dear," Lori answered calmly while continuing her perusal of the large, musty smelling book in her hands, "I understand. We have *both* been through a lot. And it is time for us to pick ourselves up and start rebuilding our lives here. Hiding away from the world won't serve any purpose. Now please get your breakfast."

"Oh my God!" Morgan exclaimed. "You are being *soooo* unfair right now! You don't know what type of *pressure* I'm under! I have to meet all these new kids, *most* of whom will probably hate me, and learn new teachers, and figure out where I'm at in relation to my new classes! This is a lot of stress!"

"Yes, it is," Lori softly answered. "There is a lot to do and there is no time like the present to get started. So please go get your breakfast. We need to leave soon."

"Okay, Mom," Morgan replied in a near pleading voice, "How about we make a deal?"

"No deal, dear," Lori answered while hiding her bemused expression. "Please get ready to go."

"But Mom!" Morgan roared back.

"I have said all that I have to say on this matter," Lori stated with a bit more forcefulness. "Now, are you going to get some breakfast, or will you be going to school hungry? Your choice."

Morgan stood behind her mother while clenching her fists. Lori could feel her daughter's seething gaze burning into her back and casually turned the page without saying a word. Finally, a frustrated Morgan yelled out "Fine! But I'm not happy about it!" while storming into the kitchen.

A few minutes later, a resigned and calm Morgan sat next to her mother on the couch while munching on a piece of wheat toast. "So, where's Grandma at?" she asked with a full mouth.

"She's already at the diner doing prep work for lunch," Lori answered while continuing to stare at the oddly scripted pages in the book that she was holding. "And don't talk with your mouth full dear. It's unbecoming."

"Whatever," Morgan said as she rolled her eyes before continuing. "You know, Grandma kinda creeped me out last night. Y'know when she was talking about all those people who have had accidents. It was almost like she enjoyed it or something."

Lori began chuckling and responded. "Well, your grandmother is a bit of an…um…well, there's really no other way to say it. She's a vindictive bitch. Always has been. If she cares about someone, then she would move heaven and earth to help them. She would do absolutely *anything* for somebody that she cared about. But if she *doesn't* like someone, well, I've never known her to actually *do* anything to anyone, but let's just say that she doesn't exactly shed any tears over their misfortune, either. She is a woman who has always been driven by pure emotion. It is not a trait that I inherited. I have always been calm and cerebral about things. I believe that there is good in everyone and that everyone can be reasoned with. We just need to find the right approach. My mother on the other hand, believes in an eye for an eye. If you do something to harm me, then I will rejoice if something harmful happens to you. I just don't see the point in that. I don't see the point in harboring all those ill feelings toward someone else. It just doesn't serve any purpose and it eats us up inside. You would do well to remember that dear. I love my mother, but there are certain things about her that I have never really liked. Do you understand?"

"So," Morgan replied in a contemplative tone. "You think that you can reason with *anybody*?"

"Yes, dear, I do," came Lori's immediate answer.

"Even Dad?" Morgan inquired further.

Lori felt her blood pressure immediately rise and her pale face turned crimson. She let out a deep breath and said with a forced calm, "Well, your father is a bit…um…well…I really don't wish to speak about him. I believe that if you *do* have somebody in your life that creates emotional turmoil for you, then it is best to just suppress those emotions and move on with your life."

"Uh-huh," a suspicious Morgan replied. "So, like, you never think about how cool it would be if he got his dick caught in a blender or something? Or his precious stock portfolio plummeted, and he was forced to live on the street? Or he tripped and crushed his head on the pavement? Are you saying you never have a moment where you think about that?"

Lori experienced a strange sense of satisfaction as her mind envisioned each of the scenarios that her daughter had just outlined. Her fingers that were laying on the pages of the book began tingling slightly. Despite her best effort, she could not prevent her lips from turning upwards in a devious little smile. She turned her face from her staring daughter, regained control of herself and said, "No, I do not. And that is all that I have to say on the subject. I have a zoom meeting with my attorney this morning and it is not helpful for my mind to be cluttered with such unevolved thoughts, so just drop it, okay?"

"Sure, Mom," Morgan answered with a slight chuckle. "So, what in the hell is this book that you're reading?"

"I'm not sure," Lori answered with an intrigued tone. "I remember seeing this once as a kid. It was left out on the dining room table. It's such a random memory. I guess I just remember it because right after I saw it, Mom came into the room, picked it up and took it upstairs to her room. A few minutes later, we received the call that my dad had been blown up on his boat. I haven't seen it since, until now. I don't know why she left this out. It was just lying here on the coffee table when I got up. But it's really interesting. It's bound in this weird leather and all the entries are handwritten in this beautiful calligraphy in this reddish, brown ink. I'm not sure what this language is, but it appears to be Latin. It's pretty cool. It's weird, but I was really upset when I first got up this morning. Then, I sat down and began reading the passages in this book and I immediately felt calm. Maybe these inscriptions are some form of meditation, huh?"

"That *is* weird," Morgan replied. "Can I see it for a minute?" Morgan took the book from her mother, and she immediately felt a wave of adrenaline rush through her body. "Whoa. I guess my coffee just kicked in," she said through a slight chuckle. She read one passage in the book before her mother said, "Okay, we have plenty of time later to look at this. Come on. Let's get you to school."

As Morgan was walking to their car, the one inscription that she had read began being repeated over and over in her mind. *Cum verba irae me moveant tua, illa ipsa verba offendes. Cum verba irae me moveant tua, illa ipsa verba offendes. Cum verba irae me moveant tua, illa ipsa verba offendes.*

Morgan was dragging her feet as she exited the car and began the torturous trek into the high school. As she walked down the hallway looking for her home room, she would lift her black-dyed head and observe the various clusters of students who were congregated in their natural tribes. *God this is so stupid,* Morgan thought to herself. *Just like every other school that I've been in. High school is nothing more than a sad microcosm of our entire society. People huddled with other people who are just like them, for the most part. There's no desire to be with different people. To learn from them. To understand their culture or view-points or worldviews. It's no wonder why distrust abounds in our world. We just naturally gravitate to those who are most like us, then allow ourselves to be brainwashed into thinking that 'the other' is less important somehow. That they are less deserving of rights and personal freedoms. They are less than citizens. They are sometimes even viewed as less than human.*

And that isolation breeds distrust. And that distrust breeds hatred. And that hatred breeds violence. All because someone is different from you. It's so damned sad. Many of the parents support this dynamic because they don't want "their kid" to be influenced by "those people," and the schools just look the other way and hope that a match isn't lit by some poor kid who's been relentlessly bullied. If no one will stand with the bullied, then the bullied have two options. They can either cower in the corner and have their dignity stripped away from them until they have no sense of self-worth. Or they can fight back and demand to have the respect that they deserve. And that can be damned dangerous. Especially if their parents let them have access to guns.

Yes, we have a gun problem. And a mental health problem. And a drug problem. But most of all, we have a civility problem. Because if all these different people were at least civil with one another, then there wouldn't be the deep suspicion that drives people to arm themselves. There wouldn't be the epidemic of depression. There wouldn't be a need to escape with drugs.

God, I sound like my mother. All rays of sunshine and shit. I know that all our problems wouldn't be completely solved. But there would be a helluva lot more people who would stand together and support one another regardless of their respective tribes. And I love my mother, but I know which way I'm going to go if someone hassles me. And it won't be cowering in a corner. But it sure as hell won't be lashing out at random, innocent individuals either. No, my retribution will be precisely targeted. If needed.

Yep, all the usual suspects are here. The brains. The popular kids which mean they can play sports or look good in a tight cheerleader outfit. The different racial groups. The group of LGBTQ kids. The nerds who are into horror and comics and role-playing games. The drama kids. The band kids. The chorus kids. The tough kids. The goths. Screw it. I have just one year here. Then, I'm free. Free to go to college and live my life. Until then, I think that I'll just keep my head down and not make waves. I don't want to be in a tribe. I just want to be left alone for the next nine months. Nope. No close group of friends. No after school hangs at the mall or wherever they go around here. And definitely no romant...

Morgan's thoughts were interrupted as she entered her assigned classroom and looked up when she heard a petite classmate say, "Hey! You're new here aren'tcha? Wanna sit next to me? My name is Naomi, what's yours?"

Aaaawwww, shit, Morgan thought to herself. *She's cute.* Morgan sat her black, baggy clothed frame down next to Naomi and smiled tentatively. Morgan then realized that her neighbor wasn't just cute. Naomi could talk. A lot.

"Um, hi," Morgan said meekly. "My name's Morgan. Morgan Cabot. My mom and I just moved here from..."

"Well, nice to meetcha, there Morgan! Like I said, I'm Naomi. Naomi O'Sullivan. I know, I know. I don't exactly *look* like an O'Sullivan, and I take a lot of shit for it, but my mom brought me here from Haiti when I was a baby then she like, died, and then I was adopted by the O'Sullivan's 'cause they couldn't have kids of their own and stuff, y'know? Anyway they adopted me and they're the only family that I've ever known and a few years ago they asked if I wanted to keep their name or use my biological mother's last name and I said I wanted their name because they are my parents and they raised me and loved me and stuff and even though I don't really care for whiskey, at least not yet, I wanted to have their last name because they are my family, y'know? That was a joke about the whiskey, by the way. Y'know, because of the stereotype about the Irish liking whiskey and…oh, nevermind. So, where did you say you moved here from? Oh, hey, I'll help you navigate this joint if ya want. It's like everyplace else. Most of the kids are pretty nice, but a few are dicks. I'll tell you who to stay away from because the dicks can be really mean and make your life here a living hell. They do it to me all the time, y'know? Call me names like 'half-breed', which doesn't even make sense but they're not terribly bright, y'know? Or Black Irish, which at least kinda makes sense. Or 'Irish Coffee', y'know stuff like that. If you don't say anything back, they eventually get bored and move on to somebody else. They finally quit picking on me all the time about halfway through my sophomore year. But you're new here, and you're fresh meat and they'll want to test you. Especially with your black hair, and black lipstick and…hey! I totally love your nose ring! I wanted to get one, but my mom said no and that I can do whatever I want when I turn eighteen and, where did you say you were from again? Anyway, like I was saying…"

Naomi's diatribe was finally silenced when the middle-aged male teacher said for the third time, "Miss O'Sullivan! Would you *please* pipe down so that I can read the announcements and get you all to your first class? Please? Are we *really* going to start the new year like this? Again?"

"Sorry," Naomi sheepishly replied before giving Morgan a knowing wink. *What the hell was that? I feel like I've been through a hurricane*, Morgan thought to herself as she settled in to listen to the teacher.

As Morgan left each of her morning classes, she thought to herself, *Wow. Based on the syllabus, this shit's gonna be easy. Even the AP classes and…"*

Her thoughts were once again interrupted. "Oh hey! That's the lunch bell!" Naomi excitedly exclaimed as she pranced down the hallway. "Oh, this is soooo cool. We have the same lunch period. It's going to be soooo nice to have somebody to sit with during lunch. I mean, I have some friends here and everything, but they don't like to sit with me during lunch for some reason. Dunno why. It's weird. Come on. I'll show you where we can sit and…"

Fifteen minutes later, Morgan was continuing to listen to the longest sentence ever spoken while gazing down dreadfully on her lunch tray of pizza, apple sauce, and green beans. She felt a glimmer of hope at being released from Naomi's verbal onslaught as she watched three girls dressed in their designer's best approaching her table. Morgan looked up at the trio and smiled. Her feelings of hope were immediately dashed.

"Hey! Irish Coffee! Shut the hell up!" the girl in the middle yelled out. Naomi immediately became quiet, and she looked down on her tray of barely eaten food. As much as Morgan had been praying for a moment of silence, she did not want it to come from an admonishment from some entitled little bitch. And she most certainly was not going to allow the one person in this school who had been nice to her to be treated with such disrespect. Deep inside, a cork had just been popped and the contents of Morgan's anger began pouring over.

"So, you must be new here, huh?" the striking brunette said in a haughty tone. "Aaawww, look girls. We have a new little goth bitch to play with. Yeah, you all are always so fun. You just stand around looking at your gross shoes, listening to your creepy music all dressed in black. What are you hiding under all those black, baggy clothes, huh? Are you really a boy or do you have tits? Are we going to find out after gym class? Oh, I bet you're really looking forward to that aren't you? I bet you really like looking at the girls in the shower, don't you? Well, don't you? Don't you have anything to say you little…dyke…bitch?"

Morgan's face was beet red, and tears began welling at the corners of her blue eyes. She wanted to lash out, but her mother's voice kept creeping into her consciousness. *Just suppress your emotions. It isn't worth it. Everyone can be reasoned with.*

Her anger intensified as she watched the trio of female bullies laughing and pointing at her. Her mother's voice was then replaced by her own. *Cum verba irae me moveant tua, illa ipsa verba offendes. Cum verba irae me moveant tua, illa ipsa verba offendes. Cum verba irae me moveant tua, illa ipsa verba offendes,* kept playing over and over in her mind on a loop. The brunette picked up Morgan's lunch tray, spat upon her pizza, dropped the tray with a clatter, and turned to make her triumphant exit.

As her antagonist took one step forward, Morgan heard a loud CRACK! The brunette fell face first upon the hard linoleum floor. There was another loud CRACK! as her nose was shattered against the unforgiving surface. Blood sprayed several feet from around her planted face and the shocked girl began wailing. Her friends lifted her up. She took one step and realized that her left ankle had been shattered. She plummeted once again onto the floor, landing squarely on her mouth and knocking out all of her front teeth.

School personnel rushed to her side. They got the wailing girl to her feet, leaving a pool of blood and shattered tooth fragments on the floor. As soon as she placed weight upon her right foot, there was another loud CRACK! as her other ankle gave way. The girl careened once again onto the floor. Her forehead landed violently, and she passed out from a vicious concussion.

Morgan watched as medical personnel were placing the battered girl onto a stretcher. Her nose was flattened. She had a bump the size of a softball on her forehead. Blood and drool were flowing from between her split lips and her eyes were dark purple and nearly swollen shut. Morgan felt the pangs of retribution creep into her consciousness. The incantation then began again. *Cum verba irae me moveant tua, illa ipsa verba offendes.* The chanting then changed from Latin to English and a sharp chill ran down Morgan's spine as she finally understood the translation. *When your words cause me anger, you shall trip over those very words.*

What the hell is going on? A shocked Morgan thought to herself as she looked upon the swollen and bloodied face of her nemesis being wheeled away.

"Wow!" Naomi exclaimed. "She's gonna have a helluva time finding a date for the homecoming dance looking like that. Oh, you're going to the homecoming dance, aren't you? Please say that you are! What are you going to wear? Do you want me to help you pick something out? Do you want to go out for dinner first? Where do ya wanna go? We'd better get our reservations. Places book up really fast around here. Who else should we invite? Oh, you're new here, so you don't know. I'll think on it and get back to you. Oh! You have to give me your number so that I can get back to you! This is going to be soooo cool! My mom has some really great jewelry that we can borrow! We can do each other's hair, and makeup, and rent a limo and..."

Chapter 4

A Rise In Temperature

Lori re-entered her childhood home after dropping her daughter off feeling a mixture of relief and dread. On the one hand, it was comforting to be back in the inviting confines with her mother and daughter. She felt safe for the first time in a long time. On the other hand, she was embarrassed to need her mother's help at the age of forty-one.

How the hell did I get here? She thought to herself as she pulled her laptop from her black leather carry-all. *How did I not see this coming? How could I not heed the warnings of my mother? My friends? I thought they were all nuts. He was such a romantic man when I first met him nearly twenty years ago. Dashing. Charismatic. Rich. And as much as it makes my skin crawl now, I found him to be absolutely hot. As did a lot of other women, as it turns out.*

All the romantic notes that he would leave for me. The flowers and sweet little gifts. The tenderness of his kisses. He absolutely swept me off my feet. To say that I swooned would not be doing it justice. I was drowning in my adoration for him. We married a year later, and everything stayed the same. They say that marriage changes a relationship. Not in my case. He was the same doting, sweet man that I had fallen for. It was a no-brainer to have a child with him. I wanted to have and raise a child with him. To me, he was the most perfect example of manhood. Responsible. Protective. Attentive. And then the most precious gift that he could have given me arrived. My Morgan. And then, things changed.

Slightly at first. Little put-downs. The dinner wasn't what he wanted. I wasn't keeping up with the housework. I was coddling our baby too much. Drip, drip, drip. And I just accepted it. He was still mostly the man that I had fallen for, and the pressures of now raising a child can change things a bit, I thought. So, I shrugged it off. His criticisms weren't necessarily hurtful, after all. They were just annoying.

But then I caught him in his first affair. Morgan was three years old, and I came back early from a shopping trip. I heard Morgan crying from her bedroom and heavy breathing coming from mine. I threw open the door and there he was. With our nineteen-year-old babysitter. He didn't even try to say, 'It isn't what it looks like.' It couldn't be anything other than what it looked like. Nobody could trip over a rug and accidentally land naked in that contorted position. I remember that look on his face. Like he enjoyed me catching him. Like he knew I wouldn't do anything. It was the first time that I truly saw who he was. Controlling. Arrogant. Cruel.

He said all the right things. That he was sorry. That it had never happened before, and it would never happen again. That it was the babysitter that had seduced him. He was too weak to resist. He was under too much pressure at work. He was driven to provide for his family. He was driven to provide for his daughter. He was driven to provide for me. That was why he was working the long hours, he told me. He was weak. He begged for my forgiveness. And I gave it to him. I buried my anger and disappointment and tried to look at the situation reasonably.

He was under a lot of pressure. I did make the mistake of hiring an attractive babysitter. And I was frequently too tired to make love. He was a good provider and had been a good husband, up to this point. People make mistakes. I understood. And I forgave him, and we decided to pretend that it never happened. And my allowing him to get away with it just increased his confidence. He was convinced that I was under his spell and that he could do anything to me...over time.

He was overly sweet and kind for the next couple of months. But then the slight jabs started again. And they became increasingly personal. I never wore the right thing to events. I was looking old. I was gaining weight. Drip, drip, drip. Until my self-esteem was shattered. It was like being slowly sucked down into an emotional quicksand of hopeless resignation. Mom would come and visit. She knew something was wrong. She asked if she could help. But I assured her that I was alright. Or at least I tried to. I'm not that good of an actress. It was drudgery. The constant criticism. And the constant late nights at work. I knew that he wasn't working. I knew who his prey was on his hunting weekends. I just ignored it, tried to look as pretty as I could, make a nice dinner that Morgan and I would usually eat alone, and retire to bed after another day as a willfully kept woman.

Every now and again I would think about leaving him. But I now knew how controlling he could be. And how cruel. He was wealthy and his family was well-connected. I had left college to marry him and hadn't held a job since I was twenty-two. I had no way to support myself. I had no way to protect my Morgan. I knew he would hire the most expensive lawyers and try to find a way to get full custody. Just out of spite. Just to hurt me. He knew I was trapped, and he loved it. He loved the control he had over me financially. He loved the control he had over my emotions. He would intentionally make racist, homophobic, or sexist remarks just to see if I would fight back. I never did. I just ignored them. Until Morgan became a teenager, and she became his target as well.

He had always played the role of the good, supportive father. Trips to get ice cream. Watching cartoons with her. Loving kisses on the top of her blonde head. That seemed to all change when she was fourteen and she dyed her hair jet black. Despite his best efforts at manipulating her, she instinctively always knew what he was. He was a fraud. A con man. A bigot. She knew that about him, and she dyed her hair just to piss him off. She began getting piercings in her ears, nose, and lips. She seemed to relish in his beratement of her. She had done this just to provoke him and despite his cruel words, she knew that she was actually controlling him. Through my stepford haze, I saw this and found it comical. But despite her amusement at tormenting her father, she was quietly living a life of drudgery as well. It isn't fun when you know that your father has no respect for who you are. All the pranks, barbed comments, and black or rainbow fashion choices could not hide a deep depression that had settled in. She was depressed at how her father treated her. And she was depressed by watching how his constant beratement affected me.

Two months ago, I came home and found Morgan asleep. I then saw a note on her bedside table that said that she couldn't stand the pain of living with him any longer. And she couldn't stand the pain of watching him humiliate me. His verbal and mental abuse kept increasing and she realized that I was incapable of protecting her because I was incapable of protecting myself. If this was what life was like living as a woman then she did not want to live anymore. God, how I remember the tears streaming down my face. Those tears turned to shock when I then noticed the empty bottle of sleeping pills on my daughter's bedroom floor.

I called him from the emergency room. He was in a meeting and couldn't be bothered. When he finally called back all that he could say was that his daughter's histrionics would catch up to her someday and that he would straighten her out when he got home from his hunting trip on Monday. I became resolved to never let that conversation happen.

I changed the locks on the door, put a bunch of his stuff on the lawn, and left an emergency restraining order on the front door. He had been served with the notice. He was too busy with his young assistant to respond. It was laughable to him. With Mom's help, I was able to hire a cheap attorney and was able to get a temporary injunction barring him from our home. That injunction expired two days ago and here I am back in my hometown. And although I may be broke, I am not broken.

I have come up with a very reasonable divorce agreement. I want nothing from him but his signature, me and Morgan's personal belongings, and my ten-year-old car. He can have the house. The luxury cars. The savings accounts. The stock portfolios. The furniture. I don't want child support. I don't want anything from him. Nor does Morgan. She hates him. So, today's little zoom meeting with my attorney should be nothing more than a formality. He would be an idiot to turn this deal down. I could take so much from him. Yes, I finally have the upper hand. It will cost me a lot, but I would pay anything for my freedom. My dignity. And, most importantly, my daughter's as well.

"What do you *mean* he's suing me?" a dismayed Lori yelled at her computer screen. "Is he *crazy*? I am letting him keep *everything*!"

"Well, I'm sorry Lori," her attorney, Anne Bulanschaser, replied. "But that isn't true. You haven't given him shared custody of your daughter."

"Because Morgan is seventeen and can make that decision on her own!" Lori roared back in a rare fit of rage.

"Well, he doesn't see it that way," the disinterested attorney replied. "He says that he has evidence that you're an unfit mother and he is filing to keep everything that you proposed plus he wants full custody of his daughter until she is eighteen. He probably won't get it and you could probably take him to the cleaners if you want, but the discovery process is going to be really time-consuming. And, um, expensive. He can file motion after motion and tie this up in the courts for months or even years. The custody thing won't be an issue after Morgan turns eighteen, but he could get a judge to order shared custody until it's resolved. And then, of course, there's his portion of the suit regarding defamation of character and mental anguish."

"W-w-*what?*" Lori screamed. "He's saying that I caused mental anguish...to *him?* Is he *crazy?*"

"Um, maybe," the attorney answered. "Again, he probably doesn't have a case, but I think his strategy is to throw so much stuff into this that it will cost you tens of thousands of dollars unless you and Morgan agree to him having shared custody. He's trying to bleed you dry."

"It's all about power and control," Lori realized. "It's all about spite. It's all about trying to take the one thing from me that he knows I most care about. He doesn't want to raise our daughter. He couldn't care less. He's barely spoken to her for three years except to insult her in some way. This is his narcissistic little ego being bruised and his trying to wield power over me. This is his attempt to continue to control me."

"Well, maybe," the attorney replied. "But whatever his motivations are, they're effective. Y'know, unless you're independently wealthy."

Lori became silent as her mind quickly ran through her various options. Her mouth began twitching and she began rapidly batting her blue eyes. She took a deep breath, placed her anger and dismay into a tiny box in the furthest corner of her soul and said flatly, "Fine. Send me the information. I'll begin putting stuff together. It will be fine. I'm sure it will be fine. I'll find an answer. I always do. Yeah, he'll reason with me. I'll just find a way for him to reason with me. It will be fine. Thank you, Anne. I'll be waiting for the petition. And on your bill."

Lori fiercely batted her blue eyes a few more times, closed the computer, grabbed her purse, and began walking towards her car in a daze.

"Well, based on that look on your face, the call with the attorney didn't go so well," Lori's mother, Sophia, said as Lori entered the kitchen of the diner.

"What?" an awakened Lori answered. "Oh, well, yeah, not perfect. But it will be okay. It always is. I'll work this out with him. It will be fine, Mom. Now, where can I set up shop for my catering service?"

As Sophia was clearing a large space in the back of the diner and showing her daughter around, she said, "So, how are you feeling?"

"Oh, I'm fine, Mom," Lori answered with a fake laugh.

"Uh-huh," an unconvinced Sophia replied. "You're getting worse at hiding your anger dear. I can see it just under the surface. Please listen to me. It is okay to unleash your emotions. Especially when somebody is doing you wrong. It is through our emotions that we find our will to fight. It is through our emotions that we protect ourselves. And it is through our emotions that we vanquish our enemies, heh, heh, heh."

"Vanquish our enemies?" Lori laughed in response. "That's a bit *medieval*, don't you think? This is just a divorce proceeding. I mean, he's an asshole but I don't think he deserves to be vanquished. What do you expect me to do? Get angry and then put him on the rack or chop his head off with a guillotine or something?"

"I don't know," Sophia said in a contemplative tone. "Why don't you just allow yourself to get angry and see what happens?"

"Oh, shut up, Mom!" Lori exclaimed before the diner's manager, Taylor, popped his head into the room. "Hey, do you have that take-out order ready?"

"Yeah, yeah, here it is," Sophia answered. "Lori, honey, would you please take this bag out to the cash register for me?"

"Sure, Mom," Lori agreed. She picked up the white bag with faint grease stains and proceeded toward the door. The door swung open, and she nearly dropped the bag when she saw who was standing at the counter.

"Oh, my lord! Lori Cabot!" Connor O'Sullivan exclaimed. Despite his thinning red hair and somewhat portly build, Lori could not keep her mind from thinking about watching his teenage frame dunking a basketball or running track or reading a book or passing her notes in class or eating lunch or sitting on the school's steps or dunking a basketball or dunking a basketball or dunking a basketball.

"Wow, Connor!" a slightly blushing Lori responded. "It's been so long. It's so great to see you. How have you been? And how is your… um…wife?"

Connor let out a deep belly laugh and said, "Well, that ended a while ago. I guess all my late nights in a patrol car finally took their toll. She moved away about three years ago. It was amicable. Some things just run their course, y'know?"

"Yeah, oh how I know," Lori replied as she looked down momentarily and shook her blonde head. "Yeah, I'm kinda going through that right now too. That's why I'm back in town. Me and Morgan are staying with mom until things get…um…settled."

"Well, I'm sorry to hear that, Lori," Connor stated sincerely. "But it's so great to have you back in town! And Morgan! Why, I haven't seen her since she was in kindergarten! Oh, we have to get together and have a beer and go down memory lane some night."

"Yeah, let's do that," Lori coyly replied. "So, you're still on the force huh?"

Connor O'Sullivan reached into his breast pocket wearing a broad smile. He proudly flipped open a leather wallet revealing a badge.

"You may now refer to me as *Detective* O'Sullivan, miss," Connor said with an overinflated bravado. He then began laughing. "Can you believe it? After nearly twenty years on the force, they finally made *this* old schlub a detective!"

"That's so great, Connor," Lori replied. "And, yeah, let's get that beer some night. I could use an evening of…um…reminiscing."

"I'll get the spaghetti started," Sophia stated as she and Lori entered their home later that evening. "Why don't you go get Morgan. This won't take long."

Lori ascended the stairs and heard an unfamiliar girl's rambling voice. She lightly knocked on Morgan's door.

"Come in!" Morgan yelled out.

"Hi, dear," Lori said as she looked upon her daughter and another young woman sitting on her bed. "How was your first day of school?"

Morgan's mind raced to find the right response. The only word that she could come up with was, "Interesting. How about your day?"

Lori's mind raced to find the right response. The only word that she could come up with was, "Interesting. Who is this then?"

"Oh, this is my new friend Naomi," Morgan casually answered.

"Hiya Mrs. Cabot!" Naomi enthusiastically introduced herself as she bounced onto her feet and extended her hand. "Or is it, *Miss* Cabot? Or can I call you *Lori*? Morgan told me about your divorce and I'm so sorry about that. I just never know how to address a divorcee, y'know? Anyway, how would you like me to address you? Miss? Mrs? Lori? It doesn't matter to me. Whatever you prefer. Oh, I just love your daughter, Miss Cabot! She's super cool! I just know we're going to be the best of friends! And we're going to go to the homecoming dance together, right Morgan? Did you pick a place to eat yet? I've already invited, like, six other kids to go with us. They said they'd get back to me. Anyway, as I was saying…"

Naomi was cut off, momentarily, by Morgan who said, "Um, yeah, Mom, this is my new friend Naomi. Naomi O'Sullivan. Is it okay if she stays for dinner?"

"Um, sure. I don't see why not," Lori answered. "So, Naomi O'Sullivan?"

"Yeah, O'Sullivan," Naomi answered cheerfully. "I know I don't look the part. I'm adopted. Anyway, how should I address you? Miss, Mrs., Lori?"

"Um," Lori began to inquire further, "Are you related somehow to *Connor* O'Sullivan?"

"Oh yeah!" Naomi shouted out. "Why, do you know him? Do you know my Uncle Connor? He's my dad's younger brother. How do you know him? Oh, did you meet him at the diner? He just *loves* that diner and he's super cool! He just loves the burgers and fries and shakes there. He takes me all the time! He's kinda hard to talk to though. He's always got headphones on when we go to lunch or whatever. Dunno why. I guess he just really likes music. And he doesn't really say much. He just smiles and nods a lot. But he's super nice and he's a cop! Did you know that? That's come in handy on more than one occasion. I probably shouldn't tell you this, but this past summer me and some friends were hanging out at the harbor and we..."

Chapter 5

Simmering

Sophia Cabot was staring in disbelief as she took another bite of her garlic bread while listening to the verbal onslaught of one Naomi O'Sullivan.

"… So, my Uncle Connor came up to us and said, oh and did you know he's now a detective? Cool, huh? Anyway, he came up to us and asked what we were doing, and we told him, 'nothin,', and he just asked if maybe he needed to call our parents and we said 'no,' and so he let us just go home 'cause we really weren't doing anything wrong, y'know, and…"

Sophia could not help but smile as she looked at the faces of her family. Morgan's jaw was wide open in disbelief as she tried to process the information that was flying at her from Naomi, and Lori was transfixed with a slight smile on her blushing face. Several lengthy, run-on sentences later, Sophia thought that the dinner and the very one-sided conversation was nearly over as the quartet were placing their dishes in the dishwasher while listening to Naomi describe in detail every appliance in her parents' kitchen. Sophia felt that there was light at the end of this dark tunnel. For the first time in over an hour, Sophia felt hope. A sharp chill of dread ran down her spine when she heard her daughter say, "So, Naomi. Tell us more about your uncle."

Two hours later, the front door slammed behind Naomi's bouncing frame. Sophia looked at her family and yelled out, "What the hell was *that*? I've seen that girl around, but I've never spent any time with her. And I don't usually see her with anyone else, either. And now I know why! My lord! That is one Category Five Hurricane Naomi! Sweet girl, but dear lord. Does she even breathe? Whatever. I'm glad you made a friend, Morgan. Just put up a hurricane warning the next time she comes over, okay? I need to be prepared for that shit. I need a drink. I'm going to the pub. I'll see you all in the morning."

"Okay, bye Grandma," Morgan stated before turning to her mother. "So, Mom, I was thinkin' that maybe tomorrow, um…" Morgan saw the intensity in her mother's eyes and decided to change tactics. "That, um, I'd better go upstairs and get my homework done for tomorrow. But before I go up, how did the meeting with the attorney go?"

Lori's protective maternal instincts overrode her daughter's genuine inquiry as she replied, "Fine, dear. Just fine. Just a few hiccups but nothing to worry about. It's a divorce so there will be a bit of back and forth for a while, but it will all work out fine, okay?"

"Okay, Mom, love you," a content Morgan stated before ascending the stairs to her bedroom. Lori was once again awash with a feeling of dread as she retrieved her computer and opened it. She found the email from her attorney. Her heart sank further as she read all the items that she would have to put together for the discovery of the frivolous lawsuit.

She began pouring through hundreds of emails, texts, financial records, school reports, and other pieces of information needed to defend herself and protect her cherished daughter from her devious husband. Her fists clenched tightly, and she fought back tears as she thought, *this is going to take weeks to get all of this together. Tonight, I'll just find everything and put it in a folder. Then, I'll organize it later. Page by page. Piece by piece. He wants discovery? Oh, I'm going to give him discovery.*

She couldn't hold back her tears as she read passage after passage from her journal that she had kept hidden on her computer for years. Her journal had been her only refuge. It had been her only emotional outlet. She had to protect her daughter and could not confide in her. Besides, it wasn't fair to burden her daughter with her troubles. It was *her* responsibility to support her daughter, not vice versa. And she couldn't confide in her mother at the time. Although she loved her mother, she did not want to hear her condescending diatribes about how she had been right all along. Plus, every time she had picked up the phone to speak to her about her troubles, it seemed as though there was this feeling of impending doom if she followed through. So, she never did. Lori had no real friends to confide in, either. All her friends were her husband's work associates or, more often, the wives of his work associates. They could not be trusted with her deepest secrets. Plus, who knew which of them he had screwed over the years. *Probably all of them*, a despondent Lori mused as she scrolled down the passages of her sacred journal. Her journal that provided a meticulous accounting of her life with this mentally abusive man. A journal that had every entry time stamped.

Dear Journal. He allowed me to have $500 today to go shopping for new outfits. He says that my clothes make me look old and that I'm an embarrassment to him when we go to dinner parties or his business events. I took the money and found several new dresses. I put each one on for him. He said nothing. When I was wearing the final dress, he said that I had bought things that made me look like a whore. Return them and try again. And try to get something that doesn't make people think that I'm married to a slut. Just another day in the great life of Lori Cabot.

Morgan came home today with a nose ring. He was furious. He threatened to rip it out of her face. She laughed at him. God, how I wish I had her strength. How I wish I could just laugh at him. His mature response was to take all of her shoes that were in the foyer and toss them outside in the pouring rain. He then told her that she wouldn't get another penny from him until she stopped looking like a freak. He called our daughter a freak. She is the most beautiful, intelligent, mature fifteen-year-old. She is my special gift. She should be his special gift. But she isn't. To him, she is a freak. How can I get her away from him before he causes too much damage to her soul? How can I get him away from her before she becomes beaten down like me?

He came home tonight. I was in the kitchen wearing my normal casual house wear. Jogging pants and T-shirt. The pool man was outside. My husband looked at me then at the pool man through the window. He accused me of trying to seduce the pool man. He said that I was in the kitchen just to tempt him. He said that I was a whore and always had been one and this proves it. There could be no other explanation for why I was in the kitchen while the pool man was just a few feet away. I guess he's losing his eyesight. I guess he couldn't see all the remnants of chopped vegetables from my preparation for his dinner.

Well, dear journal, this is a new one. Today he began his white glove initiative. He said that he would go around the house with white gloves and perform inspections. Every time he found a dusty surface or anything that did not meet his impossible standards, I would lose my allowance for one week. Like I get much to begin with. He called me a little piggie who just wants to live in a pig-stie. He called me a slob. He said that all the Cabots are slobs. That I couldn't help myself, so he would show me how civilized people keep a house. This coming from a man who doesn't know the meaning of the word 'laundry hamper.' He couldn't find any problems. Until he went to the kitchen. He swept his white glove over every surface. They were perfectly clean. He then picked up the toaster and turned it over.

A few crumbs fell on the counter. I guess I won't get my allowance this week.

Well, journal, it is official. Yes, I'm officially fat. Today he put a whiteboard up in the kitchen. I must log everything that I eat, the portions, and the calories. There is another whiteboard that I must log every time I exercise. What was the activity, the weight used, and the time or reps. He said that he's tired of taking a cow to his business events. He compared me to the other women. The women that I know he is screwing. I see the knowing glances and smiles and shoulder pats. I see it and I know. He controls my mind. He controls my finances. And now he controls my nutrition. How much more of this hell must I endure? How can I escape? I guess I'll just bide my time and wait for an opening. I'll log the food. But I'm never going to log the whiskey that I drink alone at night.

I have to do something, Journal. I don't know how, but I have to get my daughter out of here. Tonight she came home and was wearing a 'Pride' shirt. Innocent enough, right? Not to him. He screamed at her. He said that he would not have a daughter that was a Godless freak. That this ended now. I fear he may be right. I fear there may come a time when we don't have a daughter at all. I fear that there will come a time when our daughter leaves us. One way or another.

Lori wiped the tears from her eyes and went to the kitchen for a well-deserved nightcap. "Aw shit," she said softly to herself. "I can't do this anymore tonight. I knew for so long. I suffered for so long. My daughter suffered for so long. Why did I stay? I can rationalize it all that I want, but I should have left long ago. I should have protected my daughter from him just as my mother protected me. Wait. What am I saying? My father's death was an accident. A really fortuitous coincidence. Mom had nothing to do with it. But she has it *in her* to do something like that. I *know* that she does. So does

Morgan. I can almost feel it. I wish I had their strength. No, actually, I don't wish that. I have something better. I have calm. I have reason. Maybe it has taken me awhile, but my reason will win out. My path will win out. I'll just finish this slug of whiskey and scroll through my social media page for a while. That inane shit should cheer me up."

"Awww, that's nice," Lori said aloud as she saw and accepted a 'Friend' request from Connor O'Sullivan. She went to type something to him but decided against it. *Let's just get out of the frying pan before jumping into another fire,* she thought to herself. *Yes, he's single. Yes, I've had a crush on him since high school. Yes, he seems to be the same sweet man as he was as a boy. But let's think about this logically. I have a daughter to raise. I have a divorce to get through. And that divorce is getting messier by the day. I have a new catering business to get up and running. And I'm spent. Nope, I have too much on my plate right now. Maybe when things settle down. And if he's not available when I'm ready? Well, I guess that will be fate intervening. Just as it intervened when I left to go to college. No, the romance will just have to take a back seat for a while. Oh, God. Back seat. The one time we were alone together was in the back seat of his friend's car. He was making out with his girlfriend up front, and Connor just talked with me. He didn't make a move. Even though I kinda wanted him to. He was just a sweet, respectful young man. Always was. And we just talked and laughed and joked. It was nice. Well, maybe after the dust has settled, he and I can have another go at a back seat. I guess it wouldn't hurt to just say 'Hi.'*

Lori then burst out laughing as she hovered her cursor over 'Accept' for another 'Friend' request. She paused for a moment and contemplated the pros and cons of having this person connected to her virtually. She smiled and said through her laughter, "Well, I guess it wouldn't hurt to have *another* O'Sullivan as a 'Friend.'" It did not take long for Naomi to respond to the acceptance.

One hour and many, many, many sentences later, Naomi said that she had to go to bed, 'lol.' *Why is that funny?* Lori wondered. She then went to her own home page. She hadn't posted anything in months. But someone else had. Recently. It was a meme that had been forwarded to her page from one of her husband's friends. Lori's blood began simmering as she glared at the image of a middle-aged woman dressed in a provocative "cougar" costume. Her rage intensified as she read the words written over the image.

Look on the bright side. They say divorce causes weight loss. Not from the stress, but from the fact he's taking you to the cleaners and you can't afford food! So, enjoy your new figure! Now you can be the slut that you've always wanted to be!

Lori's face was beet red, and she rapidly began blinking her tearful eyes as she noticed that he had 'Liked' his own post. As had several other men. And the 'Likes' kept coming. There was a gust of wind. The old leather-bound book was blown open. An enraged Lori looked down at the page's reddish-brown inked incantation.

"So, Sophia," Vince inquired of his old friend as he leaned across the bar, "How's Morgan adjusting? How did her first day of school go?"

"Alright, I guess," Sophia replied with a slight slur. "She didn't mention anything. She's a smart girl. A wicked smart girl. She'll be fine. As long as her classmates leave her alone. And even then, she'll be fine. She takes after *this* old broad. I'm not to be trifled with and neither is she. She did make a friend, though. A girl named Naomi."

Vince burst out laughing. "Naomi? Naomi O'Sullivan? Oh, she is a sweet girl, but..." His voice trailed off as he struggled to find the right descriptive words to use. He was granted a reprieve from Sophia.

"But can that little bitch talk!" Sophia yelled out. "I mean, she just goes from one topic to another. How can somebody's mind work like that? That little thing needs to find an outlet for everything that's flying through her mind. She is positively exhausting!"

"Yes, yes she is," the chuckling Vince agreed. "Y'know, when she was a bit younger, she used to deliver papers. I made the mistake of greeting her one morning. I made that mistake once. I'm not sure what happened but let's just say that I didn't have to read the paper that day. She told me everything that was in it, whether I wanted to hear it or not. Sweet girl, though."

"Yeah, sweet girl," Sophia agreed as she searched for a way to change the subject.

"And Lori?" Vince inquired further. "I'm sure this can't be easy for her. How's she holding up?"

"Oh, she'll be fine," Sophia answered as she wore a devilish little grin. "My Lori will be just fine. She's on a journey. A journey to discover who she truly is. And she *will* discover it, Vince. She will. She just needs to be honest with herself. She just needs to allow herself to feel her true emotions. Then the healing can start. Then she can..."

Sophia felt a wave of warmth stream through her body. She gulped her final shot of whiskey, slammed the glass down on the table and muttered, "Well, speak of the devil." She then flashed a smile at Vince and said, "You know what? I'm glad you mentioned her, Vince. I think it was a sign. A sign that my daughter needs me tonight. I'll see ya tomorrow. Probably. And make sure you have my whiskey in stock! I'm tired of drinking this cheap shit!"

As Sophia swayed down the sidewalk, she thought to herself, *I think my precious daughter is about to have a bit of an awakening. I think she's found our book. And I can't wait to see who's gonna be on the receiving end of her gift.*

Chapter 6

Boiling

A seething Lori looked in on her sleeping daughter. A tear fell from her blue eye as her enraged mind wandered. Then wondered. *We had made so much progress,* she began thinking to herself. *We women certainly have not achieved complete equality with the men, but we have made so much progress. More women in the workforce. Better, certainly not equal, but better pay to do the same jobs as our male counterparts. More of us in leadership positions. More of us in elected positions. More of us in executive positions in industry. After decades, hell, centuries, of struggle we were finally being viewed by society as equal members who were just as important as men. Who were just as capable. Just as intelligent. Just as talented. Just as important. And now, I see it all coming undone. And not just for us. It is coming undone for everybody who isn't a straight, white, so-called Christian male. All of my LGBTQ, Black, Hispanic, Asian, Middle Eastern, and Indigenous brothers and sisters need to realize that we have a common enemy. And that enemy is the majority of straight, white, so-called Christian males. Certainly not all of them. But many of them. Like my husband and his guffawing, knuckle-dragging friends. They would strip our rights from all of us. Because, to them, we are less than them. We are to be subservient to them. We are here to do their bidding. It is all about their perceived right to have ultimate power over anyone who isn't in their* demographic. *It is about sex, and money, and influence, and ultimate control over everything. And they wrap themselves in the flag or the bible while they spew their hateful rhetoric. It's all very sad to see what is happening to us. Again.*

That is truly why a bunch of old, white men want to control our reproductive freedom. To control our very bodies. It has nothing to do with their so-called religion. It is the ultimate gambit for power and control. They see us gaining influence in our society and it frightens them. And that fear leads them to resent us. And what is the key to our success? Our reproductive freedom. Our ability to make choices for planning our families and lives. Not some man. Not some political body. Us. That freedom of self-determination is what has led to our economic freedom. It has led to our feelings of self-worth. It has led to our belief that we truly can achieve anything that we desire as long as we put forth the effort. And that strength scares the hell out of them. That is why there are so many societies throughout this world that keep women under the heels of men. Because there are many men in this world who are frightened of women. It happens in the Middle East, and parts of Asia, and on and on. Hell, violent persecution of women was here. That is why so-called witches were burned. Not out of some religious belief but out of men's illogical fear of a woman's strength. The fear of losing control over us and the greed to keep everything for themselves.

So, how to put us back where we belong? Back to the kitchen, and the laundry room, and the factories making half as much as our male counterparts. Out of the board rooms. Out of the halls of legislation. It is quite simple. Take away our reproductive freedom. Keep us shackled to our homes. Keep us shackled to our wombs. Keep us shackled to our husband's checkbook and stock portfolio. Keep us shackled to the houses of worship that they say we can join. Keep us shackled economically. Politically. Mentally. Hell, keep us shackled physically. Take away our right to bear children when we choose, or to not have children at all, and we are once again shackled to the resurgent white patriarchy. They see other male-dominated societies in the world, and they admire them. They aspire to turn our representative democracy into a patriarchal dictatorship. They are not Godly, and they certainly are not patriots. They are the American Taliban.

All this leads me to wonder and worry about my Morgan. What type of society will she live in? I never saw this coming seventeen years ago when I brought her into this world. How could I? Rights for all underrepresented groups, including women, had been steadily increasing for decades. It seemed obvious that that trajectory would continue until we truly had an equal society. I suppose we underestimated the number of men who silently harbored their resentment towards us. And we underestimated their ability to organize and mobilize a populist political movement designed to place power firmly back in the hands of the straight, white, so-called Christian males. And we also underestimated their ability to influence many in groups of underrepresented voters to actually vote against their very own interests. And those of their precious daughters.

Oh, my Morgan. What type of world will you live in? Will it be a world where you will have every opportunity to be the wonderful, talented person that you are? Or will it be a world where you have to battle against every asshole man out there like my husband's dullard friend who sent me that horrible meme?

Lori's angered mind instinctively began reciting the passage that she had briefly seen in the opened book downstairs. *Contra eos qui suis vocibus alios opprimunt, habebunt locutions. Contra eos qui suis vocibus alios opprimunt, habebunt locutions. Contra eos qui suis vocibus alios opprimunt, habebunt locutions.*

She felt a shot of energy flow through her body as a gust of wind blew open her daughter's bedroom window. Her blonde hair and housedress were flowing in the strong breeze as Lori fought to clear her mind from the repetitious incantation. With each passing recitation, her mind seemed to burn with greater intensity. She felt her muscles tighten and strengthen. She felt healing satisfaction in her very soul.

Wh-wh-what is happening to me? Lori thought to herself as she slowly began levitating off the carpeted floor. Her bare feet suddenly felt the carpet again and the incantation stopped when she heard the front door close. She looked down upon her still sleeping daughter. Her bewildered mind attempted to make sense of what she had just experienced as she rifled through all the possible logical explanations. She decided to settle on too much whiskey as she closed her daughter's bedroom window and descended the staircase to greet her smiling mother.

Sophia was standing at the living room coffee table looking with satisfaction at the open book. She was also looking at the sexist meme. *Huh*, Sophia thought to herself. *Yep, that asshole might send her over the edge.* She then looked up and smiled at her approaching daughter.

"What the hell have you been *doing?*" Sophia asked while still wearing a sly grin. "Your hair is a mess and why is your robe all twisted around like that?"

"Um, well," Lori began to explain. "First off, this isn't a robe. It's a housecoat."

Sophia exploded into laughter. "Housecoat? Who in the hell says housecoat? What is this? 1953?"

"Mother, it's a perfectly fine term. Please don't belittle me. Not tonight," Lori replied sternly.

"Bad night, huh?" Sophia tenderly inquired. "I'm sorry about that sweetie. And sorry to make fun of you. I know all the shit that you're going through. I know this isn't easy. But don't lose your sense of humor, dear. Don't ever lose that. When they take away your ability to laugh, then they've taken everything. Then they truly have taken your soul. Now, tell mommy all about your bad day."

Lori felt relief to be able to change the subject from the strange occurrence upstairs to something more tangible. More logical. More realistic. Although traumatic, Lori felt herself more at ease as she showed her mother the lawsuit against her. An increased calm swept over her as she proudly opened her files on her computer. Her mother looked carefully at each saved email, social media post, financial record, and text. "Shit, Lori," Sophia stated. "What are you worried about? Look at all the shit he's been talking. He's made a grave mistake, dear. You tried to be reasonable with him. Just let you and Morgan live your lives and you won't take anything from him. But, with this, he's asking for it! *He's* the one who is suing *you! He's* the one demanding discovery evidence. *He's* the one that is going to look like a *fool* in front of the court. It's time, dear. It's time to go for the jugular. You have him dead to rights. Countersue him. Countersue him for everything that you can. Bleed the bastard dry."

"No, Mom," Lori responded calmly. "It isn't logical. If I do that, then it will be an even longer, drawn out process. Maybe I'll win, maybe I won't. There are no guarantees. And I simply don't have the money to fight this. And he knows it. I'll give them discovery material alright. I'll hand over everything that I have. But not to countersue. It is my hope that his attorney will see all of this and realize he doesn't have a case and just drop it. It is my hope that he will finally be reasonable. That is all that I want. Just drop it and keep Morgan out of it. I don't want her to have to go through any more stress. I just want it done. I just want to know that my Morgan will be protected."

"Yeah, well," Sophia replied with a slight snicker. "I think that you're underestimating the strength of your daughter. I understand your position, dear, but it is impossible to protect her from everything in this world. At some point, she will face adversity, and there's not a damn thing that you will be able to do about it. Just like there wasn't a damn thing that I could do to keep you from getting involved with this spineless dick. It was *your* life. It was *your* fight. And now, here we are. At *your* crossroads during *your* fight in *your* life.

"Yes, our Morgan is much more powerful than you realize. And so am I. And so are you. We are the ladies Cabot, and the will and strength of our ancestors run through our veins. It runs through our bodies. And it absolutely *courses* through our souls."

"Yeah, yeah, yeah," Lori replied dismissively. "Whatever. Pep talks don't really mean much, Mom. Yeah, okay, we're 'Cabot strong.' Who cares? What does that have to do with anything? It's meaningless. Whatever strength that I might have will be used to just settle this thing. As simply and peacefully as I can. That's it. That's all that I want, okay?"

"Nope, not okay," Sophia strongly responded. "Not okay at all. What I just said wasn't some sort of a pep talk. It wasn't some insipid little phrase that people shout out after some tragedy then do nothing about what caused the tragedy. What I said wasn't just words. It isn't 'thoughts and prayers.' It isn't 'Cabot strong.' It isn't a worthless exercise. Because what *I'm* talking about is action. What *I* am talking about is the ability of the ladies Cabot to harness their emotional strength and take action. Action against those that wrong us. Action against those that would wrong others. Action against those who would prey upon the defenseless. Action, my dear. Quick, efficient, and *very effective* action."

"That's what I'm doing, Mom!" Lori roared back. "Don't you see that? Look at all the work that I'm putting in to defend myself in court! This is going to take hours and hours to compile and organize this shit! Take action? Just what the hell do you think that I've been doing all night?"

Sophia turned her grey head away in order to hide her slight chuckle. She realized that the tactic didn't work when she heard her daughter yell out, "What the hell is so funny?"

"Oh, my dear," Sophia answered as she attempted to extinguish her delight. "That is not the action that I am speaking about. Perhaps my words aren't enough. Perhaps you need to be *shown* what type of action I speak of. Perhaps you need to be *shown* just how your emotional strength can be harnessed and used to take such action. Yes. That is what must be done. Let's just change the subject for a moment, dear. What was it that was on your computer when I walked in?"

Lori felt her face turn red as she stammered, "Oh, nothing really. Just a stupid meme. It's no big deal."

"I see, I see," Sophia replied as she could feel her daughter's anger growing. "Could you please show it to me? I didn't really get a good look at it."

"Fine," Lori said as she opened the page on the social media account.

Sophia looked at the image of the provocatively dressed middle-aged woman and carefully read the caption.

Look on the bright side. They say divorce causes weight loss. Not from the stress, but from the fact he's taking you to the cleaners and you can't afford food! So, enjoy your new figure! Now you can be the slut that you've always wanted to be!

"Well, that certainly was mean-spirited and unnecessary," Sophia observed. "Just who is this man that sent this to you. And 'Liked' his own post?"

"He's nobody, Mom," Lori began explaining. "Nobody at all. Just one of my husband's neanderthal friends. He's just one man with some really backwards thoughts. He's nobody. It's nothing for me to get worked up about."

"Just *one man*, you say?" Sophia prodded further. "Well, this *one man* certainly seems to have quite a few followers, don't you think? Just look at how many men have 'Liked' his hurtful post. And it isn't just hurtful to *you*, dear. This is going to be hurtful for *every* woman who looks at it. This is going to hurt *every* woman who realizes just how many nean-derthals there really *are* in this world. He isn't just one man, dear. He is a microcosm of a movement. So, have you met this man, before?"

"Yeah, quite a few times, actually," Lori answered as she felt the gravity of her mother's words merging with her hatred for the simpleton. "He's a good friend of my husband, like I said. He came over to the house a bunch. Y'know, just typical guy stuff. They'd sit around and get drunk and watch sports or whatever. He's married with two daughters and a son. So, I suppose his son will turn out to be a sexist creep like him and his daughters will learn to be docile, little housewives or something. It's very sad."

"Yes, it is sad," Sophia continued to push. "Very sad indeed. Sad that such a man should have such influence over pliable children. Sad that such a hateful message should be liked by so many. Very sad, indeed. Is that all, dear? Is that the only interaction that you've had with him?"

"No," an increasingly red-faced Lori responded firmly. "No, he used to hit on me all the time. Suggest that we should do things together. He said that my husband wouldn't mind, and he was probably right about that. He was constantly winking at me and giving me creepy little smiles. One time as I was exiting our bathroom he was standing there. He pushed himself on me and started groping me. He grabbed my hair and tried to force me to kiss him while his hands were going up my dress. It was repulsive. It was disgusting. It made me feel like a useless whore."

"I see," Sophia calmly replied. "What a deplorable man he must be. And what did you do about it, dear?"

"I just got so angry," Lori began explaining in a rapid cadence. "I knew that if I told my husband he wouldn't believe me or wouldn't care. Morgan was fifteen at the time and just down the hallway. What if he tried that with *her*? I felt *helpless*. I felt *used*. I felt *worthless*. And as he continued groping me and trying to put his fingers in me and trying to kiss me, I just got angrier and angrier and I..."

Lori turned her tearful eyes away from her mother who said, "Yes, dear? Finish the story. What did you do? What did you do to this man who was *violating* you? What did you do to this man who was a *threat* to your innocent daughter? What did you do to this man who would send you such hurtful images during your most vulnerable time? What did you do to this man who has all these followers 'Liking' his repulsive posts? *What did you do?*"

"I'll *tell* you what I did!" an enraged Lori shouted out. "I kneed him in the balls! As hard as I could! And then when he bent over, I kneed him in the nose! I shattered his goddammed nose! And when he fell to the floor, I kicked him in the balls again! And again! And again! Until he vomited everywhere! *That's* what I did mother! *That's* what I did!"

Lori's convulsing body began lifting slightly off the floor as Sophia continued her targeted inquisition. "And how did that make you feel, dear?"

"I felt...I felt...*powerful*, mother!" Lori yelled out from her frothing mouth. "I felt *alive*! For the first time in a long time, I felt *empowered*! I felt *vindicated*! I felt *human*! I felt like a *woman*, mother!"

"And what do you feel *right now*, dear?" Sophia continued with her orchestrated agitation.

"I feel *angry* mother!" Lori screamed. "I feel so damned *angry* at him, and my husband, and all the men like him! I just want to tell them all! Tell them how they make me feel! Tell them how they make *all* of us feel! I feel angry and I feel helpless, and I want to feel important again, mother!" Lori once again heard the loud, repetitive chanting from the incantation of the book as her mother reached up and handed her floating daughter the laptop. *Contra eos qui suis vocibus alios opprimunt, habebunt locutions. Contra eos qui suis vocibus alios opprimunt, habebunt locutions. Contra eos qui suis vocibus alios opprimunt, habebunt locutions.*

"Then *do* it," Sophia ordered in a deep, sinister voice. "Regain your pride. Regain your power. Just one little expression of your anger. That is all that it will take. Just one little expression of your anger and you will regain your dignity."

The chanting pounded in Lori's brain as she glared at the post. She glared at all the 'Likes.' She glared at the man's name. She began cackling as she used her delicate finger to place her cursor over the choices of emojis. Her cackling increased in volume as the lights flickered in the living room. The television kept turning on and off. The microwave began beeping. And over it all was Lori's cackling.

Just before she pressed down on the computer's built-in mouse, her mind converted the Latin incantation to English.

Those who use their expressions to oppress others shall have their very expressions used against them.

The house suddenly fell into a tranquil silence. The lights remained on. The emotional chaos had ended. And Lori finally felt at peace as she looked upon her posted 'Angry' emoji with righteous satisfaction and dignified glee.

CHAPTER 7

LIKES

Lori's sweaty body went limp and collapsed upon the couch. "Oh, my God," she panted as she wiped the mop of wet blonde hair from her forehead. "That was better than the greatest sex that I've ever had! I feel exhausted and invigorated at the same time! What the hell just happened? It was like I was aware of everything that was happening but had no control. It was like I was being controlled by my emotions. No, that isn't quite right. It was like my emotions were marshalling some type of force. Almost like I was a general sending troops into battle or something. Am I crazy?"

Sophia softly chuckled before responding. "No, dear, you are not crazy. Not in the slightest. What just happened is that for the first time in your life you have experienced who you truly are. For the first time in your life, you have allowed yourself to experience your true emotions and have discovered the power that you can wield. I said it before, and I'll say it again. The will and strength of our ancestors course through our souls. Well, I suppose we have a few minutes before the show starts. The spirits that we summon aren't exactly…um…punctual. Yes, we have a few minutes before the effects of your actions are realized. So, I am going to take this opportunity to explain to you what just happened.

"Now, to start off with, don't think that you will feel this way every time this happens. The levitation. The frothing. The sweating. The...um...orgasm. That was all a result of this being your first time. Your first time truly connecting with your emotions. Your first time unleashing your emotional strength to summon them. It can all be quite exhilarating, until you get used to it. After a while it becomes just as natural as breathing. Oh, you will still feel invigorated and powerful, but certainly not to this extent."

"What the hell are you *talking about*, Mom?" Lori asked out of confusion. "I didn't summon *anybody*. I just responded to that vile post with an 'Angry' emoji. I didn't do anything *more* than that."

"Oh yes you did," Sophia replied. "To you, all you did was post a harmless little emoji. You did much more than that. You used that emoji as an outlet for your anger. You used that emoji to summon them. You used that emoji to ask them to exact your vengeance. You see, dear, when you combine that emoji with your intense anger and the summoning incantation from our book, well...that little emoji becomes anything *but* harmless. That emoji becomes your weapon that the spirits that you summoned shall use to exact your vengeance. As you will see in a few minutes, dear, that emoji is going to cause that dreadful man quite a bit of trouble. Oh, I just can't wait to see how the spirits will use it. They can be so creative at times."

Lori could only stare at her mother with bewilderment as Sophia continued. "You see, my dear, we are descendants of a long line of female mediums. Our lineage has always had a strong connection to the spiritual world. And we have always been drawn to spirits who are a bit...um...shall we say *mischievous*. Well, *mischievous* doesn't really do them justice. They are vengeful little bitches who absolutely *love* to see mortals get their come-uppance. Usually in very interesting and painful ways. For centuries, our family has created various incantations that can summon partic-ular spirits. Once we have stumbled upon one, we write them down in this book. This book that is bound by the charred flesh of one of our earliest ancestors. This book that has pages made from the skin of their would-be persecutors. This book that has our family's incantations written in our own blood. Here, let me show you one."

Sophia flipped the pages until she came across the final entry. "Yes, here it is," a reminiscent Sophia said. "I remember this as though it were yesterday. Of course, it wasn't. I created an incantation to summon a particularly nasty spirit. She really is quite fun. I wrote this incantation down on this page in my own blood. I remember watching as the page glowed slightly as it absorbed my bloody words into it. It was a rather silly incantation, I thought on that night, thirty years ago. The night that your father went out on his boat for the last time. I recited this incantation, *Imago tua cibus meus est. Meus cibus te faciet boom.* I picked up his picture and stared at it. The longer I stared the angrier I became. And the angrier that I became, the louder this incantation played in my mind. Over and over like I had no control over it. And I didn't. I had recited the incantation and that had summoned the spirit. And that spirit kept saying this to me over and over as my anger increased. Finally, my anger and my request became one. The spirit had been summoned and she now had my emotional strength to complete my requested task.

"I then could feel my eyes rolling back into my head and my soul was transported to where he was. I could see everything. I could see him bobbing in the ocean on his boat. I could see him whiling his time away looking at his girlie magazines. I could see him get yet another beer from his cooler. And I definitely saw his screaming body become consumed with flames after his boat exploded."

Sophia let out a loud, guttural laugh as she wiped tears of amusement from her cheeks before continuing. "You see, dear, the English translation of this Latin incantation is, *your image is my fuel. My fuel will make you go boom.* And that was it. Your dickhead, deadbeat dad was dead, and we left that home and moved here. Pretty simple, huh?"

"You *murdered* my *father?*" Lori exclaimed out of disbelief.

"Well, murder is such a loaded word, dear," Sophia responded calmly. "It holds such negative connotations. I prefer to think of it as

I blew the shit out of him, *literally*, and watched as his tortured body was scorched by deserving hellfire. But, potato, potawto. You call it what you wish, and I shall do the same. Do you want some popcorn? I can feel the spirit that you summoned arriving. You will be able to do that as well, over time. So, popcorn? Yes? No? Cat got your tongue? Well, I'm going to have some. You know how your mother loves a big bowl of buttery popcorn when she watches her stories."

A shocked Lori watched as her mother sauntered casually into the kitchen. Her mind raced as her analytical brain attempted to process what she had just heard come out of her mother's mouth. She was a descendent of mediums who have been creating incantations and writing them in this ancestral book made of flesh and blood to summon spirits to exact vengeance upon those that harmed us. *Right? Did I get that right? Is that what my mother just said? And she used this to murder my father? This is too freaky. But it does explain a lot. No. This can't be happening. This must be some sort of bad dream or bad whiskey or a bad joke that she's somehow playing on me. This can't be real. I can't be a descendent of witches. Witches aren't real.*

"Not witches, dear, mediums," Sophia said over the popping sound coming from the microwave. "Oh, sorry, dear, but until this little episode is over, we're a bit psychically connected, and I just couldn't help but overhear your thoughts. Yes, you heard me correctly. I couldn't have explained it better myself. And no, we are not witches. We are mediums. Witches cast spells and use potions and stuff to obtain a desired outcome. It might be vengeance, like us. Or love. Or prosperity. But their tactics are pretty hit and miss. If they don't combine their ingredients just right, their spells are useless. And there aren't very many of them. Most people who practice witchcraft truly don't have the gift. They just think it's cool and they get into the whole spiritual, connecting with nature thing. Which is fine, but most can't really cast spells.

"No, we are mediums. We have a direct line to the vengeful spirits in the universe. All we have to do is figure out the proper words to use to communicate with them. Then, we combine those words with our intense emotional energy. And the spirits are summoned and they do the rest. We are not witches. That would be just silly. And our tactics are *not* hit or miss. Our tactics are most *definitely* one hundred percent hit and hit. As you're about to find out. Do you still like a lot of salt on your popcorn, dear. And would you like a soda?"

Lori silently nodded and waited until her mother came into the room with a tray holding two bottles of soda, a saltshaker, and an overflowing plastic bowl of popcorn. "Ah, yes, the show is about to start," Sophia casually said as she positioned herself on the couch next to her dismayed daughter.

"Hey! Lighten up! This is gonna be fun!" Sophia declared as she picked up the book and flipped it to the page of Lori's incantation. She laid the book into her daughter's lap and said, "Now just place your hand over the incantation. Yes, dear, just like that. Tingles, doesn't it? Now, I'll take my hand and place it over yours so that I can be connected to you. I don't want to miss this. Now, just relax. Allow the soul of the summoned spirit to connect with yours. Yes, I can feel us being connected. We will be able to see what is going on. We shall be an invisible fly on the wall. Now this is the most important part. With your left hand, please pass me the salt. This popcorn is a bit bland."

———

"Henry! When are you coming to bed!" Henry's wife yelled to him from behind the closed door of his study.

"Yeah, yeah, yeah, I'll be there in a minute. Quit nagging me!" he yelled back before eagerly returning his delighted gaze to his computer screen. His giggling face glowed from the light on the screen as he said aloud to himself, "Oh man, that little bitch is gonna be sooooo pissed! Serves her right for divorcing one of my best friends. He always said that he knew she was a whore, and this just proves it. The little mouse got away from the cat so it could play. So, it could play with all the *hard cheese* that it wants. Doesn't explain why she always turned *me* down though. I'm still pissed about that.

And how she kneed me in the balls and broke my nose! What the hell was *that* all about? I know she was giving it up to just about everybody in the neighborhood. Well, that's what *he* thought, anyway. So, why not *me*? Hell, I've got more money than her husband. Work out more. Better hair. Don't know why she didn't just bend over like a good little girl and…wait a minute! *Now*, I get it! This little mouse doesn't want to play with hard cheese! This little mouse likes cats. *Pussy* cats! Just like her dyke daughter!

"Now, it all makes sense. She's a closeted dyke. That would explain why she didn't screw me. Or Mr. Henderson. Or …what was the name of that other senior partner again? Shit, I can't remember. Man, he had the hots for Lori though. Yeah, he always said…"

"Henry! Are you coming to bed? It's getting late!" the wife's voice bellowed out once again.

"I'll tell you what's getting late you nagging bitch," Henry muttered under his breath before yelling, "I know! I'm just finishing up a few things! Get out of my ass and give me a minute!"

He listened to his wife's angry footsteps stomp down the hallway before returning to his cruel entertainment. "Jesus, now what was I saying? Why is she always interrupting me? Needy much? Oh, yeah. Let's just go to my post on her page and see how many 'Likes' I'm getting."

Henry exploded into laughter when he saw the reactions. His ribs hurt from his immature guffawing when he saw one lonely 'Angry' emoji. "Really? That's your response? That's the best you can do? The little angry face? Jesus, Lori, where's your fight? Using emojis really doesn't do much to further civil discourse, that's for sure. Ah well, she always was pretty quiet. Maybe she can't spell or something. She's pretty, but I never thought that she was the brightest bulb.

"And speaking of pretty, what do we have here? Why we have a lovely little lady who 'Liked' my post. Well, what's *your* name darlin'? Yeah, *really* pretty. Wonder where she lives. Might have to get to know her and take one of my out-of-town hunting trips, heh, heh, heh."

The computer then made a PINGING sound as yet another 'Like' was added to the growing number. Immediately following the sound, Henry's face turned from glee to confused pain as he felt something thrust deep up into his backside. "What the hell was *that?*" he yelled out. "What the hell did she put in that pot roast? Damn. That really hurt."

Another PING was followed by yet another intensely painful intrusion. "Whoa! What the hell!" PING, "Ouch! What is going on?" PING "Oh Jesus, something *really big* keeps going all the way up my a..." PING "Jesus! Stop it!"

Henry frantically thought about what might be happening to him as he began feeling blood oozing out of his cavity. "Oh God, am I dying here?" he exclaimed before hearing another PING. "Ow! Stop it! Please, stop it!" He yelled out. "Oh Jesus. It's the computer. Every time I get a 'Like' I feel this sharp pain. I've gotta do something!"

He began lumbering toward the keyboard before another PING brought him to his knees. Blood was saturating his pajama bottoms while he crawled toward the office chair. PING. "Oh, God! I've gotta stop this! I've gotta delete that post!"

Henry was leaving a slimy trail of blood mixed with excrement as he crawled toward the computer. His disoriented, tortured mind thought that he heard the voices of two women laughing as he pulled his weakened body up to the computer. PING. "Oh my God! I'm dying!" he exclaimed as he fell back to the sticky, smelly floor.

Over and over and over, a 'Like' would be entered on his post. The computer would PING. And yet another violent thrust would enter deeply into his posterior, penetrating his intestines. Henry was sitting on his knees weeping. Every time he tried to move toward his computer there would be yet another PING and yet another painful penetration of his dark cavity. There was a final PING followed by a final vicious thrust. His battered intestines began evacuating out of his painfully stretched exit. The slimy entrails flowed out of him like a magician's never-ending scarf and pooled around his knees and feet. Henry's emaciated, pale face looked up. The last thing that he saw before collapsing forward onto his face was a glowing 'Angry' emoji. There was a loud THUD / SPLOSH as Henry's nose was broken again on the feces and blood covered hard-wood floor.

"Okay, Henry, that's it!" The wife yelled out. She threw open the door of the study and shrieked at the sight that was before her. Henry was lying face down on the floor surrounded by a pungent, brownish, red ooze. His legs and feet were encased in his own serpentine intestines. And every time the computer would PING his body would twitch forward as a two-foot-long blue thumbs up viciously buried itself into him once again.

His wife stood there in shock wondering what to do. It was obvious to her that her husband was deceased. And it was obvious, although unexplainable, what had caused his untimely death. The wife exhaled deeply and collected her thoughts. She looked up to the ceiling and smiled as a single tear rolled down her cheek. She clutched the crucifix that hung from her neck and silently mouthed, "Thank you," before saying aloud, "Wow. I knew that a lot of people liked his ass, but this is ridiculous."

CHAPTER 8

———————

TEMPEST IN A COFFEEPOT

Lori came rushing down the stairs the following morning to find her mother and daughter casually eating their steaming oatmeal. "Oh, my lord, sweetie," she said apologetically. "I'm so sorry. I've overslept. We need to get you to school."

"It's okay Mom," Morgan replied as oatmeal dribbled down her black lips. "I don't have to leave for a half-hour. Besides, Naomi's gonna pick me up. You know, this really wouldn't be a problem if my asshole Dad hadn't sold my car out of spite. We really need to be a two-car family."

"I know, I know," Lori responded as she attempted to keep her anger in check. She then thought to herself, *I really need to control my temper. I'm not sure what the hell happened last night, but it wasn't good. I think that I may have killed that man. I can't let that happen again. I need to just let things blow over. Deal with them reasonably. I believe my mother when she says we all have these powers. Now, I need to keep them bottled up. And my daughter's.*

Sophia wore a sly grin as she watched her daughter's face flush red, then return to its natural pale. "You know, I think that I might just have a car that would suit your needs, dear."

"Gramma," Morgan replied with a slight chuckle. "I love the

offer, but I would look like a complete dork driving around in that boxy sedan of yours. I mean, no offense, but it really is an old lady's car. But thanks for the offer. I can get by for a while. I'll be going off to college in less than a year anyway, so it's really not a big deal."

"Oh, but it *is* a big deal, dear," Sophia retorted. "Cars are a *very* big deal for teenagers. You need to be mobile. And you need to be mobile in something that will turn heads. And let everybody know just who they are dealing with. Something with an attitude. So, I am not speaking about *my* car, which is quite *dependable*, I might add. But it isn't for a seventeen-year-old young lady. Especially one with such…um…dark fashion sense. No, I have *another* car that has been in storage for decades. Thirty years, in fact. How about if I take this afternoon off and pick you up from school and we can go on a little test drive? If you like it, it's yours. Cool?"

"Well, what kind of car is it? It sounds really old," Morgan inquired.

"Oh, it *is* old, dear. *Quite* old. Let's just see if you like it, alright?" Sophia replied with a hint of knowing glee.

"Well, alright," Morgan said as she wiped her chin and began getting up from the table. "Thanks Gramma, I know that I will love it." She then passed her mother and mouthed; *I'm going to hate this car.*

A smiling Lori shook her head and sat at the table with her mother. "I thought that you had gotten rid of that thing years ago. I didn't think that you held on to it."

"Just waiting for the right owner, dear," Sophia replied as she got up and began rinsing her bowl in the sink. "I knew you had no interest in owning anything of your father's, and *I* certainly didn't want to drive it, but I just couldn't part with it. I've had many offers for it over the years, but it just felt like I needed to hang onto it for some reason. Probably one of our spirit friends whispering to me, don't you think? It may not have been owned by a special man, but that is one bitchin' car. And our Morgan is going to look damned hot driving around in it."

"So, Mom, about last night…" Lori tentatively began before

hearing her daughter answer her phone. "Yeah, hey Naomi. Yeah, I'm ready. Yeah, okay, I'll be watching for you. Okay, I got it. I'm hanging up now. Naomi, I'm…I'm hanging up now. Naomi…just stop…I'm hanging up now. Would you put the phone down and just focus on your driving? I'm hanging up…"

There was suddenly a loud crash outside of the home, followed by the beleaguered voice of Detective Connor O'Sullivan. "Oh, Naomi, how many times do I have to tell you to not talk on the phone…or at all, really…while you're driving? Just look at what you've done…again."

The ladies Cabot rushed outside to see Naomi's heavily dented red Mazda Miata sitting on their front lawn with their mailbox jutting out from its smoking grill. "Okay, okay, I'm really sorry," Naomi hastily said as she bounded out of her deceased car. "But I don't think that it's my fault and…oh, hi Sophia! Hi Morgan! Hi Miss Cabot or Mrs. Cabot or Lori. You never told me how to address you. I'll just call you Lori, that's okay, isn't it? You guys up and at 'em and ready for the day? Beautiful day, isn't it? Anyway, it really wasn't my fault. I was just talking to Morgan on the phone and the driveway just appeared, like out of nowhere, and its like a *really, really* sharp curve to get into the driveway and this big car is really hard to handle and…"

Naomi's relentless diatribe was interrupted by her exasperated uncle placing his hand firmly over her mouth. "Naomi, darling, please listen to me. First, this is at least the *third time* you have wrecked this car in six months. And from the looks of it, it might be the last. Secondly, this car is *not* difficult to handle. It is not much bigger than a go-cart. I'll take care of it…again. I'll put in the report that you swerved to miss a cat or something. I'll call a tow truck, but you need to pay to replace their mailbox, understand?"

Naomi began nodding her head vigorously as her stifled attempt at an apology continued. Connor's palm was wet from the onslaught of spittle as Naomi's mouth threw out a barrage of muffled words.

"It's, it's okay, Connor," a slightly irritated Sophia stated. "If you could just arrange to take this off my lawn, that would be wonderful.

No real harm done. Although I did love my mailbox. Oh well, what's done is done. Girls, why don't you climb into my sedan. I'll drive you to school today."

"Thanks for your understanding, Sophia," Connor replied as he mistakenly removed his hand from over Naomi's mouth.

"...course I'll pay for it. I'm so, so sorry. I'll get a new one that looks just like it. Or maybe I could rebuild it! How would that be? That would be a great project for me to work on. My parents always say that I need to find more projects to do with my hands and that I can do alone. This will be great! Morgan, do you want to help me? We'll have so much fun rebuilding the mailbox and..."

Naomi finally fell into silence when she heard Sophia yell out, "Naomi! Get in the goddam car! We're late!"

The nervously chuckling pair of Lori and Connor were left alone on the front lawn as they watched the sedan go down the street at the break-neck speed of eighteen miles an hour. "Oh, Lori, I'm so sorry about this," the red-faced Connor began. "Oh, that girl. She is the sweetest thing on this Earth, but she is just so...um...easily distracted."

"She's a space cadet," a laughing Lori contributed. "So, Connor, what brings you here? I must look a mess."

"Um no, actually, you don't," Connor stumbled in response. "You look really, um, well, that isn't important. I'm actually here on official business. Really bizarre official business. Could we go in and talk for a few minutes?"

Oh shit, I'm going to jail, Lori thought to herself as the pair entered the well-kept home. "Wow, that looks like a really old book," Connor said as he peered down on the coffee table. "I'm really into old books. Mind if I take a look at it?"

"Uh,uh,uh," was all that Lori could utter as she watched Connor pick the book up and begin flitting through the pages. "Wow, this really *is* old. Odd texture on this paper. And this ink is really interesting. What are all these passages written in? Latin? This is really cool. Family heirloom or flea market find?"

"Uh, uh, uh," was Lori's response before she collected herself.

"Uh, family heirloom, I think. It's my Mom's. Um, she's really pretty protective of it, so why don't I just put it up. We wouldn't want to spill our coffee on it. You would like a cup of coffee wouldn't you, Connor? Or should I call you 'Detective' since you're here on official business?"

Connor let out a hearty laugh and replied, "No, Lori, Connor will be just fine. With you, Connor will *always* be fine. And sure, I'll take a cup. Black, please."

Lori and Connor settled in on the couch. Connor took a sip of his coffee, placed the cup on the coaster on the end table and opened his notebook. "This is gonna sound really silly, Lori, but Boston PD wanted me to come by and check on something. Do you know a Henry Johnson?"

"Um, yes," Lori hesitantly answered as she averted her blue eyes from Connor's policeman's stare. "He wa..I mean *is* a friend of my husband. He's not a very nice man. I just know him through my husband. You know, the occasional dinner party and things like that."

"Well, *I'll* say he isn't a very nice man," Connor stated with a hint of anger. "I saw that post he left for you. Mean-spirited little cuss, wasn't he? Well, that's why I'm here. He's dead Lori. And, of course, Boston PD is looking into it because, well, because his death is a bit strange. You see, he died shortly after you responded to his post. You know, the little angry face you responded with. That's the least I woulda done, let me tell ya. But since you were the last person to have any negative interaction with him, Boston PD wants me to check out your alibi. So, where were you around 10:30 last night?"

"Well, I was here, with my Mom," Lori answered as Connor began scribbling in his notepad. "Uh-huh, uh-huh, and what were the two of you doing?" he asked.

"Oh, just looking at that old book actually. And eating popcorn," a nervous Lori answered.

"Sure, sure," Connor dutifully replied. "And just what experience do you have with witchcraft?"

Connor looked up and stared into Lori's frantic blue eyes before bursting into laughter. "Oh, I'm sorry, Lori, but I just can't do this with a straight face. That was, of course, a joke. It's just that the deceased's wife has a rather…um…interesting story. She said, oh I really shouldn't laugh at this. I'm sure that whatever she saw was horrible. But she said that she heard her husband screaming in his study, then silence. When she went in there, he was lying face down on the floor in a pool of his own blood and intestines and he was… um…I just don't know how to tell you this. Um, she said that she saw a giant blue 'thumbs up', um, *penetrating* him. Repeatedly. I'm sorry for the visual, Lori, but that was the story. Now obviously what she saw is impossible. We figure she's just in shock. But what is absolutely true is that he was, um, well, again, penetrated repeatedly until his, um, insides came out and he died. Most bizarre scene I've ever heard of.

"Anyway, Boston PD has to cover all their bases and since you left the little angry face, they wanted me to check out your alibi. I've already talked to the neighbors, and they said your car was in the drive all night, and it's a good hour's drive to get to that guy's house anyway, plus the wife said she didn't see anyone else in the house and the alarms were all set. So, nobody broke in. All she saw was a giant, blue 'thumbs up' screwing her husband to death. She's the obvious suspect, but so far there's no evidence. The coroner's report indicated that the approximate time of death was right before she called 911. And there aren't any weapons found so far that could have done that, um, damage. So, it's a real mystery. I'll have to speak with Sophia briefly too, but your alibi checks out. Nothing to worry about. And just between you and me, maybe it isn't such a bad thing that he isn't around anymore. Not a man that treats a woman like that. Just my two cents. Hey! Don't forget you still owe me that beer and trip down memory lane. Well, I'd better go. I have to file this report to Boston and…"

Connor's thought was interrupted as he opened the front door and once again looked upon Naomi's wreck. "Oh yeah. And I need to fill out a report for *this* and get *this* off your lawn. Oh, that girl. Well, thanks Lori. Gimme a call when you want to grab that beer, okay?"

"Uh, uh, uh, sure. I sure will," a slightly relieved Lori stammered as she closed the door and wiped the sweat from her forehead. "Oh shit," she said aloud to herself. "This is not good. Not good at all. I have to talk to Mom. Figure out how to prevent this from happening again."

Lori heard a chuckling woman's voice in her head. The chuckling turned to incessant chanting. *Contra eos qui suis vocibus alios opprimunt, habebunt locutions. Contra eos qui suis vocibus alios opprimunt, habebunt locutions. Contra eos qui suis vocibus alios opprimunt, habebunt locutions.*

"Stop it! Just stop it!" Lori yelled out. "Never again, do you understand? I will *never again* summon you! What we did was wrong! I will never again look in that book! Ever!"

The female spirit's voice let out a low cackle and responded in English. "You don't need to look in the book again, my dear. Not unless you wish to summon another spirit, which would be quite pointless because you already have me. I have been summoned. I have been connected to your emotions. The incantation is now a part of you. *I* am now a part of you. And together, you and I shall have some fun. Just like last night. But I'll leave you now. You need to get ready for work. But just know that I am always available to you. Your emotions will summon me when I am most needed. And you certainly will know when I have arrived. Have a nice day at work, Lori. Toodles."

"Cool," a profusely sweating Lori said aloud. "If it wasn't enough to have to battle my ex in court, and raise my daughter, and deal with my mother, and start a whole new career and life, now I get to deal with a vengeful spirit. Perfect. Great day. I may as well get showered and dressed. What could possibly go wrong?"

Lori returned to the living room dressed and ready to start her day. She went to pick up her purse from the coffee table and said to herself, "Didn't I put you on the shelf?" She lifted the ancient book and several folded papers fell out from behind the book's grisly cover. "What are these?" she said as she picked them up and sat on the couch. She carefully unfolded the first paper. Her eyes widened as she once again said, "What are *these?*"

———

"No, Naomi, I cannot give you a ride after school," Sophia said sternly for the third time as her parked sedan hummed in the drop-off lane of the high school. "Morgan and I are going to test drive a car. No, Naomi, I'm sorry but you cannot come with. Once again, Naomi, I'm sorry but you'll have to find your own way home. No, Naomi this is grandma, granddaughter bonding time. You cannot come this time. Naomi, would you *please* just be quiet and get out of the car!"

"Oh sure, sure, sure," the smiling Naomi cheerfully replied. "I totally understand. You and Morgan need your bonding time. No sweat. My Dad can probably pick me up. Or my Mom. Or Uncle Connor. Or maybe one of my friends, but they usually don't like me riding with them for some reason. Sometimes I get a ride from one of the teachers. They don't stay long. They just drop me off about a block from my house and go jetting off. They're probably busy with something."

"Naomi," Sophia attempted again in a controlled tone. "Please get out of my car before I rip your tongue out."

"Oh, okay, bye!" Naomi exclaimed as she bounded out of the car and stood next to an exasperated Morgan. "No worries! I'll see ya later! And...wow. That's about how fast my teachers drive off after *they* let me out. I guess your grandma's really busy too. Oh, hey Frank! How are you! I guess he didn't hear me..."

Morgan and Naomi walked down the bustling hallway of the high school heading toward their lockers. Morgan tried to tune out Naomi's relentless rambling and concentrate on what the other kids were saying as they reverentially parted and gave her a wide berth.

"Is that her?"

"Yeah, she's the one that messed Jasmine up."

"I heard she got up and threw her on the ground and stomped on her face."

"No, I heard she tripped her…um…several times."

"I heard that she cast a spell on her or something that made her ankles break and keep falling."

"Well, that's stupid, like that's even a thing."

"It *is* a thing! I've seen documentaries about it on the CW!"

"Those aren't documentaries. Those are…oh, never mind."

"I heard Jasmine's getting out of the hospital tonight and going home. Probably won't be in school for a while though."

Morgan smiled to herself as she heard the comments. She wasn't exactly sure what had happened to her nemesis yesterday, but she instinctively knew that she had played a part in Jasmine's misfortune. Her inability to control the chanting from the incantation in the book that repeated itself over and over and louder and louder as she became increasingly angry at Jasmine. And then, the accidents. Jasmine collapsing repeatedly and violently until she was battered and unconscious. Morgan did not know what had happened. But Morgan liked it. She couldn't help but look up and smile at a cute female classmate as she heard her say, "Whatever happened, I think it's cool. It's about time *someone* stood up to that bitch."

———

"Yes, dear, what is it?" Sophia said into her phone as she casually took a drag off her cigarette in the alley behind the diner. "And why aren't you at work today? Oh, you found them. Been reading them all day, huh? And your little spirit says she's connected to you, huh? Yeah, that happens sometimes. Alright. We'll talk about it when we get home. I was just about to pick Morgan up. We'll be home in an hour or so. Just don't worry about it. And don't worry about the cops. As you just read, I've had a few of these, um, incidents and have never been caught. It's no biggie. Well, I know *you* think that it's a biggie, but it really isn't dear. We'll be home in a while. And since you played hooky today, why don't you fix us dinner, alright? Okay, bye."

Morgan jumped into her grandmother's car and Sophia gunned the accelerator, allowing her sedan to speed away from the catastrophic effects of Hurricane Naomi. "Whew, made it," Sophia said as she relaxed into her driver's seat. "She's a nice girl, dear, but oh my lord."

"I know, I know," a chuckling Morgan replied. "But she's super sweet and would do just about anything for anyone. Plus, I kinda feel bad for her. Everybody pretty much avoids her because, well, you know, she just doesn't see it. She thinks that everybody is her friend and she's upbeat and sunny about everything. She doesn't hear what the other kids say about her or see them laughing at her. So, for better or worse, she's going to be my best friend."

"And *just* a friend, dear? She's awfully cute." Sophia suspiciously inquired as she wore a sly grin.

"Yes, Gramma, *just* a friend," a slightly embarrassed Morgan replied. "She may be cute, but I couldn't imagine, um, I just couldn't imagine, well, I just can't imagine. No, she may be cute, but she isn't my type. Hell, I'm only seventeen. I don't even know what my type *is*. It's kinda girls, but there have been guys I've been attracted to also. It's not like I'm attracted to any sort of body type or gender. I'm more attracted to personalities, I think. I don't know. Maybe I'm bi or something. I'm not going to get hung up on labels. I'm Morgan and I'll fall in love with whoever I fall in love with. And people can label it however they want. I just don't care. I'm not just whatever my sexuality turns out to be and I refuse to be completely defined by it. I'll get involved with whoever I get involved with and it really isn't anybody else's business, y'know? Plus, she's strictly into guys. Trust me. I think that I've heard her talk about pretty much every guy in school. Where in the hell are we going, anyway?"

"Right here, dear," Sophia replied as she pulled into the gravel driveway leading to a number of large storage garages. "Ah, yes, here it is," she said softly as her brakes squeaked to a halt in front of garage number twenty-three. *Oh please, let me like this car, Morgan* thought to herself. *I really can't hurt Gramma's feelings and I really don't want to look like a dork.*

Sophia unlocked the garage and pulled the metal door up revealing a large, sleek object covered in a green tarp. "Well, here it is!" Sophia exclaimed as she grasped a corner of the tarp. "Are you ready for this? Are you ready for the big reveal? Drumroll, please."

Morgan began laughing as she rapidly slapped her thighs with the palms of her black-nailed hands. "Let's see it Gramma!" she yelled out.

Morgan let out a gasp as Sophia whipped the tarp off the car. "Oh…my…God," a shocked Morgan stated quietly as a tear caused her black eyeliner to streak down her youthful face. "Oh, Gramma. This might be the most beautiful car that I've ever seen."

Morgan approached the monster and gently ran her fingertips alongside the jet-black steel. "I told you that you'd like it," Sophia haughtily stated. "Here it is, dear. The 1968 Pontiac Tempest. Black as the night. All red vinyl interior. Horizontal headlights. 320 horses under this massive hood. What do you think?"

"I think that it's just wonderful, Gramma," a nearly hyperventilating Morgan answered. "But why do you keep it here in storage? Why don't you drive it? This thing has got to be worth a fortune. I just can't accept it, Gramma."

"Yes, you *can* accept it, my dear," a slightly emotional Sophia replied. "This was your grandfather's prized possession. I don't know how many hours he spent waxing this thing. He loved this car more than he loved me. More than he loved his own daughter. He was such a vile man. But, hey! You gotta admit he had great taste in cars! And I just never wanted to drive it. Too much attention. And your mother wouldn't have wanted it. Not her style. But you, my dear. This car is perfect for you. This car deserves to be owned and driven by someone who cares about others. This car deserves to be relieved of the curse of ownership of that horrid man. This car deserves *you*. And *you* deserve *it*. Plus, those little bastards that go to your high school will cream when they see you in this! Come on! Let's take 'er for a spin!"

Sophia tossed the keys to her granddaughter and settled into the passenger seat. Morgan eased her trembling body behind the red steering wheel. She carefully clasped the seat belt and adjusted the rearview mirror. She looked into the mirror and saw the face of an overjoyed seventeen-year-old young lady. She felt around the steering column for the gear shift and said regretfully, "Aw shit, Gramma. I can't drive this. I can't drive a stick."

"Oh yes, you can, my dear," Sophia replied confidently as she pulled a piece of paper from her faded denim pocket. "I thought that might be an issue, so I borrowed a little saying from my book. Well, *our* book. Here. Just read this, dear. Read this and start the engine."

Morgan unfolded the paper and looked at the incantation. Her young face held a confused expression as she looked up at her smiling, nodding grandmother. She shrugged her shoulders in resignation, sighed, and said, "Habeo potestatem equi mei. et equus meus in aeternum portabit me. But what does this mean, Gramma?"

Sophia chuckled slightly and responded, "It means, 'I have full control over my steed. And my steed shall carry me forever.' Now start the car dear. Trust me. You *and* your car are in good hands, heh, heh, heh."

There were a pair of cackling female voices in a black blur streaking in and around the streets of Plymouth. Morgan was swept away with ecstasy as she effortlessly shifted her steed from one gear to the next. She squealed with delight as she would hit the third gear and the car's engine would smoothly accelerate. "Oh my God, Gramma!" Morgan exclaimed. "I feel like I'm flying!"

The black behemoth came whipping around the corner of a well-to-do neighborhood. On the side of the street, a young woman in a wheelchair was being pushed onto her newly installed ramp that ran from the curb to her front door. The Tempest's front tire was quickly approaching a large puddle. Morgan let out a sadistic laugh as she looked in her rearview mirror and saw a tidal wave of water saturating the chair bound young woman and her parents. Her maniacal laughter increased as she heard the wailing Jasmine scream out, 'WHHHHYYYY?"

Chapter 9

Unfortunate Trips

"Oh, my lord, Morgan!" Sophia yelled out. "You just soaked that poor girl in a wheelchair!"

"Yeah, I *know*, heh, heh, heh," Morgan replied with an evil sneer. "But she isn't a poor girl, Gramma. She's a little bitch who bullies everybody at school, including me and Naomi."

"Oh, I see," Sophia responded as she mirrored her granddaughter's evil sneer. She fondly gazed at Morgan's youthful face and saw herself from fifty-four years earlier. "So, did you have a run-in with this girl yesterday?"

"Yeah, it was really weird Gramma," Morgan answered. "I don't even know how to describe it. I've been wanting to talk to someone about what happened yesterday, but it's just so weird that I can't find the words. I don't think that you'd understand."

"Well, give it a try," Sophia said as the big, bad, black Tempest cruised slowly up to a stop light. "I've been around the block a time or two and I think that you might be surprised at what I may understand."

"Alrightythen," Morgan answered as the light turned green and the Tempest's engine once again roared to life. "Well, it kinda started yesterday morning. You had some old book out and I just happened to look at one of the passages. I can't remember exactly what it said." At that moment a whispering voice in Morgan's head said, *Cum verba irae me moveant tua, illa ipsa verba offendes.*

"Oh yeah, that was it," Morgan continued. The passage in the book read, 'Cum verba irae me moveant tua, illa ipsa verba offendes.' Weird, huh? Anyway, I had that passage in my head all day. It was kinda like when you get a song stuck in your head and it just keeps playing over and over, y'know? Anyway, Naomi and I were eating lunch and these three 'popular girl' bitches came over to us. The one in the middle, Jasmine, started giving me shit. Like, she was really cruel, Gramma. And the more she harassed me, the angrier I got, and the angrier I got, the louder that saying kept getting in my head until I could barely hear anything else. It was like it took over my brain or something. So, Jasmine lets out her last insult, turns to leave and her ankle just snapped! And she fell face first on the floor and demolished her nose. There was blood *everywhere*, Gramma! Her friends tried to get her up and she fell *again* and like knocked her teeth out. Then the school staff tried to get her up and her *other* ankle snapped, and she fell *again* and knocked herself out. Then, once she was unconscious, the voice in my head just laughed for a second then disappeared. I mean, it was pretty cool, but I think that I might be insane. Like, I feel like I caused that somehow, but I didn't lay a finger on her Gramma! I swear! I was just sitting there!"

"I see," Sophia calmly replied as she continued to wear a sly grin. "Well dear, you are not insane. And I understand perfectly what happened. I need to speak with your mother anyway, so we may as well kill the two birds. Turn left here, dear. We need to get back home now."

"Hi Mom!" Morgan yelled out as she entered her new home and flung her backpack onto a chair. The backpack teetered precariously on the edge of the chair for a moment before tumbling onto the floor. Morgan looked down at it, shrugged and proceeded to the kitchen. "We got any chips and dip? I'm starving!"

"Morgan," Lori replied as she picked up the abandoned bookbag and placed it neatly upon the chair. "I have dinner on. It will be ready in about a half-hour, so no snacks."

"But Maaaawm!" Morgan yelled back in a whiney voice. "I'm *starvin'*! I need *sustenance*! I'm growing *weak* from the hunger! I might pass out and *die!*"

Lori looked at her histrionic daughter with her arms folded and said, "Oh, shut up. Well, at least we know you'll never be an actress. That was pathetic. Just go upstairs for a while. I need to speak with your grandmother about something. And take your bookbag with you."

"Fine! Gaaaaawd! Why do you make me suffer?" Morgan exclaimed as she grabbed her bookbag and began stomping up the staircase. A chuckling Sophia then said, "Um, Lori, dear. I think that Morgan needs to stay and listen to our little conversation."

"No, Mom," Lori said quietly out of the side of her mouth. "You know what we're talking about. Morgan isn't to hear about that. Ever. Do you understand?"

"Oh, I understand *perfectly*, dear," Sophia casually responded as she went to the bookcase and retrieved her book. Morgan stood on the staircase and watched the scene play out with an inquisitive look on her face as her grandmother continued. "And what *you* don't understand is that our Morgan *needs* to hear this conversation. Our Morgan needs answers. Because our Morgan has *already* made a connection."

"Oh, shit," Lori stated as she fell onto the couch and held her worried head in her trembling hands. "What happened?"

Following an overly dramatic reenactment by Morgan about Jasmine's misfortune, Lori said, "Okay. Where do we start?"

"Why don't *you* start dear?" Sophia answered. "Why don't *you* explain to your daughter what is going on? I want to make sure you understand it. And then, we can talk about those papers that fell out of the book."

"Fine," Lori reluctantly conceded. "Listen, sweetie. I guess there's no way to do this except to just come out with it. We, the ladies Cabot, are descendants of a long line of female mediums. That means that we can connect with spirits and call on them to do our… um…*bidding*. And this book contains various incantations that can summon specific spirits that do our…um…*bidding* in ways that are unique to them. So, what happens is that when we get very angry and recite an incantation, then we summon and connect with that spirit. And that spirit uses our anger to exact our revenge on whoever has wronged us. And that is why sweetie, we must always keep our emotions in check. We must never allow ourselves to get overly angry. And we must never look at any other incantations in that book. Ever. This is a power that can cause great harm. That Jasmine may be a bully, but she didn't deserve that. And that man who, um, never mind. You don't need to know that. We just need to remember to keep our emotions in check and to never look in that book again and we won't have to worry about it. Okay?"

"Well, that's bullshit," Sophia muttered under her breath.

"What's that, Mom?" Lori sneered back.

"I *said*," Sophia repeated loudly, "that's *bullshit*! We have a gift, girls. We have the ability to right the wrongs that have been committed against us. Listen, we aren't able to summon and use the spirits unless we are *really* angry. And the spirits won't do anything if a person isn't *really* deserving of it. Just think! If these assholes are treating *us* this way, what the hell do you think that they're doing to *other* people in their lives? Their spouses? Their children? Their neighbors? Their employees or co-workers? An asshole is an asshole is an asshole. And we have the ability to eliminate some of them. So, we do *not* need to keep our emotions bottled up. We need to let them loose and use this book to summon the spirits who will provide just a little bit of justice in this mean-spirited, messed-up world. And may I just add, little miss reasonable, that *you* do not *need* to look in the book anymore. The spirit that you connected with likes you. She has bonded with you. She thinks that you're cool for some unexplained reason because you are the furthest thing from cool that there is. I mean, you might want to try to wear something a bit more fashionable than your sensible shoes and business slacks. Just sayin'. And now, every time you get angry, that spirit is going to come to your rescue. *Every* time. She is burrowed in your brain. She is burrowed in your soul. And there's not a damn thing that you can do about it."

"Oh yes there is," a defiant Lori countered. "As I said, I can control my emotions. I can go through life without flying off the handle. I can deal with my problems rationally. I will *not* be held prisoner by my emotions."

"Yes, you will be," Sophia retorted. "What you are describing *is* a prison. A prison where you never allow yourself to feel. To truly feel love or joy or anger. If you keep all of that bottled up, Lori, there will be repercussions. It simply is not healthy. Not for anyone, but *especially* not for us. We are not wired that way and our bodies and souls and psyches will react. And not in a nice way. You just need to resign yourself to the fact that we are mediums, and we exist to right some of the wrongs in the world.

"Here, let's just use those papers that fell out as an example. You want to know why I kept folded up obituaries with an incantation stapled to them? You want to know if I was responsible for these deaths? Well, little miss thing, the answer to the first question is because I like my keepsakes and this shit isn't exactly something you can take a picture of for posterity. And the answer to the second question is 'yes.' I am absolutely responsible for those deaths. I was wronged. I became angry. I summoned a spirit. And they did the rest. I am responsible and do not regret *anything* that I have done. Why is it that it is always the victim who fights back the one who should feel sorry? Not the asshole that wronged somebody. It's always the victim who has been wronged that is persecuted. If the dickhead wasn't an asshole in the first place, then he wouldn't have anything to worry about, now, would he? I will *not* allow myself to be victimized again for fighting back and righting a wrong. And neither should you.

"Okay, let's get started. But before I go down memory lane, why don't *you* tell your daughter about *your* little adventure last night? And Morgan, when the three of us speak like this, it's like Vegas, got it? Not one word to anyone outside of our circle. Do you understand?" A wide-eyed and enthralled Morgan nodded her head vigorously as she thought, *this is soooo cool.*

"This isn't funny! This is serious! I *killed* a guy last night!" Lori screamed at her guffawing mother and daughter who were bent over and nearly wetting themselves from laughter after hearing about Lori's victim. "But it *is* funny, Mom!" Morgan joyously yelled back. "That guy was a total creep to me and the way he died! Oh my God, getting screwed to death up the ass by a giant 'Like!' This is classic!"

"Yeah, you think it's funny?" Lori countered. "Okay, Mom. Why don't *you* tell her what you did to her grandfather. You know, the guy whose car she's now driving."

"You guys, this really isn't funny," Lori stated solemnly to the tittering pair following Sophia's final utterance of 'BOOM'! Lori could feel herself longing to laugh along with them. But she couldn't. She couldn't allow herself to feel the unbridled joy that her family was experiencing. So, she just sat there and kept the lid on her emotional boiling pot.

Sophia's stories continued. With each subsequent unfolding of an obituary, Sophia would stare at the paper for a moment with fondness, then begin. "And that's what I did to that asshole so-called "reviewer." Made him choke on his own words. Now, what's this one?"

"So, that banker messed around with my numbers so that my loan would be called in early just so some scumbag rich friend of his could buy *my diner* out from under me. Now, I must say, some of these incantations are a bit silly, but, hey, any port in a storm, am I right? The English translation of *this* one is 'Have a nice trip. See you next fall.' And, oops. Off the cliff he goes. I guess his face was barely recognizable after his little tumble, heh, heh, heh."

"Oh yeah, that dickhead meat distributor. He kept jacking up my prices and told me that it was a supply chain issue or some bullshit. But then I checked around and all the *other* restaurants weren't getting jerked around. Or, should I say that all the other *male owned* restaurants weren't getting jerked around. So, a huge pallet of frozen ground beef came tumbling down on his head. I was disappointed when I heard his neck snap when all that frozen beef fell on him. I was hoping to watch him suffocate for a bit. But que sera sera. Dead is dead, I guess. His son has been cool to deal with, though. And pretty cute. If only I were a few years younger. Screw it. Maybe he's into old broads. Maybe I should corner him in the freezer sometime and see what happens."

"Oh yes! That peeping tom! You remember him, Lori. This creepy bastard was peeping in your window when you were a teenager. And if he's doing that to *you* then he's probably doing some other twisted shit. So, once again, just a little nudge from our tripping spirit and SNAP! Right on the goddam Plymouth rock. While a bunch of tourists were watching too! What poetic justice. He liked to watch young girls at their most vulnerable and a bunch of hicks from the Midwest got to watch him twitch on granite until he died. That was a fun day."

"Your first boyfriend. You really have never had good taste in men, have you dear? Do you remember what he tried to make you do? Then how he ruined your reputation when you wouldn't? Oh, Lori! I think that I used *your* new little spirit friend for that one! Yup, here's the translation. Those who use their expressions to oppress others shall have their very expressions used against them. Same bitch that 'Liked' the guy up the ass last night. I mean, this kid *did* say that you could deep throat a javelin, so kinda appropriate don't you think? That was one messed up track meet."

"Well, may as well go down the list. Here's your second boyfriend. He really was a little freak. And how was I to know that he was into erotic asphyxiation? Hell, this one maybe wasn't my fault. But I'm taking credit for it anyway."

"Your fourth boyfriend. Easy one. Car accident. Here's the translation. Your steed will betray you. Kinda the opposite of the spirit who taught you how to drive a stick today, Morgan. Huh, we seem to have skipped one. Who was your third boyfriend?"

Lori felt as though she couldn't breathe. Throughout her mother's tales, she was struggling to control the glee that she felt from her mother's stories and the anger she felt at her for exposing her daughter to this outrageousness. When she heard her mother ask about her third boyfriend, a new emotion emerged. One that she could not stifle. "Um, that would be Connor. Connor O'Sullivan," she said breathily as her face turned red. "I'm not sure he was ever technically my boyfriend. We just went out a few times. Held hands once." Lori once again bottled up her feelings and changed the subject. "What about this last one, Mom? What about this article about the bagboy who suddenly went mute?"

"Oh yeah, that little prick," Sophia said in a satisfied tone. "Hey! I didn't kill him! He's still alive so get off my ass! He just kept calling me an old hag. A bunch of times! It really pissed me off, so one day he woke up and...he couldn't make a peep. But do you know what that little bastard did after that? He couldn't speak so he would flip me off every time he saw me! What an asshole! Well, he can't do *that* anymore either. His hands are now crippled, heh, heh, heh. Oh shit! The pots boiling over!"

Sophia sprinted out of the room and took the boiling over pot off the stove. "Shit. Mac and Cheese is ruined! Wanna get a pizza?" She then ran back into the living room after she heard Morgan yell out, "Mom!"

"Ah, shit. I thought this might happen," Sophia muttered as she looked down upon her shaking, comatose, and frothing daughter. "Yep, I guess the Mac and Cheese isn't the *only* pot that's boiling over. You see, Morgan? This is what happens to us when we try to suppress our emotions. This is what happens when we don't take the lid off the pot. We have to release the pressure or else our entire system shuts down. And just look. She's wet herself. Dammit, now I'll have to get the cushion cleaned. I guess thinking about Connor took her over the edge. Too many intense emotions to try to control.

Alright, let's drag her out to the Tempest. We'll get there faster in that."

"G-get where?" a distressed Morgan asked through her tears.

Sophia let out another sly chuckle and said, "Well, I need to get some herbs from him anyway, so it won't be a *completely* wasted trip. Come on. Let's get this pathetic thing to the car. Maybe *now* she'll listen to me. Yes, I guess it's time for you two to meet Papa Doc."

Chapter 10

Voodoo Wanna Dance?

"Gramma, she isn't responding!" a frantic Morgan yelled out as Sophia whipped the Tempest around the sharp curves of a vast cranberry bog on the outskirts of Plymouth County. "She's just staring straight ahead and sweating and frothing from the mouth! Please, hurry!"

"She will be fine, dear," Sophia calmly replied. "She isn't in any pain. She is just shut down. Again, this is what happens when we keep our emotions bottled up. If we deny and disregard our feelings, they will fight to find a way to come out. She cannot respond to you right now because she cannot hear you. She is being bombarded by her emotions. She is fighting to keep her anger and joy in check and those very emotions are battling to come to the surface. It is a stalemate. It could last for days. Weeks even. Until her emotions finally break through. But there's no sense in wasting all that time. So, we'll just go visit someone to break the stalemate. She'll be just fine in a little while, dear. Don't you worry."

"What is that sound?" Morgan asked about the sudden loud thumping of heavy bass as the Tempest glided around one final curve and pulled into a gravel drive. "And all those lights?"

Sophia chuckled as the bass rattled the car's glass and a kaleidoscopic light show was penetrating through the windows of a large wooden shack. "Oh, yes. Tuesday night dance party. Well, I guess it doesn't matter *what* night it is. Papa Doc does enjoy his dance parties. Now Morgan, don't freak out over what you're about to see. Leave your mother in the car for a moment. We don't want her to get hit in the head by some bimbo's flailing tits. And believe me, there *will* be flailing tits."

Sophia parked the car in front of the tattered building's door. She turned the doorknob and she and Morgan were immediately bombarded by thumping rhythms and blinding, swirling disco lights. In the middle of the makeshift dance floor were thirteen scantily clad, gyrating beauties. The overhead lights were glinting off their short sequined dresses, showering the room in thin colorful beams of light. Their sweaty, made-up faces were ecstatic as they writhed suggestively to the never-ending percussive beats. And their tits were indeed flailing as the thin dress fabric struggled to contain them.

Morgan's eyes widened as she saw what was in the center of this frenzied circle. There was a one-hundred-and-thirteen-year-old man who was wearing a black leather biker jacket and black leather biker cap. His hunched over torso was being supported by canes that his withered hands were gripping. His haggard face wore a huge smile as his denim clad legs were gyrating, kicking, bending, and convulsing in a perfect rhythm to the explosion of beats.

Sophia glided her way around the entranced, sweat-soaked group of revelers to the stereo. She pushed the power button, and the room was instantly encased in silence. "Aaaaaaw, what happened? Did I blow another receiver?" The old man lamented. He then smiled as he looked upon the familiar face of his old friend.

"Why, Sophia! How nice to see you my dear!" He yelled out as his ears continued to throb. "To what do I owe the pleasure? Wanna dance? It's been years since you've come to one of my soirees, so I bet you're ready to get your groove on, am I right? Come on, Sophia. Turn the stereo back on and let's boogie!"

"I'm sorry for the intrusion, Papa Doc," Sophia answered. "But this isn't a social call. I need your help. *We* need your help."

The old man looked behind him toward what his friend's eyes had focused on. "My lord," he said. "Could this be? Is this your Lori? She looks so young."

"No, this isn't Lori. This is Lori's daughter, my granddaughter, Morgan," Sophia answered.

Papa Doc raised his head as far as his bent-over frame would allow and smiled at the black-garbed young woman standing in front of him. "Why, Morgan! I have heard so much about you! And I just love your outfit! Oh, this is going to be fun! Girls! Go in the back room and pull out the short, black robes! Put on some black makeup and come back in! I'll cue up some Cure, Bauhaus, maybe a little Sisters of Mercy. We're about to throw ourselves a Goth dance party!"

Morgan's jaw was agape as her grandmother returned to her side. "I'm sorry, Papa Doc, but that isn't why we're here. You asked about my daughter. Well, she's in the car. And she needs you."

"Aaaaaw, shit," one of dancers stated as she poured herself a drink at the tower of milk carton crates that served as the bar. "Leave it to a *medium* to screw up the night."

"Listen you witchy bitch," Sophia immediately countered. "Do you *really* want to make me angry?"

"Ladies, ladies," Papa Doc stated as he pulled himself between the two near-combatants. "Come now. This is a party. And we're all friends. There's plenty of Papa Doc to go around for everybody. Let me just help my old friend out and then we'll get back to getting it on!"

The thirteen sweaty women looked into the intense eyes of Sophia. One of them shivered before saying, "Naw. Come on, girls. She isn't worth it. Let's fly up to Boston and go to a club. There'll be a better class of people there."

"Oh, no," Papa Doc pleaded. "You don't have to go. I'm sure this won't take me long. Just have a drink and cool off. Then, we'll get this thing cranked back up!"

"It's okay, Papa Doc," one of the women stated as each of them went to a dingy corner and picked up a broom. "We'll be back tomorrow night. When it isn't so *crowded*." She bent over and gave Papa Doc a light kiss on the top of his head before straddling her broomstick. The thirteen women levitated a few feet off the ground before the back door blew open. There was the sound of multiple women cackling as the women flew out of the shack and into the cooling, moonlit night.

"What the hell was *that*?" a shocked Morgan exclaimed.

"Witches," Sophia bluntly answered. "Little witch bitches. Real ones, too. Not those weekend warrior, gazing at crystals, dancing naked in the forest posers. Those are the real deal. The power to harness nature. And the arrogant attitude that goes along with it. They aren't our kind, Morgan. Just steer clear of them. You might pick up some bad habits. And you *definitely* will pick up a social disease from those skanks."

"Really, Gramma?" Morgan stated in a disappointed tone as she rolled her eyes and folded her arms in disgust. "Even you? Even in the world of the supernatural there's cliques? Rivalries? Pettiness? What is this? High School for the psychically enhanced? Why can't you just appreciate them for who they are? And why can't they appreciate us for who *we* are? Why don't we embrace each other's differences and work together? The world would be a much better place if we just put aside all the jealousy, and competition, and unjustified hatred. Why can't we do that Gramma? Why can't we stop the bigotry?"

"Because they're witches," an unblinking Sophia answered. "Did you not hear me? They are *witches*. And witches are bitches. Really, Papa Doc, why do you hang out with them?"

"You're kidding, right?" Papa Doc snickered. "You *did* see them dancing, didn't you? And you ask why I *hang out* with them? Don't be silly, dear. They may be a bit…um…high strung. And arrogant. And high maintenance. But damn, can they cut a rug! Come on, go get your daughter out of the car. Let's just see what we're dealing with here."

Morgan and Sophia laid Lori down on a large waterbed in Papa Doc's bedroom. Their dark silhouettes shifted on the walls and ceiling to the casual rhythm of a red lava lamp as black light posters gave off an eerie glow.

Papa Doc looked deeply into Lori's comatose eyes and said, "Emotional shock, huh? You always did say this would happen to her. Yep, pretty bad case of it too. Well, we'll just get her fixed right up. I believe that I have just the thing." Morgan and Sophia looked on as Papa Doc shuffled his way over to a large oak table that was covered in a disheveled array of small glass bottles, foliage, human skulls and bones, and an ecstatic encaged gerbil that was running on his treadmill.

"Oh Gary," Papa Doc said to his beloved pet. "Now where did I put that concoction? Nope, that isn't it. Not this one either. Oooooo, I've been looking for this. Oh, Sophia, here are those herbs that you were wanting. They are so good in a marinara. Ah, here it is. My own special recipe. I'll just rub a bit on her forehead and a bit over her heart, say a little something to our healing spirit, and that should be it. Sophia, I do need a bit of an assist here."

Papa Doc leaned over the bed as Sophia stood behind him and held him upright. He poured a black powder out of the bottle and onto the tip of his wrinkled right index finger. He rubbed a small amount on Lori's forehead, then under her shirt over her heart. "A little dab'll do ya," he said as he capped the bottle and tossed it haphazardly back onto the oak table. There was the clinking sound of bottles falling over before he placed one hand over Lori's head and another over her heart. "And don't worry," he said to the suspicious face of Morgan. "I am not feeling your mother up. I'm not into cheap thrills. My hands need to be placed here. Just think of me as a doctor. Because I am. I am Papa Doc."

The entire room began glowing in a dark green and there was the sound of cracking bones as Papa Doc righted his fragile frame. His brown eyes turned red and his pale, dry lips turned upward in a mischievous grin. A strong gust of wind began whipping the curtains and black light posters around the room. "Oh Morgan, would you please close the window?" Papa Doc requested. "I didn't know it was supposed to be so windy tonight."

He then stared into the wide-open blue eyes of Lori and said in a dark voice, "Je vous libère de votre prison émotionnelle. Votre tête et votre cœur sont maintenant unis et travailleront ensemble pour exploiter votre force émotionnelle. Ce jour est votre éveil émotionnel. Ce jour est le premier jour de votre vraie vie.

"Well, that should do it," he said in a satisfied tone as his spine cracked back into its original arched position. The only light was now coming from the red lava lamp and the only sound was coming from Gary's treadmill. "Anyone want a drink? We have a few minutes to kill."

"This is so freaky," Morgan said to her grandmother. Sophia smiled at her and poured her a whiskey. "Here. Don't tell your mother." She then retrieved two more glasses from the unmatched rummage sale menagerie and poured drinks for herself and Papa Doc. The three of them settled onto their respective hardwood chairs and casually sipped their drinks as they waited.

"Blech," a grimacing Morgan said as she downed her first drink. "How do you people drink this shit? And if you don't like witches, Gramma, then why did you bring Mom to a witch for his help? And what was it that you said to her, Papa Doc? What was that language?"

"Because my lovely," Papa Doc answered. "I am not a witch. Not even close. I am a voodoo priest. Been one for many, many decades. And that language was French. And what I said was, 'I free you from your emotional prison. Your head and your heart are now united and shall work together to harness your emotional strength. This day is your emotional awakening. This day is the first day of your true life.' Yup, that's what I said."

"Um," a confused Morgan replied. "I thought that voodoo priests, well, if they were actually *real*, were like, Jamaican or something. You're like the whitest dude I've ever seen."

"Well, *that's* a bit racist and prejudicial of you, don't you think?" Papa Doc answered as Sophia covered her mouth with her hand to stifle her laughter. "You know, White men can be voodoo priests just as easily as Black men. It's that very attitude that drove me out of Louisianna and to this little berg. Oh, they were nice to me to my face. Would say that 'I was one of the good ones.' But did I ever get invited to their parties? No. Out to dinner? No. Maybe catch a movie? No. They were embarrassed to be seen with me. It was quite hurtful. So, I moved up here seventy years ago. And I've been partying ever since. I've met all kinds of nice folks who aren't as biased as that closed off club back home throwing their swamp hootenannies.

"Yes, I've made all sorts of friends from all walks of life. Regular humans, mediums, and yes witches. I could care less about one's race or sexual proclivities or religion or special abilities. All that I care about is if someone is up for a good time. You wanna dance? Then you're alright by me. But if you have a stick, broom or otherwise, up your ass, then I simply don't have the time of day for you. That's why I've never understood these silly rivalries. Black voodoo versus White voodoo. Mediums versus witches. Vampires versus werewolves. It's all so pointless. I am a voodoo priest. I am a healer. That is what I do. I summon the healing spirits and with the help of a few carefully combined ingredients, can heal others.

"If only we could all learn to work together rather than against one another. Just think of it. My ability to heal. The witches' ability to cast spells and bend nature to their will. Your ability to right wrongs. Just think of what we could accomplish if we worked together. Just think of the example that we could set for the rest of humanity. Just think of the better world that we could create. But no. We are *just* as bigoted, and hate filled as our less evolved counterparts. I find it to be quite sad."

"Well," Morgan began to inquire as her mind was whirling. "What about the vampires? Are *they* real? How do *they* fit into all of this?"

"Vampires?" Papa Doc roared back in laughter. "Oh, the vampires are worthless. They are *literally* the leeches of this earth. Always skulking about in the dead of night looking for someone to suck on.

I don't say this lightly, but vampires *literally* suck. And don't get me started on the goddammed werewolves! All *they* do is exacerbate the flea problem! Vampires and werewolves. They are both just dreadful."

"Throw good parties, though," Sophia contributed. "Yeah, that's true," Papa Doc conceded. "But I have difficulty dancing on a dance floor that's covered in blood, so I haven't been to one of *those* events in some time. How do you think my back got this way? This isn't from old age. It's from doing *The Electric Slide* on a blood-soaked dance floor at some vampire rave back in '92. My ankle went out from under me, and I landed awkwardly on this delightful young lady who ended up being somebody's meal, and my lower back just cracked. I tried to use my voodoo powers to heal myself, but the spirit wouldn't do my bidding. Said that I should have known better than to party with vampires and my crippled state was my penance. What a dickhead. I've never tried to call on him again, let me tell you. Anyway, the point is, we all need to learn how to work together and combine our experiences and talents to make the world a better place. Except for vampires and werewolves. Those assholes are deplorable."

At that moment, the bedroom door opened. An invigorated Lori stood in the doorway. Her confused blue eyes darted around the room as she tried to orient herself. She saw her mother and daughter's relieved faces. She smiled, wiped the drool from her lips and said, "God, I feel *great*. I need a drink. And I wanna dance."

CHAPTER 11

TAILGATING

"So how are you feeling, dear?" Sophia inquired of her awakening daughter as an enthralled Morgan looked on awaiting the response. Lori sat down at the kitchen table and poured herself a glass of orange juice. She lifted her relaxed face and casually glanced into the blue eyes of her daughter and mother. She let out a light sigh and said, "I'm not sure I can describe it. I don't think that I've felt like this before. I don't think that I've felt this amount of emotion, both in intensity and number. I don't know. I feel relaxed. I mean, like more calm and at ease than I've ever been. I feel strong. Empowered, y'know, like I can take on the world. And I don't feel any fear. Nor do I feel any guilt. It's like I instinctively know that what was done to that man was justified somehow. It goes against everything that I've always believed, but I just don't feel guilty about it. I feel vindicated. But Mom, I can't do this anymore. I don't know what I'm doing. What if I use this power to hurt someone that doesn't deserve it? What if I abuse it in some way?"

"That isn't possible, dear," Sophia calmly answered as Morgan wiped a soggy corn flake and stream of milk from her attentive face. "The spirits won't allow it. They will not take action against somebody who truly doesn't deserve it. Nor will they take more action than is necessary. If someone deserves nothing, then they will do nothing, regardless of your request. If someone deserves a bit of come-uppance, then that is what they will receive. Like Morgan's little nemesis that got her face rearranged the other day. Sometimes, the retribution isn't all that serious. Well, *comparatively* speaking, heh, heh, heh. But there are many deplorable people in this world, dear. Horrible, malicious people who walk amongst us every day. People who hide their evil deeds from society. Underneath their shiny respectable veneer is nothing but rot. Regardless of what might seem to be a petty infraction against us that makes us angry, the spirits will know *everything* that that person has done to others. *Our* job is to summon them. *Their* job is to play judge, jury, and as you have seen, sometimes executioner.

"And the spirits may not act right away. They will bide their time and wait for the appropriate opportunity to impose their sentence. Just like your father. I recited the incantation the moment he walked out the door. But the spirit did not act right away. She waited as he walked down the street to the harbor. She waited as he pulled his boat away from the other traffic in the bay. She waited until he was all alone in the middle of the ocean where no one else could be harmed. And then, BOOM. The spirits trust us implicitly and we, in turn, trust them."

"Well, I guess that's a relief," Lori stated as she buttered her toast. "But what the hell happened? And did I hear that there are actually witches, vampires, and werewolves? I mean, *our* shit is pretty unbelievable, but that's just nuts!"

Sophia chuckled before responding. "Well, what happened was that my old friend, Papa Doc, allowed your mind and heart to be in sync. He healed you so that you are now able to reasonably assess situations and then use your emotions to take appropriate action. He allowed you to connect with your true nature, dear. You are naturally a very reasonable person. But what is *unnatural* to you is your penchant for bottling up and suppressing your emotions. The reasoning in your mind and your emotional sense for justice are now in sync. They are now one. And hell hath no fury like a medium scorned. Especially of the *Cabot* variety, heh, heh, heh. The other thing that happened is you danced *your ass off* last night!"

"Yeah," a slightly embarrassed Lori responded. "I haven't let loose like that for…um…well never. I just had so much joy in my heart. And energy. It was like a huge weight had been lifted and I could just be myself. I could do anything that I wanted to do. And then you had Papa Doc gyrating and twisting around like he was a tornado or something. How the hell does he do that at his age? And with his back all hunched over?"

"Papa Doc is a man of many talents," Sophia replied as she attempted to hide her blushing face. "Yes, many, many physical talents."

"Gramma!" Morgan yelled out. "Did you screw Papa Doc?"

"Well, *that* is a question that I will not dignify with an answer!" Sophia answered as she feigned offense. "My personal life is *none of your business*, young lady!" Her face then became flushed, and she collapsed onto her kitchen chair. "Oh, to hell with it," she stated quietly as a smile forced its way onto her seventy-one-year-old pretty face. "Yeah, I screwed him. Many, many times. And it's pretty incredible. Well, once you get past the sound of the cracking bones, that is. And then there's usually the hip displacement. Okay, that's it. Let's change the subject and get back to your questions. Are there witches? Yes. I have already told you that. The pretend witches aren't bad, just delusional. Tupperware parties by day, dancing around naked in the moonlight by night. They're just normal women who think they have the ability to connect with nature. They can't but they think that they can, and they really don't cause any harm. The rest of us just kinda laugh at them.

"Then there are the *real* witches. And yes, they can actually connect with nature through their little concoctions and silly spells and whatnot. And they are little bitches. Each and every one of them. Never did meet one that I liked, what with their flying around on their brooms so that Papa Doc could look up their little skank dresses. Once they started hanging out with Papa Doc, he lost interest in me, which makes them all little whores. Once *they* showed up, I *never* attended another one of his dance parties. What did he need *me* for when he had his buffet of tits?"

Morgan and Lori looked at one another while trying to stifle their laughter at their obviously jealous elder. "Now, vampires and werewolves," Sophia continued as her rage subsided. "They are just ridiculous. They have spent eternity battling one another. Vampires making their silver bullets. Werewolves planting their garlic. It's all so silly. It all began centuries ago when a young vampire woman, who was betrothed to another vampire, fell in love with a werewolf. The young lovers ran off together which initiated this whole feud. Legend says that they committed suicide so that they could be together for eternity. I think there was a play written about it, but the fact that it involved vampires and werewolves was taken out. Too scary for the audience, I suppose. But isn't it silly? An age-old war over something as petty as jealousy? Ridiculous. So, they just run around biting and scratching humans when they aren't busy killing off one another. This timeless war has taken its toll on them. They're both near extinction now. Which is *exactly* what should happen to those goddammed little slut witches!"

Morgan and Lori could no longer contain their amusement and burst into laughter. Chunks of half-chewed toast and cornflakes splatted onto the table as the pair embraced their pure joy in the moment.

"Well, isn't *that* nice," Sophia said as she retrieved a washrag from the sink and began wiping up the discarded morsels. "I have half a mind to not tell you your good news now."

"What good news, Mom?" Lori asked.

"Oh, I don't know if you deserve to hear it," Sophia replied passive-aggressively with a turned-up nose.

"Okay, Mom. We're sorry. What is it?" a frustrated Lori again inquired.

"Well, dear," a rebounding Sophia answered. "I have gotten you your first catering gig for this weekend. Isn't that exciting?"

"Exciting?" Lori exclaimed. "No, Mom, it isn't exciting! I'm not ready! Hell, I haven't even put flyers up yet or advertised at all! And it's this weekend? I don't have a menu ready or any supplies! There's *no way* I can be ready for this!"

"Well, first dear," Sophia said to her fuming daughter, "you really need to learn to control your anger. It isn't a good look on you, heh, heh, heh. Secondly, it isn't a big deal. It's just a football watch party this Sunday. I have everything you need at the diner. Its just going to be hamburgers, hot dogs, mini-tacos, and various salads. And for only around fifteen people. Very simple, and Morgan and I can help you. This will be an opportunity for you to get your name out there. Plus, it is being hosted by the O'Sullivans."

"The *O'Sullivans*, you say?" a smiling Lori responded as her mind wandered onto the image of a certain young classmate dunking a basketball.

The following Sunday, the ladies Cabot were greeted by the smiling, forty-six-year-old Quinn O'Sullivan at her kitchen door. "Oh, Lori, thank you *so much* for doing this!" she exclaimed. "We had a caterer, but they had a last-minute family emergency. Connor mentioned it to Sophia and, well, here you are! We're *so excited* to be your first customers and to have you he..."

Her voice trailed off as she heard her husband's voice booming from the living room. "Naomi, would you *please* not stand in front of the TV? Yes, Naomi, we all know how proud you are of your scrapbook, but now isn't the time. Naomi, no one wants to hold the cat."

Quinn held her shaking head in her hands and said, "Won't you please excuse me? I need to go rescue my husband and our guests. That girl is so loveable but can be a bit...um...much. Patrick! I'm coming!"

There was an audible sigh of relief from fifteen people that came from the living room before Morgan said, "Um, why don't I come with you? Maybe I can keep Naomi, um, occupied."

Quinn looked into Morgan's piercing blue eyes. She shed a slight tear and said, "dear, you are a saint."

One by one the guests retrieved their plates and stood in the buffet line. Hamburgers, hot dogs, potato salad, coleslaw and other tailgating fare were eagerly scooped onto their trays. "Hiya Lori!"

Connor O'Sullivan gleefully stated as he approached the counter. "Thanks so much for doing this on such short notice. My brother and sister-in-law just love to throw little things like this, but aren't really good at planning, y'know? Or cooking, for that matter. So, you are a savior!"

"Well, it's my pleasure, Connor," a blushing Lori replied as she needlessly stirred the pasta salad. "And thank you for the referral."

"Oh, you bet! You bet!" Connor exclaimed. "Well, I don't wanna hold up the line, but how 'bout a beer together at half time?"

The awkwardly hopeful moment ended as Connor's wide frame turned from the counter, revealing the short, petite form of one Naomi O'Sullivan.

"Ah, shit," Sophia muttered under her breath. "Hiya Sophia! Hiya Mrs. Cabot! Or Miss Cabot! Or…no! We settled on Lori, didn't we? Hiya Lori! Wow, that's such a pretty name. What does it mean? I bet it's something really cool. Just like Morgan's name. That name's really cool, too. Didja know ever since Jasmine fell down like a bunch of times that nobody at school bothers Morgan anymore? They don't bother me either. It's really cool. It's like I have my own personal body gua…"

"Here, try a hotdog," Sophia bluntly stated as she thrust the grilled sausage into Naomi's wide-open mouth. "Um, come on Naomi," Morgan coaxed. "Let's go find our seat. Oh, I just *love* your table on your deck. Why don't we eat out there?"

Sophia chuckled at her equally amused daughter. She then looked up and gulped when she saw their next patron. "Why, hello Vince! What are *you* doing here? I figured you'd be pourin' suds down at the pub today."

"Naw," Vince replied. "I got somebody to cover for me. And the O'Sullivan's always have a kick-ass spread, and this time is no exception. Plus, I kinda heard you would be here helping out, and I kinda wanted to see you outside of the bar. So, whaddaya say? Maybe have a little whiskey and stroll at halftime, hmmmm?"

"You're never going to give up, are you?" a bemused Sophia asked.

"Nope," Vince confidently answered. "Not until you give me my one shot. Just one little date. That's all I'm askin' for. Then, we can just go back to being pub friends."

"Alright, Vince," Sophia replied. "One whiskey and one fifteen-minute stroll. This is your shot. This is your date. Got it?"

"Well, alright!" Vince exclaimed. "How 'bout a *twenty*-minute stroll?" Vince looked into Sophia's determined blue eyes and received his answer. He then meekly said, "Or fifteen minutes. Fifteen minutes is enough time for a stroll, I suppose."

The final party guest came lumbering into the kitchen. His football jersey clung tightly to his obese frame causing the nipples on his enormous breasts to stick out through the mesh fabric. He gave off an odor that did not mix well with the food or anything else for that matter. He took a hot dog off the tray with his hairy, bare hand, wiggled it in Lori's face and slurred, "Hey baby. You maybe got some buns I could stick my hot dog in?"

"Yes, sir," Lori replied in a controlled tone. "The buns are right over there."

"Sir?" the man drunkenly replied. "No need for such formalities with me, baby. No, you and me are gonna get to know one another *real well*. I'm kinda a *big deal* in this town, so, if you play nice with me, I'll play nice with you. And since it looks like you like to play with meat, well, I think we'll get along *just fine*."

An intrigued Sophia watched her daughter's face turn bright red before saying, "Jerry, isn't it? How about I help you to fix your plate. My Lori here needs to get the dessert ready." Sophia grabbed the man's bulbous, sweaty shoulder and turned him toward the array of salads as Lori mouthed 'Thank you,' and went into an adjacent pantry.

"Well, Sophia," a smiling Vince stated as he entered the kitchen with two glasses of whiskey. "It's half-time. How 'bout that stroll?"

"Alright, Vince," Sophia replied as she rolled her eyes and smirked. "Fifteen minutes. You're on the clock."

"Hey, where's Lori?" Connor strategically asked just as Naomi was stuffing her mouth with a large piece of apple pie in the kitchen.

"Um, I think she's out back by the trash cans," Morgan quickly answered.

Connor went toward the back fence and was horrified at what he saw. "Listen, Jerry, just keep your hands off of me alright? Please, I am not interested." Lori was saying as respectfully as she could as Jerry's greasy hands were pawing her shoulders.

"Jerry!" Connor yelled out. "Time for you to go! I'll arrange a ride for you!"

"Go?" an incredulous Jerry bellowed out. "Hell, it's only halftime, and I'm just starting to have me some fun!" He then leered back at Lori and tried to plant his pudgy, purple lips upon hers. He immediately stopped when he felt a firm hand on his shoulder spin him around.

"I *said*," Connor intensely stated through gritted teeth as his unblinking cop eyes stared through Jerry's. "It's *time* for you to *go*. Now, do you want one of *your* friends to drive you home? Or one of *mine?*"

"This is bullshit," Jerry gruffly said as he pulled away from Connor, nearly tumbling over. He regained his balance, puffed out his chest and said, "Fine. I'll go. But I know people Connor. People who might be interested in cops abusing their power. You better watch your back, buddy-boy."

Connor watched the sloven, swaying frame re-enter the kitchen door, turned to Lori and said sincerely, "I'm so sorry Lori. I know that guy is one of my brother's biggest clients, but I don't see why he has to invite him to these things. He's just such a dick. Always drinks too much then gets really handsy with the ladies. Plus, he's always talking about some new tinfoil hat conspiracy theory that he's heard on some radical TV show or website. He really is a piece of shit, Lori. I'm so sorry."

"I-it's okay, Connor," a slightly disoriented Lori answered. "I-I'm fine. No harm done. Not the first guy that I've had to fight off."

"Well, he'll be the *last* if *I* have anything to say about it," Connor softly said as he fell into Lori's lush blue eyes. The tender moment was suddenly broken as the couple heard rustling coming from a nearby group of bushes. Vince and Sophia came tumbling out of the foliage laughing. They looked up, saw Lori and Connor, and immediately began reconstructing their discombobulated clothing.

"Well, sorry, Lori," Sophia yelled out. "But we gotta go. Something, um, came up."

"But Mom!" Lori exclaimed. "It's only halftime! And I have to clean everything up!"

"Oh, don't worry about it, Sophia," Connor stated as his feelings of male heroism continued to rush through his body. "I can help Lori with all that. You guys just go ahead and enjoy your, um, second half."

The sun was beginning to set behind a bank of puffy clouds as Connor placed the final serving tray into the back of Lori's minivan. "Thanks so much again, Lori," Patrick O'Sullivan said as he draped his arm around his wife's shoulder. "We couldn't have done this without you. The food was just fabulous. Believe me, we will definitely be telling everybody about your service."

"Oh, and thank you for bringing Morgan," Quinn O'Sullivan contributed. "She has been, um, well she has been, um, let's just say that she has been a godsend. This has been the most peaceful dinner party we've had since, um, ever. And don't worry about Morgan. The girls will have so much fun having their sleepover tonight and we'll make sure to have her up and ready for school in the morning. Naomi can't wait to ride in her new car."

"Yeah, it's pretty bitchin,'" Lori said as she thought *I wish I could have a sleepover tonight.* "Well, thank you so much Connor for all your help today. And, we'll have that beer and stroll down memory lane one of these nights, y'know, when my life gets a little more, um, organized."

"Alright, Lori, looking forward to it," a smiling Connor replied as he thought, *Well, a little booze and stroll seemed to work for Sophia and Vince.*

Naomi came bounding out of the front door followed by Morgan. Lori immediately panicked, jumped into her minivan, and said, "Okay! Thanks! Good night, everyone!"

"Wow, your mom sure is in a hurry," Naomi said to Morgan as they watched the minivan fly down the street. "That minivan sure can move. What kind of engine does it have? Not as large as yours, I bet. This thing's a beauty. Come on, let's get your overnight bag. Oh! Can I sit behind the wheel? Pleeeaaase? Just once? I promise I won't..."

Lori returned to an invitingly empty, silent house. She kicked off her sandals and collapsed onto the couch. She opened her laptop and noticed that she had a notification on her social media account. Her eyes began blazing and the chanting of *Contra eos qui suis vocibus alios opprimunt, habebunt locutions*, began pounding in her brain. She stared in angered disbelief at Jerry's post on her page.

HEY BITCH! WHY DON'T YOU DO SOMETHING USEFUL AND TAKE A LESSON FROM YOUR FOOD AND SUCK!

She noticed that he ended his post with a 'Laughing' emoji. "Oh, you think that's *funny*, do you?" Lori said aloud through a twisted little grin as she felt her intense anger consume her soul. "Well, let's just see how funny you think *this* is," she said as she pounded her finger down on the mouse to post the 'Angry' emoji. She sat back, let out a deep breath and waited for her spirit to lift her spirits.

CHAPTER 12

LAUGHING

She did not have to wait long. "Hello Lori," she heard her invited spirit's voice say to her. "It's nice to work with you again. Your timing is perfect. Now just close your eyes, sit back, and enjoy the show. I promise that I won't disappoint you, heh, heh, heh."

"I told you I'd leave right after I make this post! And now I'm done! Happy now? I'm leaving! I guess there's *no* place to watch this game in this town!" Jerry bellowed out to the bartender following his third warning to leave. "And you'll never see me in this dump again! The beer's always, um, watered down. And gay! You serve gay beer here, don't you? Yeah, I know you do. You're probably all a part of the deep state aren'tcha? I bet you're puttin' microchips in the beer to turn us all gay, right? Just like you put microchips in the covid vaccine. Yeah, you all worked with China to create that pandemic so you could put microchips in the vaccine and turn us all gay! Well, I'm not fallin' for it! I didn't get that damned vaccine, and no one can track me! And I never got covid neither! I don't care what everybody told me, I never had it! Just a bad cold or something! Then you put something in the beer so that I can't smell or taste right! And made my muscles ache! That's it isn't it? It's in the beer! Yeah, you probably got one of those pedo rings in the basement too, don'tcha? Just like that pizza place in DC! I know the truth! I know what you libtards are trying to do to us God-fearing patriots! You won't even let us watch our team play! You hate this country so much that you won't let us God-fearing patriots watch our Patriots!"

The muscled bartender rolled his eyes as his fully tattooed arm wiped Jerry's third spilled beer off the worn oak counter. "Yeah, Jerry. That's it. We put stuff in the beer to make you gay. Because *lord knows* we want someone as hot as *you* on our team. Just go home, Jerry. I'll forget about what you said. There's no point in arguing with a bigot."

"Bigot?" Jerry roared back. "Why you little…" Jerry took a wide swing at the amused bartender, spun completely around, and fell over two barstools. "I'm okay! I'm okay!" Jerry yelled out. "Don't you touch me with your faggot hands! I'm leaving! And believe me I'm gonna talk to Vince about this and you'll be out on your ass, buddy-boy!"

"Yeah, okay. Bye Jerry," the bartender replied as he began fixing a mixed drink for a new male patron. "Wow, what an asshole," the patron stated. "Yeah," the bartender replied. "He's such a Jerry. He usually keeps his bigoted shit bottled up, but once he gets a few drinks in him, his true, insane self comes out."

"Why do you guys put up with his shit?" the patron asked.

The bartender smiled at the patron and strolled over to the area of the counter where Jerry had been sitting. He lifted a wad of soggy twenty-dollar bills and said, "Because he's a helluva tipper. He gets drunk, forgets what he owes and just throws everything that he has in his wallet down on the counter. He drank, or spilled, about twenty bucks' worth of beer. And he left, hmmm, let's see here." The bartender counted the wet bills, looked up at the patron and smiled. "One-hundred and sixty dollars. I guess I can put up with his shit for a one-hundred-and-forty-dollar tip. That'll buy us a nice dinner. What do ya say? Wanna grab a bite after I close up?"

"Goddam libtards," Jerry was muttering to himself as his bulbous frame lumbered through a wooded area near a park. "Ow! Damn branches keep getting caught in the mesh in my jersey. Can't even walk down the street like a normal person. Hafta go this back way, so the cops won't find me. God-fearing Americans can't even have a few beers in this woke town. Public intox, my ass. And if that Connor tries to take me in, I'll kick his ass too! Just like I'm gonna do to that fag bartender. And that little caterererer bitch. Who is *she* to turn me down? She's nothin' more than a servant and I needed to be served! Well, I told *her* dyke ass off too, heh, heh, heh."

Jerry thought about his post and his laughter increased. He clutched his sides as his hysterics became uncontrollable. He looked around the forest through his watery eyes. Everything was funny to him. Every tree. Every bush. Every blade of grass. He found everything that he saw to be absolutely hilarious. Including the two dark forms that emerged from the woods and began walking towards him.

"What's so funny, fat man?" the first ruffian said. "Yeah, you laughing at *us*?" The second delinquent added. Jerry looked at the intense faces of the approaching forms, pointed at them and burst into another fit of uncontrolled laughter.

"Well," the ruffian said. "I guess he *is* laughing at us. I guess he finds us *funny*. Well, let's see how funny he thinks *this* is." The ruffian pulled out a sixteen-inch club and smashed it into Jerry's face, shattering his cheek bone. And Jerry laughed. The delinquent put on a pair of brass knuckles and said, "Huh, I guess he didn't learn his lesson. Maybe he'll find *this* funny too." The delinquent rapidly struck Jerry in the mouth three times. Blood, saliva, and teeth plummeted onto the grass. And Jerry laughed.

"You sonofabitch, stop laughing!" the ruffian said as he wielded his club in a frenzy against Jerry's side. The sound of ribs cracking echoed off the trees with each subsequent blow. And Jerry laughed. Jerry laughed through the barrage of kidney punches from brass fists, causing him to urinate all over himself. Jerry laughed as his ears were meticulously cut off by a pair of switchblades. Jerry laughed through the blood and drool as his tongue was pulled out and sawed off. Jerry laughed as his legs were snapped at the kneecaps by the thunderous kicks of heavy boots. And Jerry laughed as one of the switchblades mercifully tore through his triple chin and sliced open his gelatinous throat.

The murderous pair looked down and listened to the final gurgled chortles of their victim, shrugged, and departed through the dense woods. "Man, I'm *never* gonna start drinking," one of the young men said. "Nope," the other agreed. "Not if that shit makes you *that* crazy. Come on. It's getting late. Mom's gonna be furious. We're late for dinner."

Lori opened her eyes and was awash in sweat. Her immediate thought was one of fearful dread. Her frantic eyes looked back down at Jerry's post. She glared at the 'Laughing' emoji. She looked at her angered response. She took a deep breath and exhaled. She felt all her fear, guilt, and dread float away with her exhalation. She then laughed. Lori laughed while she showered. She laughed as she slid into her pajamas. She laughed as she turned down her bed. And she laughed as she opened her computer once again to review the documents that she would be submitting to her attorney. The faint light of the computer screen illuminated Lori's overjoyed face as she laughed.

The sun's brilliant orange hue began to rise over the calm waters of Plymouth harbor as Detective Connor O'Sullivan looked down at Jerry's shattered body and sliced face. Teeth were dripping out of his broadly smiling, swollen purple lips as congealed blood hardened around his stiff body.

"Where do you want to start, sir?" an officer inquired of her superior. "Should we start by seeing if he had any enemies?"

Connor let out a light chuckle and said, "Sure. Let's see if he had any enemies. I'll start at the front of the phone book, and you start at the back. Once we get through it, that should eliminate about ten percent of this town from suspicion. Enemies? This asshole was awash with them. People just put up with him because he was rich. Naw, let's just track his movements. I was with him yesterday afternoon at a football watch party. He was getting unruly, so I had someone take him home. We'll start there, because obviously he wasn't dropped off at home. We'll talk to his ride right after we talk to this witness."

"Yes, ma'am and you live just beyond that tree line? And you couldn't see anything, but you heard a disruption. Around six-thirty or so? Alright, please tell me what you heard. Two male voices yelling. Uh, huh. And another male voice laughing. I see. No screaming or hollering for help or anything? Just the yelling and laughing. Strange. Well, thank you ma'am. We'll be in touch."

"Okay, you took him from my brother's house to a drive through then to the Sand Dollar? Alright. Any issues at the fast-food joint? He called her a *what?*"

"I'm sorry to bother you miss, but did you have a customer here around three o'clock yesterday that was a bit rude to you? Uh-huh. Yes, ma'am, that wasn't very nice of him. No, I don't think you look like that at all. So, where were you around six-thirty last night? Still working your shift, huh? And I assume there's security footage of you being here? Did you call anyone? No? Can I take a look at your call history on your phone, please? Thank you, ma'am. We'll be in touch if we have any further questions. Oh, and one last thing. Is my breakfast sandwich ready?"

"Made a real ass of himself, huh? Practically cleared the place out? Yeah, I know. I bet the place was packed. It was a good double-bill yesterday. Yeah, that was an amazing catch. Kind of a bullshit interference call at the end though. Oh well. There's always next week. So, what was he saying that drove everybody away? Right, right. Typical homophobic shit from him. Oh, and accused you of running a pedo ring, huh? That one's new. What time did he leave? Around 6:15? Huh. That's about when I left my brother's watch party. And what time did you leave here? Around eleven? Alright. And this young man can vouch for your whereabouts? Really? All night? Just left a half-hour ago? Well, I'm glad you at least met some-body out of this whole ordeal. That's nice, I guess. Did he make any phone calls? Just the Governor's office? Why? Oh, the gay beer thing. Right. Did you happen to see his phone? It wasn't on his body. A patron found it on the floor, huh? Well, that's kinda too bad. We find the phone; we might have found our suspect. Well, can I have it? Besides the Governor, any other calls? No? But he said he left a post? For who? Could you say that again please? A 'catererer bitch?' Oh, he was so drunk he couldn't say 'caterer.' Gotcha. And what time was that? Right before he left, huh? Well, let's just see if I can take a peek at his phone here. Oh yeah. I know his password. It's the same password he uses for everything. DEEPSTATE. And he bitches about cyber security. Idiot."

Connor looked down at the post that Jerry had left for Lori and said, "Ah, shit. Why in the hell were you harassing her?" He read the post one more time then looked at the 'Laughing' emoji. A sharp chill ran down Connor's spine as he immediately flashed back to the huge smiling face that was found on the battered victim. He experienced yet another sharp chill when he looked at who had left the 'Angry' emoji in response and said again, "Ah, shit."

The front door of the Cabot home flew open, and Morgan came running in. "I just forgot my book bag. No one talk to me. Please. No more talking." She picked up her bag and she immediately left the home wearing a drowsy, dazed expression.

"Wonder if she got any sleep last night?" Sophia mused as she was clearing the breakfast table.

"I don't know," Lori replied. "I mean, Naomi has to shut down *sometime*, right? She *can't* have all that energy all the time. I bet when she shuts down, she crashes. Speaking of sleep last night, Mom, how about you? Get much sleep?"

"Yeah," Sophia replied with a haughty tone. "I did. I slept like a rock."

"You didn't get *home* until rather *late*," Lori playfully chided. "I heard you creeping in around *eleven*. So, what were you *up to* for, like, *eight hours?*"

"Oh, wipe that shit eating grin off your face and grow up!" Sophia roared back. "I'm not some little schoolgirl running around mommy's back. And you know what I was up to. I was getting laid! Repeatedly! I mean, I thought Papa Doc was talented, and he is, but that Vince, um, well, let's just say that they might need a mop every time I watch his brawny hands grip a beer tap. Yes, I may have underestimated him. For such a mellow guy, he has *a lot* of pent-up energy. And he knows how to use it. Might just let him have a second date. Maybe. I think I'll string him along for a while though, just to keep him revved up. Any *other* questions little miss inquirer?"

Lori laughed as she answered. "No, I think that you've said enough. More than I wanted, actually."

"Hey, if you don't wanna hear this shit, then don't ask!" Sophia exclaimed through her laughter. "How about you? Did you have a gentleman caller last night? It looked like you and Connor were getting rather cozy by the trashcan. That's not a *thing* for him, is it? I mean, I've participated in some kinky shit, but I think that I'd draw the line at screwing in trash."

"Oh my God, Mom, gross," a repelled Lori replied. "Please don't talk like that. And no, that isn't one of his *things*. Well, I mean, I hope not. I wouldn't know. He helped me load my car, we said goodnight and that was it. I'm not ready for any entanglements at the moment and I sure as hell don't want to drag him into *my* mess right now. No, hopefully my divorce will get settled soon and *then* maybe I'll start seeing people. Maybe it'll be him, maybe it won't. I'll just take a look at my options on the menu. And yes, I actually slept great. Mom, I need to talk to you about something. You know that Jerry guy from the party yesterday? You know, the guy that was all…"

Lori's sentence was interrupted by a knock on the front door. "I'll get it," Sophia stated as she went into the living room. "Oh, Loooooriiii!" Sophia yelled out. "It's for you! It's one of your menu options!"

"Oh, hi Connor," Lori said as she swept her blonde hair from her face and blushed. "What can I do for you? Would you like to come in?"

"Thanks Lori," Connor said as he looked down and tried to hide his red face. "I'm sorry to bother you, but…wow. You look *amazing* this morning. I mean, you *always* look amazing but there's something different about you. You just look so, um, I don't know.

Refreshed or something. You're like glowing like you could take on the world."

"Well, thanks Connor," the still-blushing Lori replied. "That's so sweet of you to say. Now, what can I do for you?"

"Well, it's another one of those silly things that I have to check out Lori," Connor sheepishly replied. "I mean, I'm sorry to bother you with this, but, um, well, you know Jerry, right? The guy who was getting kinda handsy with you, or, oh, who the hell am I kidding? The guy who was making an ass of himself at the party yesterday and was mauling you. You remember him, right?"

"Uh, huh," Lori answered with a surprising calm as Sophia's ears began to perk up. "Yeah, he's kinda hard to forget. Why is it that nice guys kinda fade out but you always remember the assholes in your life?"

"Yeah, well, that *is* something, Lori," Connor replied as he continued to search for the words to conduct his investigation. His gaze traveled from her sparkling blue eyes to her golden hair that was cascading down her bare shoulders. He chuckled lightly, put his pen and notepad in his breast pocket and said, "You know what? I'm not even gonna bother you with this. I just wanted to tell you that Jerry got himself into some trouble last night and, well, he's, y'know, kinda dead. But that's not your problem. I just thought I'd tell you personally before you heard it through the grapevine. Well, in these parts it's more like the coconut telegraph, but you know what I mean. I just didn't want you to hear it from somebody else and get all weird about it since you just saw him yesterday, that's all. And quite frankly, between you and me, I think that this town will be a nicer place without him around. But don't tell anybody I said so, alright?"

"Of course not, Connor," the smiling Lori replied as she wrapped her arms around his slightly expanded frame. "Thank you for telling me personally. That's very sweet. I hope you find whoever caused him this, um, trouble. Have a nice day Connor. And how about you come to the diner for lunch? I'll fix you a burger on the house for a thank you for my catering gig, okay?"

"Yeah, okay," Connor answered as he could feel himself becoming lightheaded. "Alright, well I'll see ya at lunch then. Have a nice day, Lori. Bye, Sophia!"

"Bye Connor!" Sophia yelled back in a singsong, playful voice. She then turned her bemused face to her daughter and said, "So, do you have anything that you want to tell me?"

Lori flashed a huge smile and began prancing up the stairs as she exclaimed, "Yes! I think that I've made my selection from the menu! Oh, and I killed that asshole Jerry last night. It was really cool. Just give me a minute! If Connor's coming in today, I want to find something *really cute* to wear!"

CHAPTER 13

INTELLECTUAL PROPERTY

"Hey, Morgan. Do you have your short story assignment finished yet?" Morgan's classmate, Hermes Mendes asked at the lunch table. "Um, yeah," Morgan answered through her half-chewed corn dog. "Yeah, I finished it last night. Why?"

"Well, can I take a look at it?" Hermes inquired. "I heard that you're a pretty good writer and I just wanted to see what I'm up against when we present them next week."

"You're not up against anything, Hermes," Morgan replied through her slight laughter. "I know you're in a heated competition for Magna Cum Whatever, but *this* is not a competition. Writing isn't competitive. Or at least it *shouldn't* be. You'll write whatever you write, and I'll do the same. Then we'll present our unique perspectives to the class next week, along with everybody else. It's really not a big deal. But sure. You can take a look at it if ya want. Let me know what you think. I'd appreciate the feedback."

The following Monday, Hermes approached Morgan in the hallway as she was heading to her Fiction Writing class. "Hey, Morgan. I really loved your story. It was really intense. You really are a good writer. I'm looking forward to seeing how the class responds to it when you present it today."

"Hey, thanks, Hermes!" Morgan excitedly replied. "I really appreciate that. And I'm looking forward to hearing what you came up with as well."

A fuming Morgan sat in the third row of desks next to a shocked Naomi. As the pair were listening to Hermes's story, Naomi would frequently whisper to her best friend. "Oh my God, Morgan! This is *your story*! He *totally* ripped off your premise and your character! Female vigilante serial killer? Check. Balancing her lust for vengeance with her work and romantic life? Check. Wears a black hoodie? Check. Even the *title* is taken from a line in your introduction! Oh my God, Morgan. What are you going to do?"

"I don't know, Naomi," an increasingly infuriated Morgan said coldly as her blood pressure rose with every subtle wink and conceited smile that Hermes flashed at her. "Nobody will believe me. He's Mister Popular around here. Everybody loves him. Nobody's gonna believe that he's a rip-off artist and I don't have anything else to present. I'm screwed."

The class roared in applause as Hermes took his seat in the front row following another knowing smirk in Morgan's direction. "Morgan?" the teacher stated. "Are you ready?"

"Um, yeah," a beet-red faced Morgan stated as she reluctantly slinked out of her seat and cautiously approached the podium at the front of the class. She looked down at her work and wanted to burst into tears. It was *her* work. It was *her* character. Her mannerisms. Her premise. He had made some strategic changes to "his" story, most notably "his" character's motivation to become a serial killer. But other than that, the foundation of "his" story had been *her* creation.

Her character, Maddy, had been created from her heart and from her hands. She had never been prouder of anything that she had created in her life. And *her* work of passion had been stolen by a fraud. A hack. A young man who had stabbed her in the back while smiling at her. He had no ethics. And, apparently, he had no original ideas either. She realized that his academic success had been achieved on the backs of others who were more creative and more decent than him. She felt tears of both anger and embarrassment well up as she began presenting her well-crafted, original story.

Following her reading, Morgan folded her paper over and looked up at the astonished faces of her classmates. She wanted to crawl under a rock. The uncomfortable silence was broken when the teacher said, "Morgan, may I please see you after class?"

"How did it go?" Naomi asked as the pair were briskly walking toward the Tempest as groups of her classmates were laughing and pointing at them. "About how I expected," a despondent Morgan answered. "I tried to explain that I had finished writing my story last week and that *he* had read and ripped off *my* story. I even offered to show her my time stamp on my computer that proved when I had finished the first draft. She didn't listen. She just kept saying how Hermes was one of the brightest students to ever come out of here and how damaging such a charge could be to him. Then she said that she would let this slide this time, but that she will recommend suspension if I ever plagiarize anyone's work again.

"He has them all wrapped around his little finger and there's not a damned thing that I can do about it. But he's taught me a valuable lesson. There are a lot of snakes out there impersonating nice people, so trust *no one*. Not until they have *earned* your trust, at least. I'm just going to go home and crawl in bed. I want this day to be over. And he may have stolen my character, but there's *no way* he can steal what I'm going to do with her in the future. And he has *no idea* how *he* is going to fit into this story, heh, heh, heh."

Sophia and Lori arrived home that evening and heard sobbing coming from Morgan's bedroom. They rushed upstairs to find black streaks of mascara running down their precious family member's delicate face. "Well, these aren't tears over some boy or girl," a concerned Sophia stated as Lori sat by her daughter's side on the bed. "These tears represent something deeper. I can feel it. What happened, dear?"

"Yep, I knew it was something deeper," Sophia stated following Morgan's explanation of her grief. "So, what are you going to do about it?"

"Oh, what *can* I do?" Morgan replied as she sat up and dangled her legs over the side of her bed. "It's just one of those things in life. Sometimes people screw you over. You experience it, it hurts you, you learn from it, you move on. He *might* just find some garbage in his locker or something. But other than that, I really can't do *anything.*"

"Oh yes, you can," Sophia replied as she wore a devilish smile.

"No, Mom," Lori stated. "Let's just let this blow over. We don't need to do that. We don't need to kill him."

"Who said anything about killing him?" Sophia replied through a fit of laughter. "Lori, I've explained this to you before. The spirits will *only* do what is necessary to right a wrong. Nothing more, nothing less. We summon them through our anger and then *they* will determine the sentence. I highly doubt that this dick will end up dead. Not unless there are even *darker* secrets that he's keeping. Why don't we just have a little look-see, hmmmm?"

"Ah shit," Lori stated as she watched her mother turn toward the door. She then looked at the beleaguered face of her beloved daughter and said, "Well, I guess a little look-see wouldn't hurt anything."

Sophia returned to the room a few moments later and sat in between her family members on Morgan's bed. She opened the book and there was an eerie green glow that illuminated the room. "Well," Sophia stated gleefully. "I believe that you've *already* got the spirits' attention before you have even summoned any of them. You are quite powerful, my dear. More powerful than your mother and more powerful than me. Just keep thinking about what this little snake did to you and let your anger intensify. I'm going to casually flip through the pages. I'm quite sure that the appropriate spirit will reveal herself to us, heh, heh, heh.

"Hmmmm, not on that page either," an increasingly frustrated Sophia said as she turned yet another page in the ancient book. She began scanning the various incantations on the newly opened sheet made from human flesh. Thirteen rows down, an incantation began glowing red. As did the room. "Ah, here it is," a relieved Sophia stated. "Oh, she *will* be interesting. Now Morgan, just touch the words and let your anger flow through you. When you hear the incantation pounding in your brain, you will know that you have made contact. And you will know that you will be avenged."

Morgan placed her black-nailed fingertips upon the dark crimson words. She felt her anger flowing out of her soul, through her arms and into her tingling fingers. She began hearing a woman's voice in her head repeatedly saying, *Si a me surripere potes, ego a te surripio. Si a me surripere potes, ego a te surripio. Si a me surripere potes, ego a te surripio.* Morgan opened her eyes and said in a dark voice, "Oh yeah. I've definitely made contact. Let the games begin, heh, heh, heh."

Ten minutes passed in awkward silence as the ladies Cabot waited for something to happen. "Um, hey Gramma," a confused Morgan stated. "Why isn't anything happening? Shouldn't I be transported to where he's at and be watching whatever the spirit has planned for him by now?"

"Not necessarily, dear," Sophia answered. "Just be patient. As I have explained, the spirits wait for the opportune time. Or perhaps *create* the opportune time. Like your mother's spirit did last week to that wretched man. It was not a coincidence that he was walking through those woods and stumbled upon two teenagers capable of murder. She summoned them to be together. Just a little whisper into one of their ears to lead them on a path towards one another. And then, she acted. Made the man do nothing but laugh, which she knew would infuriate those specific boys. Sometimes they lead, sometimes they wait. It seems as though they are waiting at the moment. Just be patient. This young man will receive his come-uppance in due time. Now, who's up for some Chinese take-out? I've been cooking all day and don't even want to step foot in the kitchen tonight. A little Ming Dynasty, anyone?"

Hermes Mendes climbed the stairs of the stage to deliver his portion of the school assembly. He bowed slightly as most of the faculty and students applauded the arrival of their Student Council

President, Future Magna Cum Laude, and all-around swell dude. Or so they had all been led to believe.

"Good morning everybody, so great to see you all," Hermes began. "I am once again just so humbled to be elected as your Student Council President and to be up here to lead our first assembly of what I'm sure will be the best school year in the history of Plymouth High!"

"It'll be *eventful,* anyway," Morgan muttered under her breath as she could feel her anger rising. Her emotions grew in intensity as Hermes winked at her and began discussing the difficult topic of plagiarism in the school. *Are you kidding me?* Morgan thought to herself. *He is lecturing us on plagiarism? On stealing somebody else's work? What the hell, man!* She balled her hands into tight fists and bit her lower lip to resist the urge to scream out. Her mind then was taken over by a forceful, evil sounding woman saying, *Si a me surripere potes, ego a te surripio. Si a me surripere potes, ego a te surripio. Si a me surripere potes, ego a te surripio.*

Hermes was in mid-sentence when his fake sincerity was suddenly silenced. The entire assembly was staring at him as he began sweating profusely and his panicked eyes darted around the room at the confused faces of his classmates. He opened his mouth to speak. All that came out was the gibberish that had suddenly begun rattling around in his mind. "Foreskin houses ranch dressing killer prostitute makeshift car parts grass orange blossom exclamation!" He exclaimed.

There was hushed silence followed by laughter. Lots and lots of laughter. Even the faculty could not contain their amusement at this unexpected turn. He besieged them to stop laughing at him. "Telephone parameters biology water bottle tape!" He yelled out, which only resulted in a greater amount of amusement from the audience. His mind was frantically trying to place the appropriate words with the appropriate meanings. "Consultation academy fish sticks purple scrotum!" He yelled out while trying to say, 'Please stop laughing at me!'

He was awash in embarrassment as he was experiencing the first moment of public ridicule in his life. He realized that he was no longer able to string even the simplest sentence together as he once again tried to implore his classmates to stop their guffawing. "Mouse dress table frame pizza slice rain!" His once-proud frame wilted behind the podium, and he held his anguished face in his trembling hands. He looked up and saw the smiling face of Morgan Cabot who had climbed onto the stage in support of her fallen classmate.

"It's okay, everybody!" Morgan yelled into the microphone. "Just a little stage fright. I'm going to take him to the nurse's office. I'm sure he'll be just fine!"

As Morgan was walking Hermes to the nurse, she began whispering into his ear in a soft, sinister voice. "You are *not* going to be fine. I can tell you this because there is *no way* you can ever tell anyone else. For the rest of your life, you will be plagued with the inability to match your words with their intended meaning. You will know exactly what you want to say, but you will *never again* be able to express yourself. Not in speech. Not in sign. And certainly, not in *writing*, heh, heh, heh. You will not graduate. You will not go to college. You will not be able to perform even the most basic communication with another human being. Even your facial expressions will betray you. When you feel pain, you will smile. When you feel joy, if you ever do, you will frown.

"Do you know why this is happening to you? Because *you* stole *my* intellectual property, that's why. So, *I* stole *yours*. Every original thought that you may ever have will be worthless to you. Every thought that you have from this point on is now controlled by *me* and is *mine*. How does it feel to be stolen from? To be violated like this? To have someone smile at you while they're screwing you over? Frustrating, isn't it? Well hotshot, turnabout is fair play and as the saying, or incantation, goes, 'If you can steal from me, I can steal from you,' heh, heh, heh.

"Have fun in the nurse's office. And with your new shrink. And at the homecoming dance. I can't *wait* to see what you might say to some hot to trot chick when you want to ask her to dance. What will it be? 'Hemorrhoid eggplant two-face asswipe?' Oh man, I can't wait.

And don't think that you can communicate with gestures, either. If you try to ask some girl out by simply extending your arms to communicate an invitation, you will do the opposite and punch her in the face! Or worse! And your expressions will be completely random, with no discernible patterns so that you can invent your own language or something. Nobody will ever again understand *anything* that are trying to communicate. Face it. The only way you will *ever* feel anything close to normal is if you are in complete isolation from other human beings. Everywhere. No talking. No letters. No social media posts. Not even a casual glance from across a room. Nothing. That is your punishment. To be banished from interacting with any other human being again. Maybe dogs will understand you, but I doubt it. Well, here we are at the nurse's office. I gotta get to class. I'm really excited to hear about our new writing assignment. I already have a few thoughts rattling around. And, hey. I *really* enjoyed the vindictiveness and tenacity of the character in your story. I found her to be, um, *inspirational,* heh, heh, heh. Morgan out!"

Chapter 14

Sorry For The Miscommunication

Morgan and Naomi were met with a brisk late October breeze as they exited the Tempest in the high school parking lot. They were also met by brilliant blue and red flashing lights. "Whoa! What's going on?" Naomi exclaimed. "There's Uncle Connor! Uncle Connor! Uncle Connor! What's going on?" she asked as she ran up to her uncle who was accompanying two hand-cuffed delinquents to an awaiting police cruiser.

"Not now, sweetheart," the sullen Connor replied. "I'm busy. Just go to your homeroom. I'm sure you'll hear all about it in there." Connor ignored his beloved niece's peppered questions as he placed each of the young suspects in the cruiser, returned to his car, and drove away. The flashing lights disappeared around the corner as Morgan said, "Wow. Those two musta done something really bad. Come on. Let's see what the gossip is."

The pair of now inseparable friends entered the school to a buzzsaw of teenage chatter. As they walked along the hallway towards their respective lockers, they picked up bits and pieces of what had just occurred. *So, they finally caught the guys that my mom's spirit sent to kill that laughing emoji jerk a few weeks ago. Well, I guess everybody gets what they deserve,* Morgan thought to herself as she opened her locker and hung up her jacket. She then noticed the incessant chatter take a turn.

She cocked her head in the direction of everybody's astonished stares. Her heart sank as she witnessed the sea of kids part to make way for the return of the Queen of the school. Jasmine was dressed in a long, flowing gold princess gown. A diamond studded tiara sat regally on the top of her perfectly curled blonde locks. Her two casts had been painted with gold glitter and adorned with plastic jewels while her crutches were wrapped in an elegant fine golden silk. She beamed at her subjects and exposed her perfectly white dental implants. The school's plebes were in amazement before bursting out into uproarious applause.

"Oh puke," Morgan muttered to herself under her breath. *Don't they know how nice it's been without her around?* She thought to herself. *Without all the drama? The constant ridicule? The tyranny? Once she went down, her little toadies kinda became quiet and left everybody alone. They were nothing without their so-called leader. They have no personal convictions. Just suck up to whoever can give them the immediate gratification that they crave and feel entitled to. Boys. Popularity. Whatever. They're spineless. They don't care about her, and she most certainly doesn't care about them. It's all transactional. Once she was out of the picture, there was nothing that she could provide to them, so they abandoned her. But now that she's back, well, just look at them surrounding her with their fake smiles and probably fake tits. And the rest of these morons just mindlessly fall into line. The Queen is back. All hail the Queen. And what a stupid, gaudy Halloween costume. Gee, arrogant much? All right. She's back. I'll just have to deal with it.*

Morgan's mind instinctively began flying through the pages of her family's book. Each memorized incantation glowed in her mind briefly before another suddenly appeared. *Nope. Just calm down Morgan,* she thought. *No need to harm her anymore. I've already made my point with her. She just better not piss me off.*

At that moment, there was yet another gasp as another popular, fallen classmate entered the school for the first time in weeks. Hermes Mendes slunk into the hallway with his head covered in a grey hoodie. His despondent eyes glanced upward occasionally to see where he was as he tried to navigate his way to his personal classroom where he would watch his teacher's lectures on a computer screen in isolation. The school administration understood his affliction and determined that he would be able to graduate if he simply sat through his lessons. The doctors had told them that he could perfectly understand what he was being taught either through lecture or by reading, but he was completely incapable of communicating that understanding in any comprehensible way. It was also determined that he would be isolated from his classmates to prevent any sort of violent miscommunication, but that being out of his home could prove to be therapeutic over time. So, he would be out of his home but isolated from his classmates within the school building. Except for each morning and each afternoon. At those times he would be amongst his peers and faculty as he went to or from his secluded bubble.

Hermes glanced up once again and saw Jasmine's pretty, smiling face. His manipulative charisma intuitively took hold, and he rushed up to his friend. "Hello, Jasmine. It is so good to see you. How are you?" he intended to say as he gave her a big hug. Instead, what came out of his mouth was, "Ass crack calculator doll face jumping cornflakes prison!" He then violently punched the unsuspecting cripple with an uppercut to her jaw. Jasmine spun completely around sending streams of blood onto the dresses of her entourage and fell face first onto the hard floor. Her newly installed implants sliced through her gums and clattered onto the polished linoleum. Her other newly installed implants exploded in her chest leaving the top of her gown looking like a pair of deflated balloons. Jasmine's bloody saliva was once again exposed for all to see as the horrified Hermes stood above her. He looked down at the bloody result of his unintended attack, began applauding, and laughed.

School officials quickly made their way through the traumatized throng of teens. Two employees rushed Hermes out of the building while two others attended to the wailing Jasmine. The only other sound besides Jasmine's hysterics was laughter. Completely unbridled laughter from one Morgan Cabot as she looked at the glinting diamonds that had been shattered out of their tiara's housing and were now resting in a dark red stickiness. The infuriated school's principal grabbed Morgan by her black-clad arm and began dragging her to her dark office.

"I'm suspended," Morgan stated flatly to Naomi as the pair trudged back to the Tempest. "She's also going to write a letter to my mother. So, that should go well. And no Halloween dance, either. Sorry. And I got all dressed up for it." Naomi looked at her black-clad, gothic friend and thought, *but she always looks like this*. Then, a miracle happened. For perhaps the first time in her young life, Naomi decided not to say anything. The pair remained silent as the Tempest roared out of the parking lot, leaving rebellious black skidmarks on the pavement.

"I see," Lori stated as she tried to remain composed following her daughter's sheepish explanation of the day's events. "Well, it sounds like you had quite the productive day, Morgan. Quite productive, indeed." Lori looked into the amused eyes of her mother, daring her to laugh before continuing. "There was no need for you to do that. There was no need for you to rub salt in their wounds. And there was no need for you to risk exposing your involvement in their, um, misfortunes. You are mature beyond your years in many ways, but you are still a child in others. And maybe those two had what was coming to them, but I don't think that relishing in somebody else's misery is very becoming of you. I'm quite disappointed. So, congratulations. Not only are you suspended, but you are also grounded. Now go to your room. I just *can't wait* to hear from your principal."

Morgan opened her mouth to protest then thought better of it as she saw the intensity in her mother's eyes. She shed a tear and began dragging herself up the stairs to her room. "Wow, that was a bit harsh," Sophia stated as she put on a fringed vest to complete her 'hippie' costume.

"Mother, please don't start with me. I have enough to deal with. I have my catering business that is keeping me busy. I am trying to go slow with Connor. Just be friends for the time being. I have a court hearing coming up soon with my dick ex. I do not have the time or constitution at the moment to deal with her immaturity. She can sit up there for the next few days and stew about what she has done. In the meantime, I have other things to do. So, stay off of my ass, old woman."

"Well, alrighty then," Sophia replied in an offended tone. "God forbid you listen to the wisdom of your mother. Fine. You're not the *only* one who has better things to do. I'm going to The Sand Dollar for Vince's Halloween party. Don't wait up. I'm gonna see if I can't get some magic out of his wand tonight, heh. And don't be too hard on her. Whether you want to admit it or not, what happened to those two entitled little assholes is damned funny. And maybe they've learned a lesson that will make them better people as adults. But I doubt it. Ah, our spirits. The gift that keeps on giving. Well, toodles. See ya in the morning."

Lori poured herself a shallow whiskey, sat cross-legged on the couch and began unwrapping a piece of candy that was intended for the small ghouls that would soon be rapping on her door. She opened her computer and saw that she had received an email from Beatrice Patterson. "Ah shit," Lori stated aloud. "Here it is. Okay, Miss Patterson. What do you have to say about my daughter?"

Lori's face was bright red by her third reading of the lengthy and unnecessarily cruel letter. She knew that her daughter's actions were, at a minimum, inappropriate, but this was personal and mean-spirited.

Ms. Cabot,

As I hope that your daughter has told you, we had a rather unfortunate incident at the school today. One of our brightest students who has recently been inflicted by a rare communication disorder injured another of our students. It was a tragedy. As was your daughter's response to it. As our other children stood mortified by what they had just witnessed, your daughter laughed. And she did not laugh out of being nervous or in shock. She laughed because she actually thought that this student being horribly injured by another was funny. As our dear Hermes was traumatized over his actions and being rushed out of the building, she laughed. As our sweet Jasmine was laying in her own blood on the floor, she laughed. It was the most disgusting sight that I have ever witnessed in my 25 years as an educator. And it was the most disgusting sight that I have ever witnessed as a life-long Christian.

But I shouldn't be surprised, I suppose. As the saying goes, the apple does not fall far from the tree, now does it? And I am guessing that you, Ms. Cabot, probably know quite a bit about eating tarnished apples. What am I to expect from a young woman who wishes to lie with other women in the most ungodly of manner. What am I to expect from a young woman, if that is how she "identifies," that dresses as though she were a vampire risen from the grave. What am I to expect from a young woman whose grandmother is the town whore. What am I to expect from a young woman whose mother fornicates outside of wedlock, as I have heard from your charming ex-husband. I can truly understand why your marriage didn't last if this is the product of your loins. Yes, your offspring is a mean-spirited, cruel, sinful person who will do nothing but sully our school, our town, and our world. She is an abomination. You are an abomination. Your mother is an abomination. The 'ladies Cabot,' as I've heard you refer to yourselves, are an abomination. An abomination against our one and true God.

Tomorrow I will be submitting a letter to your ex-husband's attorney recommending that your offspring be placed with him. Perhaps his influence can turn her around so that she can be a somewhat worthwhile member of our society. That seems to be her only hope. Also tomorrow, I will be submitting a letter to the school board requesting that your offspring be expelled permanently from our virtuous halls. We do not want her toxicity. We do not want her sinfulness. And we do not want her cruelty. I suggest that you contact me Monday morning and voluntarily withdraw your vile offspring. It will save you both some embarrassment. But it won't save your souls. That is between you and our God. And may our God have mercy upon you and your heathen daughter. You will need his mercy. I will pray for you.

Lori glared at the 'Praying Hands' emoji that the principal had ended her letter with. Her rage intensified as the incantation began throbbing in her brain once again. *Contra eos qui suis vocibus alios opprimunt, habebunt locutions. Contra eos qui suis vocibus alios opprimunt, habebunt locutions. Contra eos qui suis vocibus alios opprimunt, habebunt locutions.* Lori was sweating profusely and began to elevate slightly from the couch as her intense rage matched the eerie red lights encasing the Cabot's living room. She continued to glare at the emoji as her lithe finger swept across the computer's mouse pad. Her deep, gravelly voice said, "Pray for yourself, bitch," as she sent a reply email that contained only the 'Angry' emoji. Lori collapsed back onto the couch, wiped her brow, and yelled up to her daughter. "Morgan! I've changed my mind! Maybe what happened to those two little shits was funny after all! You can go out tonight if you want! Why don't you give Naomi a call! I think that I would like to be alone for a while!"

"I wish you were real, Larry," Morgan was saying to her illustration of a happy-go-lucky, bright yellow and black spotted leopard that was to be the star in the children's book that she had begun writing. 'Larry the Leopard' was her most recent creation that represented peace, love, friendship, and inclusion in the jungle that he lived. He would be a complete contrast to her brutally violent "Maddy" character that had been stolen from her by Hermes. He would be her way of trying to find peace through civility and understanding. He would be her way of finding balance in her soul. The balance between knowing when to stand your ground and fight back and when to turn the other cheek and compromise. Larry would never harm anyone. Maddy sure as hell would. Brutally. And they were both her creation. They were both a part of her soul. The outline of Larry's book was in her head and now his brilliant image nearly leapt off the page on which he had just been drawn.

"I wish I could be more like you. No ill-feelings towards others. No judgement. No hostility. Just understanding and happiness. How I wish you were real and could teach me that. How I wish I could feel you lick my face at night. How I wish I could feel your soft fur as you purr next to me. How I wish I could have your strength to find goodness in everyone. But I don't. I simply don't have it in me. Just like today. Mom's right, Larry. I was cruel to have laughed at them. I guess I deserve this punishment. Maybe someday I'll be more like you. Maybe someday I can invent my own incantation that will bring you to life. You will be my closest friend and confidant. Maybe. Someday."

Morgan's thoughts were interrupted when she heard her mother's voice yell out, "Morgan! I've changed my mind! Maybe what happened to those two little shits was funny after all! You can go out tonight if you want! Why don't you give Naomi a call! I think that I would like to be alone for a while!"

Morgan flashed a wickedly broad smile as she looked back at her creation. "On the other hand, maybe those two got *exactly* what they deserved for being pompous pieces of shit! And maybe it was *just as funny* as I found it. And maybe, just *maybe*, me and Naomi can salvage something out of this Halloween. Yeah, maybe we'll be able to raise a little hell. Thanks for listening, Larry. You're the best. And if I ever think of a way to truly bring you to life, you'll be the first to know."

"Thanks Mom!" Morgan yelled out as she reached for her phone. "Hey, Naomi, it's me. Yeah, I know, but. Yes, but...would you please just...Naomi! I'm not grounded anymore! You wanna hang out on cemetery hill tonight? We can just wander around with flashlights and look at all the tombstones and get really creeped out, okay? Okay, I'll be over in fifteen. Yes, I'll be over in...Naomi, I'm hanging up now...I'm...Naomi, I'm hanging up!"

CHAPTER 15

PREY FOR YOU

Lori retrieved her family's ancient book from its shelf the moment she saw her daughter fly out of the house. She immediately opened the book to the page which held the incantation that she had just used to summon her vengeful spirit. Her fingers began to tingle slightly, and the living room became enshrouded in a dark red hue as she laid her hand upon the passage. She smiled, let out a relaxed breath, closed her eyes, and peered into the home of one Beatrice Patterson. She couldn't help but giggle to herself as she wondered what entertainment her summoned spirit might have in store for her this evening.

Beatrice Patterson was going around her house meticulously locking every door and window and shuttering the blinds. Three deadbolts clacked shut on the front door and the front porch light was shut off. "There," she said to herself with pompous satisfaction. "That should give the little hellions a clue that I will not be participating in this abomination of a so-called holiday. Every year I see parents gleefully walking their children down the street to beg for candy. And those children are dressed up as ghosts and ghouls and witches and even as the devil himself. Even members of my own church participate in this travesty. This so-called holiday that teaches children to worship Satan and the black arts and death all while learning how to be welfare recipients.

"Have these children done anything to earn this candy? Of course not. They just go around banging on doors bothering peaceful strangers and beg them to give me, give me, give me. It is self-absorbed and it is wrong. No wonder our country is in the condition that it is in. These children are raised to believe that worshipping evil is righteous. They are raised to believe that they are entitled to anything that they want without having to work for it. And they are raised to believe that if they don't get what they want, then they have the right to retribution in the form of one of their 'tricks.' Give me candy or I will harm you. All in the name of Satan. That is what this accursed evening teaches them. And then they grow up believing that. That they are entitled to anything that they want without subservience to our flag, or our laws, or our savior. It is disgusting and something that I have never, nor shall ever, participate in.

"That is why I have never attended one of these dances being held in my school. Every year I try to put a stop to it, and every year these blasphemous bleeding hearts on the school board vote me down. They vote for these hormone fueled children to gyrate on the dance floor while dressed in provocatively evil costumes. Then they are all surprised when a bunch of these whorish girls get knocked up. What do they expect? We have allowed these children to sin, and that sin leads to a burden that they must now carry for nine months. And then raise. Yes, that should be their penance. They should *have* to care for that child. That child that is the product of Satan himself. That child that should serve as a constant reminder to look towards our savior for guidance. Year after year these children are drawn further away from the light and into the darkness. And it all begins with their 'trick or treating.' Well, they will receive no treats from *me* this evening. And should one of these little bastards try one of their little tricks against me again this year, well, that is why I have *you* Gabriel."

The ninety-pound black Doberman looked up from his meal,

growled understandingly at his owner, and returned to his ravenous feeding on a bloody steak. "Yes," Beatrice said snidely as she retrieved her Bible and sat upon her flowered couch. "They won't be expecting *you* this year. No more eggings. No more toilet paper in my trees or soap on my windows or slashed tires on my car. No more. If any of them try anything they will be met with your glorious fangs, my Gabriel. And we *both* shall have our just desserts, heh, heh, heh."

Lori's transported soul watched with anticipation as Beatrice Patterson opened her Bible to a random page and began reverentially reading. Lori's mind was then bombarded by flashing images that Beatrice was suddenly experiencing as the incantation began pounding in both of their brains. Beatrice began trembling uncontrollably as an onslaught of vivid projections played in her mind. The images depicted Beatrice at various stages in her life interacting with other people while always clutching her Holy Bible. The images then became intermingled with the emotions that Beatrice's victims had felt during those brutal encounters. Beatrice began feeling the intensity of the pain that she had inflicted upon innocent others.

The embarrassment that a young Hispanic girl had felt after being pushed down and called a derogatory name by a ten-year-old Beatrice. The self-loathing and guilt felt by an impregnated teenage classmate following Beatrice's public ridicule of her in the lunchroom. The fear and physical pain of a young gay college classmate after Beatrice outed him causing a group of insipid homophobes to beat him mercilessly. The hopelessness felt by one of her teenage African American students as Beatrice failed her in her class, ruining her chances for a much-needed scholarship, and dashing her dreams of a college education. The feelings of disempowerment that a black-clad, gothic girl felt when she was needlessly suspended from school. Similar scenes and their associated emotional aftermath played out over and over, covering Beatrice's forty-eight bitter years upon the Earth.

Beatrice stood and began searching for Bible passages to ward off the bombardment of vicious images and all-encompassing emotions. Every time that she would be able to briefly focus on a Bible passage, another vile image of her hypocritical actions from her past would penetrate her soul causing her to cry out in agony to her unresponsive savior. She began shouting out prayers to her savior as her essence was being battered by her victims' anguished feelings of guilt, fear, embarrassment, and worthlessness. She desperately yelled out one final time, "Oh my Lord! Please! I pray of you! Please! Make this stop!"

And it did. Beatrice's prayers had been answered. The images of her anti-Christian actions and the intensely painful emotions suddenly stopped the moment that a lunging Gabriel's vicious fangs penetrated her jugular.

Lori opened her eyes and wiped drool from her dismayed mouth. She heard a loud pounding at the front door. She shook her blonde head, got up from the couch, and carefully opened the door. She gasped as she was confronted by three blood and ooze covered zombies who had apparently just been resurrected from the grave. She then began laughing as the pint-sized post-apocalyptic trio yelled out, "Trick or Treat!"

"I'm getting' a weird feeling, Vince. Maybe I need to go home," Sophia slurred slightly across the bar at her sort-of, kind-of boyfriend of two months. "Oh, don't go, Sophia," Vince replied in a slightly pleading tone. "Is it because of Papa Doc and his friends? Hell, I'll ask them to leave if they're bothering you."

"Naw, it isn't that," Sophia replied after sticking her tongue out at the thirteen young women who were writhing their bodies around an ecstatic Papa Doc. "It's a public place. They have the right to be here, I suppose. This is really the only night of the year that they can go out and be themselves. The rest of the year, they have to hide that they're witches."

"What's that you say?' a surprised Vince inquired. "What are you saying about witches?"

Aw shit, I shouldn't have said that, Sophia thought to herself. *This is the problem with getting too close to somebody. You let your guard down and then end up saying shit that they won't understand.* She then began laughing and said, "Witches? Yeah, they're dressed as *witches*, but I said '*bitches!*' This is the one night of the year that these *bitches* can go out and be themselves and get away with being *bitches!*"

"*What* did you just call us?" a slight blonde dressed in a very revealing black chiffon gown said as she strutted toward the bar. The pair glared at each other for a moment before Papa Doc planted his hunched-back frame between them. "Now ladies," the ever-diplomatic healer began. "No need for any problems. Especially not tonight. This is *our* night. The night where *all* of us who like things a bit *dark* can come out of the shadows and play. And here we are. Playing together. In a *public place*. You two babes catch my drift? So, how about if I just buy everyone another round and we get back to boogying, okay? Vince, my friend! One more round and let's crank the tunes! Maybe something a bit more rockin' this time. I want to hear some pounding drums!"

Sophia and the blonde continued their unblinking glowering at one another until another slight witch came over to whisper something into the blonde's ear. The blonde nodded, looked back at Sophia, and gave her a devilish smile. "Okay, It's your lucky night, old woman. We have something to attend to. But we'll meet again. I guarantee it." The thirteen women then picked their brooms up from the corner of the bar and began sauntering toward the exit.

"Yeah, that's what I *thought!*" Sophia yelled out after them. "You talk a good game, but when it's time to throw down, you're all just a bunch of spineless little *bitches*! Yeah, that's right! I said it again! You are all a bunch of *bitches*!"

"Oh, Sophia," a disheartened Papa Doc said as he stared forlornly at the floor. "Why must you ruin my good times? I care for you deeply, but this is twice now that you've interrupted one of my soirees."

"Oh, *she* isn't the reason we're leaving," the blonde witch stated just before exiting. "She can believe that if she wants. But it isn't. We have been summoned to perform a little deed. And that *bitch* sitting at the bar is going to be grateful that we did. See ya soon, *bitch*. And we'll see *you* back at *your* place Papa Doc. We are *far* from done partying tonight." The patrons of the bar were either too intoxicated or too inattentive to notice the silhouettes of thirteen female figures on broomsticks flash across the brilliant face of a full moon.

———

"Wow, look at the date on *this* one," Morgan stated to Naomi as her flashlight swept across yet another ancient tombstone on cemetery hill. "Yeah, wow!" Naomi exclaimed. "You know what would be fun is to make a list of a bunch of these people then find out how they died then pick out like the best deaths then write short stories or a book or something about them starting from when they died a horrible death but write it backwards from death to birth but use the way they died as a jumping off point to make stuff up about their lives that's really gruesome. Wouldn't that be fun? Oh, hey! How about this one? Can you read the date? Can you? Um, Morgan?"

Naomi pivoted and her flashlight beamed down upon her unconscious friend lying in the damp brown leaves that covered the cemetery. It was the last thing that she saw before feeling a fierce blow to the top of her head.

"Blech!" Morgan yelled out as she pulled her head away from the foul-smelling salts. "What the hell is going on?" she yelled out at three of her female classmates who were ominously standing over her. "Listen, guys, this isn't funny," she then said as she realized that she and Naomi were bound back-to-back to a large tree. She could feel the jagged bark digging into her spine as she struggled to release her wrists from the tight ropes.

"Oh, it isn't funny?" one of the young women said. "But Jasmine getting beaten up is, *right*? You found *that* funny didn't you? I guess we all have our own sense of humor. You found *that* to be funny, and we think that *this* is funny. *Really* funny. We think it's *really funny* to have you two little dykes all tied up and helpless. We think it's *really funny* that after this, you're both going to drop out and go to dyke school or some shit. Because we think that you're going to look *really funny* with shaved heads. And brands. And busted open lips. We think that's going to be *really funny*."

"Come on you guys," Morgan began pleading as she tried to focus on an incantation that would provide her escape from this terrifying situation. "Listen, I know you hate me for some reason. Your beef is with me, okay? You can do whatever you want to me, but just leave Naomi out of this, okay? Please? I'll do whatever you want. Please just leave her alone."

"Huh," the leader of the ghostly gowned women said. "Yeah, maybe. She's still out cold. Lucky for her. If she wakes up and starts her babbling, we're going to rip out her tongue. But we'll make a deal with you, Morgan. If you let us abuse you and you don't scream and wake her up, then we'll leave Irish Coffee alone. Okay? Then, you drop out of school, and you don't tell anybody who did this to you. Because if you do, we'll come back for you. And for your little gabbing girlfriend. You got it? Not *one sound*, Morgan. If you wake her up, the deal's off. Got it?"

Morgan began weeping and solemnly nodded her head before she felt fists crashing into her cheekbones, eyes, and mouth. Morgan said nothing as she endured blow after blow from the trio of tittering assailants. With each subsequent strike, she could feel trails of blood limping their way down her grief-stricken face. She then felt her black sweatshirt sleeve being ripped open. She looked through her swollen eyes and saw one of the macabre figures approaching with a glowing iron. "P-p-please. No," She stated through her bloodied mouth before feeling the white-hot fury of the brand on her shoulder. She stifled her screams as her mind began to black out from the excruciating pain. Just before losing consciousness, a woman's voice could be heard in her head saying, *In tuo tempore necessitatis societas componenda est. In tuo tempore necessitatis societas componenda est. In tuo tempore necessitatis societas componenda est.*

Morgan felt a wave of angered adrenaline sweep over her, and she opened her bleary eyes. Through the blood and tears, she saw the images of thirteen black clad women approach her attackers from behind. The grim women said something softly in unison and their eyes began glowing red. The three young assailants screamed when they turned around and saw the terrorizing vision. Their squeals intensified as tree roots burst out of the soggy ground, wrapped around their ankles, and began dragging them into an opening in the earth. An astonished Morgan said nothing as she watched the hysterical young women desperately claw at the ground in a vain attempt to prevent their descent into a premature and very cold earthly tomb. She watched in silent awe as their faces became covered in worms that had begun slithering into the women's nostrils, mouths, and ears. There were three more high pitched shrieks before the tormentors were completely sucked into the ground and buried alive.

Morgan was hyperventilating as a scantily clad black form approached her. The blonde woman leaned over, looked Morgan in her eyes, and began wiping moss onto her wounds while whispering something indiscernible. Morgan immediately felt the swelling on her face dissipate and her burning shoulder turn cool. Three other women then untied the bound captives, looked down at them and smiled.

"Th-thank you," Morgan stuttered to the bemused coven. "Thank you for saving us."

"Yeah, well," the blonde began to reply. "Don't thank *us*. Thank your spirit that you summoned. We were kinda compelled to come here and help you out. Plus, we didn't do it for you. We did it for Naomi. We don't let *anyone* screw with one of our kind. Listen, Morgan. We really don't have anything against you or your mom personally. But why don't you tell your *grandmother* who it was that helped you tonight. *That* should really piss her off, heh, heh, heh."

As the moonlight illuminated the thirteen women's frames straddling their brooms, Morgan said, "But, I don't think that I used an incantation or summoned a spirit. How did you know to come here?"

"Yeah, you did," the now hovering blonde answered. "Just before you passed out, you came up with just the right incantation. Your recitation combined with your fear and anger and pain summoned the spirit who, in turn, summoned us. What you said was, 'In your time of need, an alliance shall be forged.' And an alliance *has* been forged, Morgan. You looked after our Naomi, and we will now look after you. You suffered in silence to protect her, and that is a debt that is not easily repaid. So, consider us to be friends or allies of a sort. But just you and your mom. We owe *nothing* to your bitch grandmother."

"But what does Naomi have to do with any of this?" Morgan asked.

"You'll find out in due time," the blonde stated. "You *both* will find out in due time. Until then, thanks for being her friend. We'll be seeing ya. We gotta go get our drink and dance on!"

Five seemingly eternal minutes later, Naomi looked up into the piercing blue eyes of her friend. "Wh-what's going on?" she asked groggily as she sat up from Morgan's lap. "Oh good. You're okay," Morgan answered. "Um, nothing much. You just tripped over a branch or something and knocked yourself out. You may have a pretty good bump on your head. We'd better get you home. Oh, and I don't think that you should tax yourself, so how about we just don't talk for a while, okay?"

CHAPTER 16

OSCAR CLIPS

"What the hell is going *on* in this town?" Detective Connor O'Sullivan asked his deputy as a team of police officers trudged through the soggy leaves that covered cemetery hill. "A high school student who mysteriously breaks her ankles and falls. Repeatedly. Another one who suddenly can't communicate in any coherent fashion and attacks that other student. Jerry's brutal murder by those two other teens. Then, not that it's a part of *my* beat, but that guy in Boston who his wife said died by being 'Liked' up the ass. Bizarre. And now this. Three of the most popular girls in the high school have been reported missing. Their friends said they were planning on surprising somebody at cemetery hill after the dance last night. And sure enough, one of their cars is at the entrance. But where are the girls? Deputy, have you had any luck with your interviews? Do you know who these girls were planning on meeting?"

"Yup," Deputy Gigi Holloway replied. "But you aren't going to like it. Several kids in their clique said they were pissed off after their friend, Jasmine, was laughed at after she was, um, attacked by the Mendes boy. They said that the person they were pissed off at was Morgan Cabot."

"Aw, shit," Connor stated as he pulled his hand down his weary face. "Are you sure? So, why did they end up here?"

"Yes, sir, I'm sure," the deputy responded. "Apparently one of their friends saw Morgan's car enter here and these girls went to confront them. And here's the car and there are no girls. What's next, sir?"

"Well, what's next is I have to recuse myself from this case. Or at least not be the one to conduct the interviews," Connor replied in a beaten-down tone. "I'm going to leave that up to you, Deputy. And you'd better start with my niece. If Morgan's involved, I'm sure my Naomi wasn't far behind. Any interview material that you have will be run through me *and* the captain, understand? This is a missing persons case involving three affluent families. I don't want there to be any hint of conflict of interest, understand?"

"Yes, sir," the deputy dutifully replied. "Um, there's just one more thing that we have just found out."

Deputy Holloway's thought was interrupted by another officer who was rapidly approaching the pair. "Detective, I think we've found something. There's a large tree about fifty yards over there. We've found traces of what we believe to be blood on leaves around the tree, rope fragments and pieces of black fabric in the bark. It kinda looks like someone was tied up there and maybe beaten or worse. There's a lot of blood."

"Okay, first things first. Officer, collect all the evidence and let's get that to the lab right away. Let's see if we can't do some DNA testing on the blood to find out whose it is. Let's start with the missing young ladies' blood type. If there's no match, then we'll know it isn't their blood. If there *is* a blood type match, call their parents and get whatever the lab needs from them. Blood samples, medical records, soiled laundry. Anything that we can get to compare the samples. If they don't match any of our missing girls, then we'll see if we can't run tests on Morgan and Naomi. But let's interview them first. See if there are any inconsistencies in their stories. Start with Naomi. It will take a while, but that girl is incapable of lying. Then, talk to Morgan. God, how I pray that those two aren't involved."

"There's one more thing, sir," the officer stated. "Near the tree, we found three long drag marks on the ground. The leaves have all been cleared away and there are definitely three distinct drag marks. And claw marks in the earth. Then, they just stop. It appears like three people were clawing the ground to keep from getting dragged. But then, nothing. Just the ground that doesn't appear to be disturbed. Maybe they were carried away at that point, but there are no shoe impressions. We did find a few pieces of straw too. Like from a broom, maybe."

"Okay," Connor replied as his mind was whirring. "Then let's get a backhoe and dig that spot up. Let's eliminate all possibilities. And I pray we don't find anything. Now please get on it, you two and thanks. I have a bad feeling about this. Now, Deputy Holloway, what were you about to tell me?"

"Well, not that you really will want this information, sir," the deputy reluctantly replied. "But Beatrice Patterson was found dead in her home this morning. The mailman thought that something was off because her new Doberman wasn't chained outside, so he looked in the window and found her on the living room floor, um, being eaten by her dog."

"Ah, shit," Connor stated. "Okay, I'll go check that out. Have animal control and the coroner meet me over there, then I'll come back here when the backhoe arrives. At least that is one tragedy that might be easy to explain. That Doberman's nuts."

"Yeah, me and Morgan were at cemetery hill last night," Naomi was enthusiastically answering the deputy. "We were just walking around looking at the headstones and stuff and trying to creep each other out, y'know? Like, we'd hold the flashlights under our faces and laugh really evil, or we'd hide behind trees and tap each other on the shoulder, y'know? It was super fun! Morgan's totally my best friend and we have such a great time together! Oh! We came up with a new way to write a book, maybe. You see, what you do is find out some really creepy way that somebody died, then you write the book backwards starting with their death and you…"

"Thank you, Naomi," the deputy interrupted before showing her pictures of three young women. "Do you know these girls?"

"Well, sure I know 'em! I go to high school with them. They're kinda snotty and call me names and stuff, but that's okay. I'm used to it, y'know? They're super pretty and super popular and…"

The deputy interrupted once again. "And when was the last time you saw them?"

"Oh, at school yesterday," Naomi replied. "Hey! Do you wanna see my science project I'm working on? It's really cool. It's gonna be a real-life working volcano! Wanna see?"

"Thank you, Naomi," the deputy responded, "but *no* thank you. I'm here on official business. It looks wonderful though. So, you didn't see them at the dance?"

"Nope," Naomi gleefully answered. "Didn't go to the dance. See, Morgan and I were supposed to go together, but then Morgan got in trouble for laughing at Jasmine, so she got suspended from school and grounded by her mom. But her mom changed her mind and let her go out, so we just went to cemetery hill, like I said. You sure you don't want to see my volcano? It's really cool and works and everything!"

"Um, no thank you, Naomi," the increasingly frustrated deputy replied. "Now, Naomi, I need you to think really hard. Did you see these girls, or anyone else, at cemetery hill last night?"

"Nope, just me and Morgan," Naomi answered. "We were just being creepy to each other like I said and then I fell over a branch and knocked myself out for a while. When I woke up, my head was in Morgan's lap. She made sure I was okay then we came home. Here! Let me show you how my volcano works!" Naomi jumped off her bed and plugged her volcano into an outlet near the deputy. She flipped a switch and fake lava exploded out of the top of the volcano, saturating everything in Naomi's room in a dark red goop. Including Deputy Holloway.

"Um," an embarrassed Naomi said. "I'm sorry. I guess it still needs some work, huh?"

"Well, I would say so," the deputy answered through tightened lips as she began wiping red mucus from her blonde hair. "That's okay, Naomi. Thank you for your time. We'll be in touch if we need anything more, okay?"

"Okay! Hey, you don't have to go!" Naomi exclaimed. "I'm going to bake cookies! You want some? I make the *best* cookies. I've *always* been good at combining ingredients and stuff, y'know? It's like I just know the perfect amount of everything to put into a dish to make it delicious! My mom says that I make the best cookies on the whole planet!"

Twenty minutes later Deputy Holloway was finally safely back in her cruiser. She double-checked the next address and started her car. "Okay, one down one to go. I sure as hell hope Morgan isn't as, um, verbose. And I sure as hell hope she isn't taking science."

———

"Allies?" Sophia yelled out to her beloved granddaughter. "We are *not* allies with those little bitches!"

"But Gramma!" Morgan countered. "They helped me and Naomi out! Those girls were really *hurting* us! They may have even *killed* us if they hadn't shown up! Plus, I guess I summoned a spirit, and it was the spirit who forged this alliance. One of *our* spirits, and you say they *always* know what's best!"

"Well, not in *this* case!" Sophia roared back. "Nope. Mediums and witches were never meant to be allies. And sure, they may have helped you get out of the frying pan, but don't you see they've flung you into the fire? The cops are going to figure out that you two were there with these dead girls. They're going to come snooping around, and if we're not really careful about what we tell them, then we'll be exposed. Okay. Just go through your story one more time and I'll tell you the exact parts to tell them, and the parts to conveniently leave out. It's not like we can tell them thirteen witches drug these little skanks into the ground and now they're a part of the tree's root system, now, can we? And Lori, don't give me that look. It's not like *you* have anything to brag about today, either. I mean, sure I've offed some people, but I've spread it around over time. You two are like a paranormal hit squad! Okay, Morgan. One more time. And we need to do something about your face. I'm sorry dear, but you've got to get your face beaten again. I know just the spirit to summon to retrieve your wounds. I'm sorry dear, but this is going to hurt a bit."

Thirty minutes later, Deputy Holloway knocked on their door. "Well, isn't *this* convenient?" Sophia stated as she opened the door. "Why, we were just about to call you. Just look at what those girls did to my Morgan's face! Deputy, you have to do something. We are definitely pressing charges. Bullying is *one* thing, but *this* is assault. Assault? Hell, it's attempted murder! Morgan, show the deputy your shoulder."

Deputy Holloway entered the home and looked upon Morgan's beaten face and branded shoulder. Morgan looked down and began crying. "Oh, my lord, child," the deputy stated. "What in the world *happened* to you?"

"Um, please, do I *have* to answer?" Morgan asked in a pleading tone. "Can't we just let this go? Please? I'm okay. Naomi's okay. I just don't want anymore trouble." Lori lifted her performing daughter's forlorn face and said sternly, "Morgan dear. What these girls did to you and threatened to do to Naomi is criminal. They must be brought to justice. Now you tell the officer everything that you told us. You don't have anything to worry about. Those girls will never harm you or anyone else ever again, okay?"

Morgan had to bite her slit lip briefly to keep from laughing as she said with fake resignation, "Yeah, okay. But I sure hope they don't come back for us for telling on them. Here's what happened Deputy Holloway. Me and Naomi were just hanging out at cemetery hill. Those three girls came up from behind us and knocked us out. When I woke up, me and Naomi had been tied up back to back around a big tree. They were standing over us. They were pissed because I laughed at their friend, which I guess I can understand because it wasn't very nice of me, but I didn't deserve what they did to me. Naomi was still out, and they said they were going to beat me and if I screamed and woke Naomi up, they would hurt her too. So, I just sat there and took it. They punched me in the face a bunch of times, then they branded my shoulder. It hurt so bad, but I didn't make a sound. I just wanted Naomi to sleep through it. After they branded me, they, um, just left us there. I was finally able to get free from the ropes. When Naomi woke up, I told her that she had tripped and knocked herself out. It was really dark and I kinda hid my face from her so she couldn't see it really well. I didn't want her to know what really happened. I was trying to protect her. I took her home. When my mom and grandma saw me this morning, I of course, had to tell them what happened. They were just about to call you when you arrived. *Please* don't let them hurt me any more officer. And *please* protect Naomi. *Please?*"

"Of course, dear," the sickened deputy replied. "May I have a sample of your blood and the top you wearing last night? We will need that for our investigation. Excuse me for a moment. I need to make a call."

The deputy went back out to her patrol car and made the call to Detective O'Sullivan. "Yes, Detective. I think that I know whose blood was on those leaves and the fabric that was in the bark. And I'll bet we find that same fabric's fibers in the rope. This isn't going to help find those girls, but here's what happened to Morgan and Naomi last night."

"Jesus, okay thank you Deputy," Connor replied after hearing the dastardly report. "Well, if these three turn up, we've got an assault charge on our hands. At a minimum. Maybe attempted murder. Terrorism. Kidnapping. Perhaps a hate crime. Put it in your report and we'll meet with the captain back at headquarters." He walked over and peered into the large hole that had been excavated in the cemetery. "So, you fellas find anything?" he yelled down to the two men who were searching. "Nope. Nothing Detective. Just a really vast root system for this tree. If someone had been buried here, we would have found them. There's nothing, so I guess *that's* good news.

There's still hope that they're okay out there somewhere. We're coming up." The two men pulled themselves out of the hole as the backhoe's engine began to rev up. Dirt was returned to fill the gaping hole. Dirt was returned to cover the literally petrified faces of three teenage girls that were embedded in the tree's tangled roots.

"*Now* what?" Connor finally exploded after hearing that the Doberman had run away. "So now we have a murderous *dog* on the loose? Find him, goddammit!" Connor wiped his frustrated face, sat at his desk, and opened Beatrice's computer. "Well, unless dogs have learned to use computers, there shouldn't be anything here, but may as well cover all the bases. Although, the coroner said that the cause of death was a canine bite to the jugular. It's amazing how they can determine that stuff. That poor woman looked like a pile of stew beef after that dog got to her. Her legs and arms were chewed down to the bones. And her face was, well, not there anymore. Just mangled gristle. One of the most disgusting sights that I've ever seen. Well, besides seeing Jerry in his filthy tighty-not-so-whiteys at that party. That was even worse. Okay, Beatrice. Who have we been talking to?

"Let's see here. The last email that you received was from..." Connor's thought halted abruptly as his heart immediately sank. "Aw, shit. Lori Cabot. At around the approximate time of death. And all she replied with was an 'Angry' emoji. Lori, my love, this is beginning to look like more than a string of coincidences. Well, *this* should be a fun date night."

CHAPTER 17

NOT THE BEST WAY TO A WOMAN'S HEART

"Or not," Connor concluded his thought out loud before turning his attention to his inner voice. *No. Too many unexplained questions. Maybe my love life needs to take a back seat for the moment until I can make sense of all this. As fantastical as all this might seem, there's no way to deny it. It seems as though anyone that crosses the ladies Cabot meets a dire fate of one sort or another. Sophia's husband and a couple of her business associates. Even a couple of my classmates back in high school met untimely deaths right after harassing Lori in some way. And that peeping Tom she had. I was gonna beat that bastard up myself, but he died before I had the chance.*

Then Lori's husband's friend who sent that horrible meme. And Jerry. And the school principal right after she sent Lori that appalling letter. And what was the common denominator in those three? Their last interactions were with Lori. The timelines all line up. Lori reads something terrible that they sent her. Lori gets upset. Lori sends the 'Angry' emoji. A short while later, they're dead.

And then there's Morgan. Jasmine picks on her and she suddenly starts breaking her ankles and falling all over the place. A classmate steals her work, and he is stricken by some sort of communication affliction. Three classmates beat her up and now they're missing. Every single person that crosses their path ends up beaten, missing, or dead. Every single one.

But what am I saying? This is ridiculous. Let's look at this logically, Connor ol' boy. Yes, it is true that all those people crossed one of them and every single one of them has met a less than desirable fate. But those ladies were never around when those things happened to them. All of Sophia's associates' deaths were investigated. They were all deemed accidents. I mean, she didn't go to Boston and shove chicken down that reviewer's throat and choke him to death, now did she? Her husband's boat wasn't rigged. It was just a fluke accident. Piles of frozen meat falling over and crushing that guy. She wasn't there when that happened. I know. She was serving me personally at the diner when I received the call about the accident. The javelin. Slipping and falling on Plymouth Rock. Falling off a cliff. She wasn't near any of those scenes. None of them. They were investigated. They were deemed accidents. No foul play. Not even a hint of it.

And then there's Lori. It was impossible for her to go to Boston and kill that guy. And what did she do? Stick a giant blue thumb on her hand and ram it up his ass repeatedly? It's ludicrous. No, that was definitely done by some sex freak. And Jerry was murdered by those delinquents. And the principal? I don't think that Lori has the ability to turn a family pet into a man-eater. No evidence of her involvement whatsoever. She got angry and responded in about as benign a manner as possible. Hell, she didn't even tell 'em off. She just sent a message that they had made her angry. And there sure as hell is no law against getting angry. Plus, she's the most peace-loving, down to earth woman that I've ever known. She wouldn't hurt a fly. And finally, the best piece of evidence that I have that she has had no involvement is her ex. Yes, he's still alive and kicking and if there's one man that Lori would have some justification for retribution, it would be him. Now, should something happen to him, maybe I'll need to rethink this a bit, but until then... No, there is absolutely zero evidence that Sophia or Lori was in any way involved with any of these mishaps. None. Maybe they have some sort of guardian angel. Maybe Gabriel himself comes down from heaven and strikes down anybody that pisses them off. And if that's the case, well, that's just a bit out of my jurisdiction. And speaking of Gabriel, I wonder if they've found that dog yet? I just hate having to put animals down.

But, shit. Morgan, on the other hand, was personally present at all those kids' misfortunes. But, so what? We have tons of witnesses that say she was seated several feet away from Jasmine and she didn't lay a hand on her. She certainly isn't responsible for weak ankles. And Hermes? The doctors have no idea what happened to him. Some sort of weird seizure or chemical thing. Certainly not Morgan's fault. But the three missing girls. Morgan and my unconscious niece were the last known people to have been with them. But, if anything, Morgan and Naomi are the victims here. All the evidence supports Morgan's story of being tied up, beaten, and branded by those girls. That poor girl. What they put her through. But then, where are they? Where are the missing girls? Morgan certainly has the motive and she's the last known person to have interacted with them. I know what I need to do. I need to clear this silliness up right now. I need to prove that Morgan had no involvement in their disappearance. So, I'm back to square one. This is going to be a fun date night. Or not.

———

A beaming Lori Cabot enthusiastically opened her front door and yelled out, "Hi Connor! Ready for our date?" Her face turned from glee to confusion as she saw a number of forensic technicians standing behind her beau wearing grim expressions.

"So, here's the thing, Lori," a red-faced Connor began explaining. "Um, yeah, I know we were supposed to go out tonight, but, um, listen. I'm obviously still investigating those missing girls. And Morgan was the last person to see them. And she sure as hell has a reason to have a beef with them. So, I just wanna get her name cleared so that I can move on from her, okay? This was gonna happen one way or another. It would be so much easier if you would allow us to search the premises and her car. If you allow us to do that, it'll look a whole lot better than my having to come back with a search warrant. I know you and your daughter have nothing to hide. But the rest of these folks don't. And I know it'll be a pain in the ass.

They'll probably take some of her stuff for evidence. But it'll be gone through quickly and then she'll get it right back, okay? I'm sorry, Lori. I can't tell you how sorry I am. But I have to do my job. And the more quickly we can do this, the more quickly Morgan will be in the clear, okay?"

"Um," a shocked Lori began to reply before Sophia yelled out from the kitchen, "Sure! Let 'em in! Do whatcha need to do Connor! I think those girls are little hellions and they probably realized how much trouble they're in for what they did to our Morgan and are on the run! Didja check to see if their credit cards or anything's been used? Hell, I bet they're halfway to Mexico by now! They know what they did and they're going to disappear so that they don't go to prison! But sure, come on in and disrupt our peaceful lives!"

"Um, okay. Thanks for your understanding, Sophia," Connor sheepishly replied as he thought, *Shit. That actually makes sense. They realized what they had done and knew they would be in trouble. Maybe they didn't have it in them to kill the girls, so they panicked. Leave their car there so it won't be traced and maybe have somebody take them to the train station or something. Or maybe they walked there. Get the hell out of Dodge before they get arrested for assault.* "Um, Deputy Holloway? Why don't you start checking the bus and train stations. Sophia's right. Those three might just be on the run."

"Of course, I'm right!" Sophia roared. "I'm *always* right! Now get your asses in here, do your thing and get the hell out! I'm *already* missing some of my stories!"

"Well, why don't you and your friends come on in Connor," Lori stated. The sharpness of her tone sent a regretful chill down his spine. "I guess I won't be going out tonight, so I had better fix myself something to eat. I would offer you something, but seeing as how you are here on official business, I wouldn't want to be accused of bribery or impeding an investigation or some such nonsense. And I suppose this pretty dress isn't needed so I guess I'll just go upstairs and put on something a bit more…uncomfortable."

"Ah, shit," Connor said under his breath before ushering his investigative troops into the well-kept home of the ladies Cabot. The latex gloved army moved from room to room, meticulously assessing every item in every cupboard, shelf, drawer, and trinket box. Luminol was sprayed on doorknobs, flooring, and walls. Any item that was slightly suspicious was carefully placed in a plastic bag, sealed, and removed from the home. The living room carpet was vacuumed as was the interior of the Tempest following the fingerprinting of the car's interior.

The most concentrated activity occurred in Morgan's room where she sat on her bed in dismay as her seventeen-year-old life was literally being turned upside down. Her computer was taken. Her phone. Her bedding. Her clothes. Any item that might contain a hair, blood, or skin sample was bagged and removed. Every surface of the room from the floor to the ceiling was sprayed with luminol and checked for blood stains. A powerless Morgan seethed as she watched this unjust violation into her life. Her seething intensified when Connor lifted a notebook out of her desk drawer.

"So, what's this then, Morgan?" Connor asked light-heartedly. "My notebook. Duh," Morgan tersely replied as she clenched her fists within her tightly folded arms.

"Well, sure, I can see that, heh," Connor stated cautiously. "But is it okay if I take a look in here?" "Of course it's okay, Connor," an unblinking Morgan coldly answered. "It is obviously okay for you to look at and take anything that I own. I really have no say over it. So please just finish your tearing my room apart and leave."

"Aw, shit, Morgan. I'm sorry about this," Connor replied softly as he began flipping through the pages. "Say, what's this then? This looks really cute!" Connor exclaimed as he tried to lighten the mood. "That's my latest creation," Morgan replied through her clenched teeth. "That's 'Larry the Leopard.' He's all about peace and love and bringing people together and not bullying people or invading people's privacy and shit like that. Maybe you should read it when I get it done. You might learn something."

"Um, yep, I sure will!" Connor replied with fake enthusiasm. "Really looks like a must-read! And what are these notes at the bottom of the page? Looks like Latin."

"Yep. It's Latin," Morgan answered. "Any law against practicing Latin?"

"Nope, nope, none whatsoever," Connor quickly replied as he turned the pages until he came to another long entry. "Huh, is this your short story?"

"Why yes, Connor, it is," the stoic Morgan answered. "That is *my* short story and *my* character. *That* is the character that was stolen from me."

"I see, I see, well I bet she's a really cool character," Connor replied through a forced chuckle.

"Eh, she has her moments," Morgan dismissively replied.

"Well, let me just take a little look-see here and…" Connor's eyes began to widen as he skimmed the vivid descriptions of Morgan's character viciously murdering rapists, terrorists, and bullies. He abruptly closed the notebook when he read about a pedophile getting an arrow plunged into his ass and out his penis. "Wow, she's a bit different from Larry now, isn't she? I think we'll just take this as well. You know. Just to be safe. But you'll get it back real soon."

"Go ahead and take it," Morgan replied in a chilled calm as her face began turning red. "Take it all. Analyze it. Bring it back or don't. What difference does it make? I have no say over this. I have no control over this. So, take my precious notebook. Take my creations from me. But just know this, Connor. You can take what I've written down, but you can't take what is in my brain. You can't take what is in my soul. And if I never see those pages again, I can recreate them. Because they are a part of me. Larry. Maddy. All of the others that are swirling in my brain. Each and every one of them are a part of who I am. So, take them. I will recreate them. And that is something that *nobody* can steal from me."

A dumbfounded Connor stood for a moment before placing the notebook into a plastic bag. "Okay, then. Um, thanks for your, um, cooperation Morgan. Um, maybe you can join me and Naomi for some ice cream or something one of these days, huh?" Morgan lifted her piercing blue eyes and glared directly at Connor in response. "Or not. We'll just see how it goes. Okay. Thank you, Morgan." He reached the top of the stairs and whispered to one of the forensic investigators, "Let's get the hell out of here. I think we've done enough damage."

Just before the intrusive group was to leave, one of the investigators said, "Hey Detective? What about this old book?"

Connor looked over at the official who had just bagged the oddly bound, antique family heirloom. He reluctantly turned his gaze toward Lori's rigid, sweat suited frame. His eyes were drawn upward until his eyes were locked on hers. Her glowering penetrated his heart as he said with resignation, "Yeah. Let's take that too. I'm so sorry Lori. You'll get this stuff back real soon. I promise, okay?"

His attempted contrition was met by three pairs of electric blue eyes staring at him defiantly. "Yep, okay. Once again, I'm sorry. And Lori, I'll be in tou...um, I'll cal...um...I'm just really sorry. Okay gang. Let's get out of these ladies' lives. Probably forever."

The ladies Cabot stood in grim silence as they watched the marauders' cars slink down their quiet residential street. "Mom," Lori stated in a concerned tone. "They have the book. They are going to read the book and it's not like it's that difficult to translate Latin. What if they read it and figure it out? It'll blow their minds, but they could still figure it out."

"Not to worry, my dear," Sophia calmly replied. "They *can't* read it. Connor can't read it. Only those who are gifted can read it."

"That's not true!" Lori yelled back. "Connor has seen the book before! He asked if it was written in Latin!"

"And just how long did he have it open, dear?" Sophia asked.

"Um, not long. He just went through a few pages really quickly. He mentioned the color of the ink and asked if it was in Latin, then I took it from him."

"Good," Sophia said. "He glanced at it and that's all. Had he kept it open and tried to read it, the book would have recognized that it was being handled by unauthorized personnel and the ink would have disappeared. It can actually be a fun little parlor game for Halloween parties. Spooks the kids. They open the book and see the writing. Then, the ink disappears. After they freak out, I just tell them that it's ink that disappears after being exposed to light for a few seconds. But every now and again, the ink doesn't disappear for someone. That is how we know that we have someone that is gifted on our hands. So don't worry, dear. He'll call us up with his mind blown, we'll laugh and tell him it's a trick. Works every time."

"So, only mediums can read the book, right?" Lori inquired.

"Well, only mediums can *use* the incantations to summon the spirits," Sophia answered as she began putting her disheveled home back in place. "Others who are gifted can read the passages, but they can't use them. It is how we mediums know that we are in the presence of a gifted one. They can read it, but they can't use it because they do not have the emotional connection to the spiritual realm as we do. Papa Doc, for example, can read it. And I suppose so can witches. The real witches. But not vampires or werewolves. They're a bunch of idiots."

"Okay, well I guess that's one less thing to worry about then," Lori stated after she let out a sigh of relief. She then went through the house, opened the back door, and whistled loudly. From the darkness of nearby shrubs, a large, black Doberman came bounding through the door, pounced up on Lori and began licking her face. "It's nice to see you too, Gabriel!" Lori exclaimed as she finally allowed herself a moment of levity. "Now, let's get you a snack. All the bad people are gone. They will *never* get you Gabriel. They will *never* get *any* of us. I promise you that."

"So how long are you planning on keeping that dog here?" Sophia asked. "Forever," came Lori's immediate reply. "He was used by a summoned spirit to help our Morgan. And he came here after escaping the animal control unit. He came directly here as though he knows that he belongs here. And he does. We owe him. He protected us, and now we shall protect him. And that, mother, is final."

"Fine!" Sophia yelled out as she trudged her weary frame up the stairs. "But you and Morgan are taking care of him! And if I step in dog shit one time, he's gone!"

Lori sat on the couch with a slobbering Gabriel laying on her lap.

She heard her daughter's final whimpers come from upstairs as Morgan had finally drifted off to sleep. Lori picked up her laptop from the cushion and placed it on her chest, just above Gabriel's snoring snout. She opened her emails, and her newfound calm was immediately replaced with unbridled rage as she read the message from her ex.

Just wanted to drop you a quick line and tell you how excited I am for our hearing next week. Yep, it should be a really good time. The judge that we drew is going to be really fair. Now, don't you worry that she receives a lot of contributions from my father. I'm sure that won't sway her in the slightest. And don't worry about Morgan. Once I get her back to her real home, I'll take really good care of her. I'm sure the judge will be impressed that I've already set her up with a therapist for her conversion therapy. Yes, we're going to turn her into a fine, young, heterosexual lady. Oh, and just in case you're wondering, this is a picture of what I'll have on my arm at the hearing. Have a nice evening.

Lori glared at the provocative picture of a voluptuous twenty-something barely covered in a revealing negligee. She then glared at the 'Drool' emoji that he had posted next to the young woman's image. "You son of a bitch," Lori said aloud with a dark determination. "You picked the wrong night to screw with me."

CHAPTER 18

DROOL

Lori's soon-to-be ex-husband flashed a devious grin as he looked at the number that was calling his phone. He enthusiastically answered the call from his attorney. "Hey buddy, give me some good news. Really? *She's* the judge? That's the perfect draw. I'll call my dad and make sure his latest donation is ready to go. You did? Already had a backchannel consult with her through an aide? Perfect. What do you think? All of it? All of her discovery evidence is getting thrown out? This is better than I could have dreamed! The only thing that she's considering is financial information and Morgan's school record? Well, I sure as hell make more than her. Ten-fold, at least. And this has historically been Morgan's home. Plus, she just got suspended from school. I know she's going to take off in June right after she turns eighteen, but that gives me several months to screw with them.

"Several months to pay them back for their betrayal of me. Plus, getting Morgan away from under her mother's spell will give me a chance to maybe make her into a God-fearing, patriotic young lady. One that likes men and gets married and becomes a good little wife the way God intended. She's got the obstinance of her mother and the mouthiness of her grandmother. That shit is going to end *now*. I am going to break her. She will either conform to what she is naturally supposed to be, or she'll end up in a nut house. Either way, her mother will be broken too. Hell, she might just come crawling back after I take Morgan. I haven't decided how I'm going to handle that yet. But if I *do* allow her to come back it will be under some rather harsh, um, shall we say *stipulations*, heh, heh, heh.

"Well, thanks buddy. Hey, is it going to hurt me if I send Lori a little message gloating a bit? I want her to be completely sleepless this next week of her life. Then, after the hearing, her nightmares will *really* begin. And my daughter's. No? The judge won't even look at it? In the bag, huh? Well, perfect. Thanks buddy. Let me know if there's anything that comes up. I think I'll go in the bedroom and, um, celebrate. Bye."

The ex cackled with wicked glee as he opened his laptop and began typing an email. "Yeah, this'll get her going. I can just see her eyes bulging out when she reads this," he proudly said aloud to himself. "God, I love screwing with her. All the mind games I played on her throughout our marriage. She was too stupid to even realize it for the longest time. And then, the manipulations. Calling her a whore just to beat her down. Then call her fat to reduce her even further. If it wasn't for our dyke daughter, I would still be ruling over her. But her maternal instincts to protect Morgan were stronger than my beratements.

"So, she left me. Embarrassed me in front of my friends and work associates. But no longer. Everybody is going to see who wields the power in this family. Everybody is going to see how weak and pathetic she is when all her evidence is thrown out and all the money that she has spent on an attorney is wasted. She'll be broke, lost, heartbroken, and completely shattered once the judge rules in my favor for Morgan's custody. She will have no choice but to return to me if she wants anything to do with her daughter over the next several months.

"But that will give me plenty of time to beat them both down. They'll be nothing but spineless jellyfish. They'll be ruined for any future relationships. They'll be ruined for the rest of their lives. Unless, of course, they become subservient to *me*. Yes, I will allow them to remain with me. They can then have a home and a place in this world. And their place will be to serve *me*. Just like my mistresses. Oh, that *will* be fun. Screw other women right under Lori's nose. Or maybe, I'll make her watch. Yeah, that gives me an idea. This might be just the salt in the wound to send her over the top tonight."

He got up from his desk, strutted across the hall and entered his master bedroom. "Hey, get up!" he yelled out to his most recent buxom conquest. "And what are you wearing? I'm not hanging out with a hot chick like you to see you in these frumpy pajamas. Here. Put this little negligee on. Yeah, that's it. Now lay back in bed *really* suggestively. Put one arm under your tits. Yeah, really stick 'em out. Yeah, that's it. The perfect picture. Oh baby, you look so delicious you're makin' me drool. Now just stay right there. I just need to attach this picture and send an email. I'll be right back for my dessert."

The young woman rolled her eyes, looked at the clock and turned the TV to her favorite housewives "reality" program. She turned the TV up when she heard loud laughter coming from across the hall. "Hey! Are you gonna come in here and screw me or what? I'd like to time it for during a commercial break! I don't wanna miss my show!"

"Yeah, yeah, yeah! I'll be there in a minute!" the chortling misogynist yelled back as his amused stare was fixated on the tiny 'Angry' emoji that his soon-to-be-ex-wife had responded with. "Oh, ouch, Lori! Wow, if *that's* the best you have for rebuttal, then this case *will* be easy to win. Yes, get angry, my former love. Get really, really angry. Come into court and make an ass out of yourself. Yell and scream and prove how unfit you are to raise Morgan. Get angry, bitch! And once you've thrown everything that you have at me and lose, you will realize that you have no power over me. You will have no power over your own life. And you will have no influence over your precious Morgan. Yes, get angry. Savor your anger. Because after next week you will be a shell of your former self. You will be drained of all your fight. You will be as listless as a deflated balloon. And speaking of balloons, heh, heh, heh."

He ran into the bedroom and pounced on top of his paramour. He opened his mouth wide and aggressively stuck his tongue as deeply into her mouth as he could. At that moment, a soft chanting began in his head. *Contra eos qui suis vocibus alios opprimunt, habebunt locutions. Contra eos qui suis vocibus alios opprimunt, habebunt locutions. Contra eos qui suis vocibus alios opprimunt, habebunt locutions.*

"Ew, wipe your mouth, wouldja? You're all slobbery!" the woman exclaimed. "Oh, sorry, baby," he said as he wiped the drool from his chin. "You just get me so excited. Here, let's try this again." The chanting increased in volume as he opened his mouth once again to greet his lover with a lustful kiss. Instead, she was greeted by a quart of spittle that cascaded out of his mouth and into hers. She clutched her throat and began coughing up the thick liquid that was flowing down her esophagus.

"Oh Jesus! Gross!" she screamed out through her gagging as she shoved him off of her. She grabbed the corner of the blanket and began wiping the thick mucus off her saturated face and hair. "I don't care *how* rich you are, this is just *gross*! God! See a doctor! Look at me! I'm absolutely covered in your...in your...oh *gross*! I'm leaving!"

"Wait baby! Come back!" He pleaded, sending a wave of drool against the closing bedroom door. "What the hell is happening to me?" he said aloud causing more drool to splash upon the portrait of his smug father. He heard a woman's laughter echoing throughout the room. "Who, who is that?" He yelled out as a waterfall of thick slobber ran out of his mouth, down his pajamas and pooled at his feet on the carpeted floor. The laughing continued and the chanting became louder as he frantically looked around the room. He could feel his salivary glands draining his body of water like an overactive sump pump during a torrential rainfall.

He looked in the full-length mirror and began to weep from his drying eye ducts as he looked upon his shrinking mucous covered body. He cried out in anguish as the pain of dehydration began setting in. Every few seconds he would be forced to open his mouth so that another torrent of drool could explode out of his overflowing cavity. His body ached intensely from the sudden loss of fluids and his weakened frame collapsed upon the flooded carpet. The laughing and chanting continued as a waterfall of slobber poured down the bedroom walls and collected along the baseboards like primordial ooze. Before gurgling out the final ounce of fluid from his wringed out body, he looked up into the mirror. There he saw his wife's brilliant blue celebratory eyes looking down at him.

The young woman opened the door, re-entered the room, and yelled out, "I forgot my purse!" She grabbed her bag from the vanity, then screamed and ran out of the room as she was being pelted by drool droplets that were pouring from the ceiling. She looked down at her former lover with dismay. His still body was lying in a lake of thick, clear drool. His once taught frame was wrinkled, shriveled, and dark purple resembling a very large raisin. The anguished expression on his face was barely visible under its thick gelatinous mask.

She reached into her purse for her phone and said in a disinterested tone, "I guess I better call the cops. I mean, I told the guy that I liked it when men got me wet, but this is ridiculous. I wonder what Benny is doin' tonight? Yes, hello? Um, I want to report a, um, well, I'm not sure *what* I'm reporting. But this guy I've been seeing is lying here dead. How did he die? Damned good question. I'll let you cops figure it out. I've never seen anything like it. Oh, and you may want to tell the responding officers to wear raincoats. And galoshes. This is a real mess."

———

"Oh gross, I need a shower," a sweat covered Lori stated through her deep breaths. "And I need to change my pajamas, too," she added as she peered down at her drool covered pants that were lying under the mouth of the slumbering Gabriel.

"So, *that* was fun wasn't it, Lori?" she heard her summoned spirit whisper into her soul. "I really do like this incantation. And your use of this new-fangled technology. It makes me creative. I must say, I've never dehydrated someone before. Well, not in *that* way. Tied down in the desert for days? Sure. That's been done. But this? This was quite amusing. I do feel bad for that poor girl, though. Oh well. Maybe she'll learn to make better choices in who she mates with."

"Okay, since you're still hanging around, a few questions here," Lori said as she slid her damp body from underneath the slumbering Gabriel and carefully rested his head on the cushion. "First off, I thought that I had to be connected with the book's incantation to be able to see the effects of my summoning. How was it that I was able to see that? I don't even have the book right now."

"Oh, that," the spirit replied. "No, I can take you there if I choose. If you are touching the incantation in the book, then I am *compelled* to take you there whether I want to or not. But once we are connected, I can allow you to see what I see, book or no book. It's up to me. And, quite frankly my dear, I enjoy hanging out with you. That *is* the proper term today for spending time together, isn't it? I sometimes get lost in all of the changing jargon."

"Um, yeah," Lori answered. "Hanging out is fine. Okay, and I know I was really angry, but did you have to kill him? I mean, he's an ass and everything but you've denied my daughter the opportunity to have a relationship with him someday. I mean, who knows? Maybe as he got older, he would have a change of heart. Maybe he could turn into somebody that my daughter could respect. But now, she won't have that chance."

There was dead silence for a moment before both Lori and the spirit burst out laughing. "Oh, who am I kidding," Lori said through her chuckles. "He's a dick. Or he *was* a dick. And he would have *always* been a dick. Morgan has no respect for him now, nor would she *ever* have any respect for him. He burned that bridge a long time ago. But still, now I have to tell her that he's dead. Whether she loves him or not, he's still her father. This isn't going to be easy."

"No, I suppose not," the spirit replied. "About as easy as it was for *your* mother to tell *you* that *your* father had been killed. My, you ladies Cabot seem to have a bit of a problem with who you choose as mates. I suggest you take your time with the next one. Make sure he respects you for who you are. Make sure he wants to contribute as much to you as he wishes you to contribute to him. These relationships have been so one-sided for the longest time. The woman is always expected to serve the man, but not vice-versa. And when we stand up for ourselves and dare to have an independent thought, do you know what happens? Well, I can *tell* you from personal experience. You are branded a witch and burned at the stake! And I most *certainly* was never a witch! Oh sure, I knew some who were, but I was like you! I was a medium! And did I have an opportunity to make my case in that penile-filled courtroom? Noooooo. The men branded me a witch and that was it. Me! A witch! Like I would *ever* lower myself to even share a sip of tea with one of those bitches. That really was the most hurtful part. It wasn't so much being burned alive, although that was less than pleasant. It was my name being associated with those little tarts for all eternity. But that's water under the bridge I suppose. Water under the bridge that witches who were chained to rocks were thrown off of and drowned. I know those Puritans were hateful cusses and they *did* burn me alive, but it *was* always fun watching one of those uppity witches go glub, glub, glub. Anyway, it seems now that you will have a better day in court than me. In fact, there will now be *no need* for your day in court. You and your Morgan are free. And speak of the little devil, here she comes. Good-night Lori. I hope to play more games with you soon. Toodles and good luck with your daughter."

"Mom?" a drowsy Morgan asked as she lumbered down the stairs. "Who are you talking to?"

"Well, that's a loaded question," Lori answered as she sat back on the couch and searched for the proper wording for her explanation. "Here, dear. Let me show you what your father sent me this evening."

Morgan read the email then stared at the 'Angry' emoji. "Is he...?"

"Yes, dear. He is," Lori softly replied. "Are you okay?"

"Yeah," Morgan answered. "I mean, I really don't feel anything.

Well, except relief. I had no connection to him, and he was so cruel to us. And I know that you've been downplaying this court thing with me, but I think that was a bigger threat than you were letting on. Am I right?" Morgan took her mother's silence and blushing as an admission. "Uh, huh. I thought so. He was going to try to take me. Just to make you suffer. To make us *both* suffer. He was a cruel man, Mom. He was never going to change. I feel nothing for him. In fact, I hope he's burning in hell right now. Do we have to go to the funeral?"

The pair looked at each other for a moment and then simultaneously said, "Eeeeewww!"

Lori then stated, "Yes, I think that we should. If for no other reason than to keep up appearances. Plus, it might be fun to watch his father and all the other sexist men in that family suffer a bit. God, how I hate those assholes!"

"That's my Mom!" Morgan exclaimed. "Always looking on the bright side of things! Okay, I'm tired. I'm going back to bed. See ya in the morning."

"Alright dear," a relieved Lori replied. "But before you go to bed, do me one favor. Go into the bathroom and wipe your chin. You have a bit of drool on it."

CHAPTER 19

─────────

BE CAREFUL WHAT YOU WISH FOR

"Here's the final report from the contents found in Morgan's room, Detective," Deputy Holloway stated as she laid a pile of papers in front of the bleary-eyed Connor. "Anything in this one?" he asked as he began skimming the findings. "Nope," the deputy replied. "Same as every other room. There were tons of fibers, hair, skin, nails, and other assorted stuff. Nothing that links to the missing girls. We have fingerprints and hair and stuff from Morgan, Lori, and Sophia, of course. And you, but that's to be expected since you've become rather, um, close to this family. Lots of evidence that Vince was there. Most of that was found, um, in Sophia's bedroom. Well, in her bedding actually. And no blood whatsoever, except a trace found near the kitchen sink that turned out to be Sophia's. Not much of it. She probably just cut her finger slightly. And Morgan's room is *really* clean. The only other person who left any trace of themselves was Naomi. Not a trace of evidence that those missing girls ever came into contact with that car, that house, or anybody living in that house. There was one interesting thing, though."

"Oh yeah, what was that?" Connor asked as his eyes continued to scan the documents.

"Well, I didn't think they had a dog, but there was a lot of dog hair found on the carpet and the couch cushions. It's the hair from a Doberman."

"Huh," Connor replied. "Well, I've never *seen* a dog there, but I'll check it out. No law against having a dog visit, I suppose. Thank you, Deputy. You have been just wonderful with this. I'm going to go through everything one more time, then I want you and the captain to go over it again. I want to make sure I haven't missed anything. A couple more questions and you can knock off for the night. Any luck with the girls' credit cards or anything? Any indication that they're on the run?"

"Well," the deputy began. "Although that is a very plausible theory, there's nothing to indicate that. We've gone through surveillance tapes from the bus and train stations. No tickets have been purchased by them. Their credit cards haven't been used and there's been no activity on their phones. No contact, that we can determine, with any of their family or friends, either. There's really only two explanations at this point, from my perspective. Either they had a bunch of cash ready and are using fake names and fake identities and maybe had some arrangement with someone to drive them out of here so that they could disappear. Or something *really bad* happened to them after they left the cemetery. And whatever bad happened to them, wasn't caused by Morgan. That's my two cents, anyway."

"Yep, that's where I'm at too," Connor replied as he stretched his aching neck back and forth. "It's really not likely that they had pre-meditated their escape. If they're on the run, then they made that decision on the fly, and they'll end up making a mistake at some point. The latter is much more plausible. But who? Who was it that lured them away from their car? I'm betting it's somebody that they knew and trusted. A classmate? Family member? And maybe nothing bad has happened to them. Maybe they're being hidden by someone. Maybe they're on the run right under our noses. Alright, once you and the captain give Morgan her final clearance, let's start looking at these girls' closest friends and relatives. I'm really glad we didn't find anything, but damn is this case getting frustrating. Okay, just one more question. What do you think of this?"

Connor handed Morgan's notebook to the deputy who began reading the short story. "Wow, she can really write," the enthralled deputy stated as she turned another page. "These kill scenes are really vivid and this Maddy character is a real hoot. Yeah, I can see why she was pissed that Hermes ripped her off. Oh wow! I didn't see *that* one coming! *That* kill was pretty funny. And gross."

"So, you don't find this a bit disturbing?" Connor inquired further. "I mean, it certainly isn't evidence that she was involved in this, but doesn't it point to a tendency towards violence?" The deputy began laughing and said, "Nope. Not at all. Listen, you old prude. I'm really into scary stuff that goes bump in the night. And *somebody's* gotta write this shit, right? I think that for the Morgans of the world, it's a coping mechanism to deal with all the crazy shit in this world that she has no control over. Somebody pisses her off? Eh, have this Maddy chick kill them. She gets her tension out and nobody is harmed. Well, not in real life. If this Maddy were *real*, then that would be a different story. That would be murder and I'd be the first in line to lock her up. But this is just a story. A *brutally violent* story, sure, but still just a story. A way for her to live vicariously through her creation.

"And a way for her *readers* to live vicariously too. You know why I think people like this slasher stuff? I think it's training. You know how cats play with toy mice? They aren't really playing. They're actually working on their hunting skills. They are working on their *survival* skills through their play. That's what I think *we're* doing by reading this stuff or watching those violent movies. On the one hand, we're practicing our survival skills. We're processing every move that every victim makes that ends up getting them killed through our own primitive fight or flight response and we're learning from it. On the other hand, we're living vicariously through the killer. Whether we want to admit it or not, we all have really dark thoughts. We think about what we would like to do to some-body that we hate. Most of us don't act on it, of course, because we are beholden to common decency and civility. Even to those who are *indecent* and *uncivil*. We *still* don't harm *them*. But we *want* to, don't we?

"So, there's a part of us that is rooting for the victims to get away and a part of us that is rooting for the killer to finish off that annoying babysitter who reminds us of somebody we hate. On a certain level, we actually admire these killers because they aren't bound by any sense of societal norms. In their minds, what they are doing is justified. And we *admire* that level of personal freedom and strength. On some level, we wish *we* could be them. So, take the stick out detective. I'd be *much* more worried if she was dressed in drab little dresses, wore no makeup, and sat reading the Bible every waking moment. It's *those* uptight bitches that you *really* have to worry about. They're wound so tight from suppressing their normal human thoughts and urges that they eventually snap. And then people *really* get hurt. I'm not worried about girls like Morgan. They know who they are and don't give a shit what other people think. And when somebody pisses them off, well, then, that's just the latest chapter in our little book, now isn't it? There is *one* thing in here that's kinda weird, though."

"Oh, yeah? What's that?" Connor asked. "Well," Deputy Holloway answered. "It's nothing to do with the case, but how does this twisted little mind also come up with 'Larry the Leopard?' I mean, talk about split personality! Weird. And what are these four phrases under the picture? Is that Latin?"

Connor nodded his head and said, "Yeah, it's Latin. I have no idea what she's doing because she's not taking Latin in school. I translated the phrases. They don't make sense. Here's what they say."

Come to me out of my dreams and into my life.

From these pages you shall be born.

You will appear to me as I created you.

"And this last one seems incomplete. It just says, 'From my heart and from my hands.' It's weird. Maybe she's just playing around with titles or captions or something. Maybe using Latin to stand out in a crowded market? I dunno. Who wants to try to figure out the mind of a teenage girl? Anyway, certainly nothing incriminating. And speaking of Latin, I just have this old book to go through, then I'll be done with this stuff. You can take off after you and the captain clear Morgan. Then, we need to get this stuff back to the ladies Cabot. Please pack it up neatly and I'll take it to them. But I'm not looking forward to it."

The deputy left the room and Connor carefully retrieved the ancient book from its plastic bag. He opened it up to the first page. The dark reddish, brown ink seemed to glow for a moment. Connor adjusted his eyes and began reading. The words on the page suddenly disappeared. "What the hell?" Connor stated as he turned the page. "My eyes must be playing tricks on me. Here. Let's see what this page says." The page said nothing to him as those words also dissipated into a blank canvass. "What in the hell is going on here?" Connor yelled out. The frustrated detective's anger intensified as the words disappeared on page after page after page the moment he tried to read them. "Goddammit!" he yelled out as he slammed the book down on his desk, exposing the final empty page.

"Alright, I'm going to get to the bottom of this right now! I don't care *how* sweet the Cabot's are, this seems like some real voodoo shit here," he roared as he dialed his phone. On the other end of the line came Sophia's voice. "Well, hello there Connor." "How, how did you know it was me?" Connor asked. "Caller ID. Duh," Sophia answered through an exasperated giggle.

"Alright, Sophia, enough with the jokes," Connor demanded. "Listen, I've been going through that old book of yours. It smells really funky by the way. Almost like burnt chicken or something. Anyway, tell me *right now* what this book is. Every time I turn the page, the words disappear. Just what type of stuff are you up to, anyway?"

Connor was greeted by brief laughter before Sophia said, "Gotcha." "What do you mean, 'gotcha'?" Connor yelled out. "Oh, Connor," Sophia replied through her chuckles. "I wanted to tell you when you took that book, but you were so intrusive and I was just a bit annoyed with you, so I thought I'd go ahead and let you look through it. Kinda freaky, isn't it?"

"Hell yeah, it's freaky!" Connor uncharacteristically screamed. "This isn't funny Sophia! I think that you're involved in something! Something that I can't explain! Like voodoo or something! Now tell me what's in that book!"

"Oh, Connor," Sophia calmly replied. "Yes, it's freaky. It's *meant* to be freaky. It's an old blank notebook I found years ago. I wrote all this gibberish in it in Latin. And I wrote it in ink that will disappear after being exposed to light for a few seconds. I use it to trip people out at parties. Pretty fun, huh? So, I know you said no more games, but Connor. *Gotcha*."

Connor's mind began whirling before he let out a loud laugh. "Oh, my lord, Sophia. I'm so sorry. This case is really getting to me. I think I'm losing my mind. Listen, just forget about it. I'll have this book back to you very shortly. In fact, I'll have *all* your stuff back. It's going through the final clearances but, just as I thought, there's nothing there. There's no evidence of those three girls having been in your home at all. So, Morgan's going to be cleared here within the hour and I'll bring all this stuff back to you. Um, is Lori home? Maybe I could get a chance to speak with her, y'know, if she isn't still too upset."

"Connor, are you a wealthy man?" Sophia playfully inquired. "Um, no, not really," a confused Connor replied. "Well," Sophia countered. "If I were *you* I'd scrape up enough money for a *very* expensive piece of jewelry, perhaps a nice bouquet of flowers, and an *exorbitant* dinner. Because, my friend, my daughter is *still* very pissed at you."

"So, go through my savings, huh?" a despondent Connor asked.

"Every goddam penny of it," an amused Sophia answered. "Alright, but hey before I let you go, did you ladies get a dog? We found some hairs on the..." Connor began to ask before hearing Sophia say, "Goodnight Connor. We're looking forward to having our belongings back." CLICK.

"What the hell is *wrong* with me?" an embarrassed Connor said aloud to himself. "*Voodoo*? I'm accusing them of *Voodoo*? Jesus, now I know why it took me so long to make detective. I'm such a sucker." His thoughts were interrupted by the bubbly voice of a teenage girl.

"Hiya Uncle Connor! Whoareya talkin' too? Talkin' to yourself? I can understand that. I talk to myself all the time, especially when people tell me to go away. Then, I don't have anybody to talk to, so I just talk to myself, y'know? It can be really fun! I've learned that I'm a great listener! I talk to myself about all sorts of things. Y'know. Homework. Boys. Well, actually that's about it. Hey, what are ya workin' on? Those missing girls? I'm sorry I couldn't be more help. I was knocked out. Do you really think Morgan did something? There's no way, Uncle Connor. She's like the sweetest person in the world and would never harm anyone. Anyway, Dad was watching his game, and I was in the living room with him helping the announcers do the play by play and Dad said that you might be hungry and why don't I bring you something to eat? So, here I am with a meatball parm! And hey! You guys need to lower your curbs in the parking lot. I think they scraped my dad's bumper up pretty good."

Connor was trying to find a way to delicately excuse himself from his niece. Only a few words that Naomi rattled were being registered by his exhausted mind. Meatball parm piqued his interest. So did his brother's bumper getting scraped. But Connor became completely engrossed in every syllable that Naomi uttered when he heard her say, "Oooooh, what's this old book? Is that Latin? Weird looking paper and ink. I took Latin for a couple years; I think that I can figure out some of this stuff!"

"Wait! You can read this?" Connor exclaimed. "Uh, yeah," a confused Naomi answered. "I mean, it's in Latin, but it's right there on the page." "Okay, Naomi," a nearly hyperventilating Connor stated. "I'm going to turn to the first page and leave it open for a few seconds, okay? Then, I want you to look down at it and tell me what you see. Okay. Look down. What do you see. Nothing right?"

"Are you okay, Uncle Connor?" a genuinely concerned Naomi inquired. "I think that this case is getting to you, and you need some sleep. Do you know what helps me sleep? Well, I used to count sheep, but I outgrew that so now I..."

Naomi was cut off by her uncle's exasperated voice. "Naomi, please. Just tell me what you see." "Um," Naomi answered. "Well, it looks a lot like the back page. Just a bunch of phrases written in Latin. What's the big deal? Do you want me to try to translate it for you? I wasn't very good at Latin, but I might be able to recognize a few words."

"No, no, that won't be necessary, Naomi," Connor replied as he wiped his saturated forehead with his sleeve. "No, I can translate it on the computer. That'll be, um, faster. What I need *you* to do is take this notebook and write down every word just as it appears on each page, okay?"

"Sure, Uncle Connor, I'd be happy to!" Naomi squealed out. "But why don't *you* do it? Are you having trouble with your eyes? I bet you're having trouble with your eyes. Uncle Connor. You're getting older and whether you like it or not, you need to start taking better care of yourself. The next time I bring you dinner it's going to be a salad and steamed vegetables and not a meatball parm, 'cause I love you and I want you to be around forever, okay?"

"But, but, I *like* meatball parm subs," Connor whined before shaking his head vigorously. "What am I saying? That's not important. Yes, Naomi. My eyes are just a bit tired, and you would be a *huge* help if you could do that, okay? I'm just going to go to the lounge and lay down for a bit. You just let me know when you're finished. Naomi, I don't think that I've ever been happier to see you. Thank you."

"No prob, Uncle Connor!" a beaming Naomi replied. "You just go get your rest. I think that's a good idea. Like I was saying, you're getting older now and rest is very important for an aging…okay bye! I'll let you know when I'm done!"

Deputy Holloway dragged her fatigued frame back into Connor's office several hours later carrying the book. "Okay, I got the results back," she said wearily. Connor looked up from the translations that he was pouring over. "Oh, Deputy. Thank you so much for staying. This is probably nothing, but it's just really strange. What do you have?"

"We found traces of Sophia and Morgan all over this book. Skin cells, mostly. Lori's was only in three places. The front cover, the back cover and in one spot on page twenty-three."

"Show me!" Connor demanded. Deputy Hollway opened the book to page twenty-three. The pair stared in amazement for a moment as the once-present inscriptions disappeared. "Right here," she pointed to a spot in the middle of the blank page. "Ok, just keep pointing to that exact spot," Connor said as he grabbed the notebook and opened it to page twenty-three. He compared the spot in the ancient book to what Naomi had transcribed. "Contra eos qui suis vocibus alios opprimunt, habebunt locutions. Okay, what the hell does *that* mean?" He retrieved another notebook that held the translations. "Those who use their expressions to oppress others shall have their very expressions used against them. This is so weird."

"Oh, and there's one more thing, Detective," the deputy stated reluctantly. "We just found out that *another* person that's associated with Lori died last night. Her husband, or soon-to-be ex-husband. Or, well, ex-husband now, I guess. He was found wringed out. I mean, literally wringed out. His body looked like a prune It had been drained of all its fluid and the room was covered with, um, well, this sounds insane, but it was covered in saliva."

"I see," Connor said regretfully. "Anything else?" "Um, yeah," the deputy answered. "It seems as though the last person to have contact with him was his new mistress. She's the one that called it in, and she said that he started kissing her then he just kept slobbering all over the place. Like, he was shooting slobber all over the room from his mouth. But the *next to last person* he was in contact with was via email."

"And was that person Lori?" Connor asked hesitantly of the nodding deputy. "I see. Did she just happen to respond with an 'Angry' emoji?" The deputy continued nodding. "Thank you, deputy. Why don't you call it a night and thank you."

Connor sat down and propped his heavy legs on the desk. His eyes repeatedly darted between the inscription and the translation. He felt his mournful heart sink to its lowest depths as the words played on a loop in his addled mind. *Contra eos qui suis vocibus alios opprimunt, habebunt locutions. Those who use their expressions to oppress others shall have their very expressions used against them. Contra eos qui suis vocibus alios opprimunt, habebunt locutions. Those who use their expressions to oppress others shall have their very expressions used against them. Contra eos qui suis vocibus alios opprimunt, habebunt locutions. Those who use their expressions to oppress others shall have their very expressions used against them.*

Trick book, huh? He thought to himself. *I don't know why Naomi could read this thing and the rest of us can't, but that's a mystery for another day. But I now know this isn't a trick book. And these inscriptions aren't gibberish. Sophia lied to me. Made a fool of me. Lori's skin is only on this one spot on this one page. And now her husband is dead. Also from unusual circumstances and also after getting an angry response from Lori. Maybe I was wrong about this being voodoo, but there sure as hell is something very strange going on. I'm convinced of it now. The ladies Cabot aren't just ladies. They are murderers. All three of them. And I'm not sure there is a damned thing that I can do about it.*

C H A P T E R 2 0

W I T C H E S B R E W

"Our newest member has been awakened sisters," Victoria stated to her coven. She lifted her black hood from off her golden locks and looked at the other twelve members of her sisterhood with glowing pale blue eyes. "We must go to her. I sense that she has done something. Something unwise. I fear we might just have a problem. And I fear we're going to have to go speak with those damned mediums. Let us go consult with Papa Doc."

The thirteen black-garbed women went outside, straddled their brooms, lifted their index fingers toward the sky to test the wind speed and direction, and whisked away toward a vast cranberry bog.

"I see," Papa Doc began following Victoria's explanation. He lifted his bent spine from off his chair and dragged himself over to a disheveled bookshelf. After knocking over two stacks of dusty books, he retrieved the one that he had been searching for. "Ah, here it is," he said with satisfaction.

"What is that book, Papa Doc?" Victoria inquired. "Will that give us instructions on how to work with the mediums?" "No," Papa Doc replied. "This book is much more important than that. This book contains a very special recipe. I was thinking about making gumbo for tonight's dance party, and this book contains the absolute best recipe. No, your problem isn't as complicated. First, Victoria, as the leader of your little coven, I suggest that you do this alone. You need to approach Naomi first, then talk to the ladies Cabot. I fear that if you do this as a group, Sophia will feel ganged up on, and nothing will be accomplished. She can be a bit, um, well…"

"She's a bitch," Victoria interjected. "Now, now," Papa Doc scolded. "That will be quite enough of that talk. If it is true that a police officer has found out about one of us, then we are all in grave danger. And this will take all of our efforts. Sophia will need to summon a spirit. You will need to cast a spell over the heart. I will put a little something together to open Naomi's eyes as to who she is and what she can do. Yes, Naomi will be the icing on the cake. The love she has for Connor should be enough to make this work. I hope. But I said it before, and I shall say it again. We must work together. A truce must be called. And adhered to. Do you understand my dears?"

"Yes, Papa Doc," the thirteen women reluctantly replied. One of the other witches then said, "But, if you and Victoria are going to go get Naomi and speak with those Cabot bitc…um, I mean, the Cabots, then what are the rest of us to do?"

"Oh, my dear," Papa Doc answered as he scurried his hunched backed framed over to a makeshift desk of stacked wooden wine crates and began scribbling instructions in a notebook. "Why *you* twelve lovelies play the most important part. Yes, we would not be able to pull this off if it weren't for you. I will be a bit preoccupied for the next few hours so this is what I will need you to do. First, go to the grocery store and pick up everything on this list. And don't get the generic stuff. Get the best that they have. Then, go to the packy and get what's on *this* list. We are running quite low on our libations. And don't forget my cigars. When you return, follow this gumbo recipe to the letter. Any slight variation will ruin the dish. Especially the onion. You must use the exact amount of onion called for. Then, go to my record collection and begin pulling out every Ted Nugent album that you can find. Build a fire in the fireplace and toss those records into it. I've been meaning to get rid of his insipid shit for some time. Then go back to the records and put together a playlist. I'm thinking seventies disco tonight, ladies. And finally, if you would be dears and sweep up a bit. I mean, you *are* all quite good with brooms. Then, we'll be ready for tonight's dance party! After today, I'm gonna be ready to boogie! Alright then, let's have at it! Let me just grab my home visit bag and I'll be ready to go. Victoria, let's go pick up Naomi first. Then, on to Sophia's. Why isn't anybody moving?"

Papa Doc lifted his bent neck and found twelve pairs of defiantly folded arms and angered witch eyes staring at him. "So, what are we now, your personal *servants?*" one of the irritated young ladies inquired. "Yeah! We didn't break the shackles of the male patriarchy centuries ago to cook and clean for *you*, Papa Doc," another roared back. There was then a chorus of, "Yeah! That's right! We're *no* man's servant! Cook for yourself! Down with the patriarchy!" Before he knew it, Papa Doc was surrounded by twelve protesting young women. One of them took off her bra and burned it near his right crutch in a traditional display of independence. Papa Doc was sweating profusely as the circle of enraged estrogen began to tighten around his crippled frame. He pleadingly looked over at Victoria who merely flashed a sly smile and shrugged.

"Ladies, ladies, ladies," Papa Doc implored. "Please, listen to me. I did not mean to offend. Please ask yourself, who is it that always prepares our little nocturnal feasts, hmmmm? Who is it that puts together our kick-ass play lists? Who is it that mixes our nasty little cocktails? I believe that the answer you are looking for is me. And I do all of that almost every night so that you, my guests, need to do nothing but come here and enjoy yourselves. It has nothing to do with gender roles. It has to do with all of us pitching in so that we can have a cool time together. Now, all that I am asking for is a little assistance so that tonight's soiree goes off without a hitch. Is that really too much to ask for?"

The twelve young women looked at each other for a moment before one of them said, "Nope, I guess not. Okay, where's the list? Let's put a party together, ladies." *Witches*, Papa Doc thought to himself. *So high-strung. All the back and forth emotional drama. It's almost like dealing with a group of mortal men. Anger followed by contentment followed by whining and on and on. They really could learn a bit from the mediums. The mediums may be deadly, but they are so much more focused and grounded. Aw well. They both serve their purpose, I suppose.*

A joyful Naomi was talking to Morgan on the phone. She was lying on her stomach on her bed, kicking her feet up in the air as she chatted with her best friend. "Yeah, and then Uncle Connor had me read this really old book that belongs to your grandma. His eyes were really tired, I guess, so he had me read it and...yes, I could read it. It was all in Latin and stuff and...yes, he had me write down all of these passages exactly as they appeared in the book and...no, I don't know what he was doing with them. I heard him talking to Deputy Holloway and they were saying that you were going to be cleared and get your stuff back real soon, so there's nothing to worry about. Except for our classmates that hurt you. They're in a *ton* of trouble when they are found and...okay. Well, if you need to go talk to your mom, that's okay with me. I mean, all you have to say is that you need to go and that's it. I'll just shut up. Yep, shut up and hang up the phone. That's just what I'll do. All you have to do is tell me that you have to go and I'll...okay bye!"

Naomi pounced off her bed and yelled out her bedroom door. "Okay! I'm off the phone with Morgan! Hey, do you guys wanna play a game tonight or something? We haven't done that in a really long time. That would be really fun and..." She was cut off by the sound of her mother's weary voice. "Um, maybe later, dear. Is there anyone else you would like to call tonight? Or perhaps you could recheck your recheck of your homework?"

"Okay!" Naomi responded. She went over to her desk and pulled out her chemistry assignment. She looked at her smiling reflection in her bedroom window. Her eyes then refocused past the window-pane and onto the sight that was floating outside of her second story bedroom. Naomi's jaw dropped and she began taking small steps backwards as she stared at the young blonde woman who was suspended in the air on a broomstick while smiling and pointing at her. "Who are *you*?" a shocked Naomi asked. Her window blew open and the blonde woman said, "I am a friend. *Your* friend, Naomi. There is nothing to be afraid of. I need your help. Your friend *Morgan* needs your help. Just tell your parents that you are going out. I'll meet you on the front lawn. Oh. And bring a broom."

The entranced Naomi put her tennis shoes on, walked downstairs, told her relieved parents that she was going out, took a broom out of the kitchen closet, and dutifully met the strange woman near the bushes in the front yard. From behind the bushes came a hunched-over old man. He looked up into Naomi's amazed expression, smiled at her and said, "Voyez qui vous êtes. Devenez qui vous êtes. Soyez qui vous êtes."

"What did you just say to me?" Naomi asked in a soft voice. Papa Doc chuckled and replied, "What I said, my dear, is 'See who you are. Become who you are. Be who you are.' Now just breathe deeply. Let Papa Doc send you on a little trip." Papa Doc lifted his right hand from his crutch and exposed his palm. Victoria then poured a white powder into it. He smiled up at Naomi, lifted his hand under her nose, and blew the powder into her face.

Naomi felt as though her lungs were about to explode as her twitching body collapsed upon the browning lawn. Her eyes rolled back, and her mind was suddenly bombarded by intense words, images, and emotions. She witnessed her ancient ancestors being chased, hunted, torn apart, drowned, and burned alive. She felt the fury, pain, and fear of each persecuted woman. And she heard spell after spell being repeated over and over in her overwhelmed mind. The plight of her ancestors was becoming a conscious part of her. As were their abilities. Their abilities to connect with and marshal the forces of nature. Fire, water, wind, plant life, and animals. Naomi's soul was now connected with the nature that surrounded her and that was now under her dominion.

Naomi let out a loud gasp and sat straight up. Whoooooaaaa!" She yelled out. "Man, that was trippy! I saw all this stuff. Really bad stuff that happened to my ancestors. It's so weird. I just know that they were my ancestors from Haiti. I now know that my ancestors were witches. And I now know that *I'm* a witch! I can like, combine herbs and stuff and cast spells and control stuff. Like this bush. Check this out!" Naomi reached down and grabbed a handful of dirt. She rubbed it into her hands, pointed toward the bush and said, "We are now one my arboreal friend. We are both sustained by the same earth. Do my bidding and I shall do yours."

A branch began extending from the bush. It creeped through the air towards Papa Doc. "Um, what are you doing, Naomi?" he asked as the tip of the branch made its way under his right arm. Papa Doc then began giggling as the leaves on the branch vibrated, tickling his underarm. "Oh, please stop it!" Papa Doc yelled out. "I'm very ticklish, please, please stop it!"

A beaming Naomi said, "Okay. Thank you my friend. Back to your place of rest." The branch receded back into the bush and Naomi squealed with delight. "That was soooo cool! So, like, are both of *you* witches *too*? Is that why you're here? To show me that I'm a witch? Oh my God! Can I do magic tricks for my friends or is this whole thing like, hush, hush. I can understand if it's hush, hush, and I won't say a word if it is. If there's one thing that I can do it's keep a secret. Yep, not one word from me about being a witc…"

"Naomi," Victoria stated sternly. "Please listen. You have *already* said something. You have *already* let a mortal know of your powers and of our existence. You were able to read Sophia's book because you are gifted. That is a book of incantations used by mediums. Your friend and her entire family are mediums. They can combine their anger with an incantation and summon a spirit to commit retribution against someone that has wronged them. That is what happened to Morgan's classmates. She got really angry, used the incantation to summon a spirit, and they did the rest."

"So, Morgan really *did* do something to those missing girls?" Naomi yelled out. "Naw," Victoria answered as she filed one of her long nails. "That was us. Me and my coven. I mean, I guess *technically* Morgan is responsible. I mean she got angry and used an incantation to forge alliances. So, the spirit that Morgan summoned got in touch with us and well, we had to protect *you anyway*, so we *kinda* had the tree drag them into the ground and make them a part of its root system. No biggie.

"Anyway, back to the main point. So, the Cabots are mediums. And no, you cannot use the incantations in that book, but you can read them. That way, the mediums know if they're dealing with someone who is enhanced. Your Uncle Connor, on the other hand, *cannot* read them. No mortal can. They do not have enhanced abilities. They're pretty boring, actually. Only Mediums, Witches and Voodoo Priests can read what is in that book. Oh yeah, this is Papa Doc. He's a Voodoo Priest. And a helluva dancer. Anyway, your uncle now knows that you are special. He now knows that the Cabots are um, well, I don't want to say *special*. I mean, they're just *mediums*, but your uncle now knows that they're involved with deaths and disappearances and all kinds of shit. So now, we are *all* at risk of being exposed and having to guard against the judgement of mortals. And we're not used to playing by their rules. If mortals knew that we were real, we would be hunted and persecuted once again, and *that* shit just isn't going to fly.

"So, we all have to come together to nip this in the bud with your Uncle Connor. And *you* are the key. You are a witch as you now know. You can cast spells and compel the forces of nature to assist you. And that is what we need your help with tonight. To compel the most powerful force of nature to convince your Uncle Connor to accept this and to not expose our secrets. We need *you* to harness the human emotion of love."

"But, but," an astonished Naomi began to inquire. "What if we don't succeed? What if my Uncle Connor arrests Morgan and her family? What if I can't help you?"

Victoria placed her pale hand under Naomi's ebony chin and lifted her head until their eyes met. She then said in a deep voice, "Well, Naomi, you had better *hope* that we're successful tonight. Because if we aren't, well, I don't care *who* it is. We won't allow *anyone* to expose us. Not even your uncle. And you sure as hell don't want to see what the vampires and werewolves might do to someone who is a threat to them. Got it?" The speechless Naomi could only gulp and nod in response. "Now, straddle your broom and let's get going."

"Um, straddle my broom?" Naomi asked. "Yes, your broom," Victoria tersely responded. She then let out an exasperated sigh and said, "Oh, new witches. Such a pain in the ass. As can be these brooms, so you want to pick one without any, um, splinters. Naomi, you are a witch. Witches ride brooms. Duh. It's in like every cartoon for like, ever. Just straddle the broom. Focus on the spell that makes you lighter than air. Can you feel it? Now just let the spell lift you into the air. Good. You're a natural at this. Now, point the broom in the direction that you want to go and, um, go. That's it. Easy, right? Now just follow me." Victoria floated in front of Naomi for a moment before jetting into the sky toward Morgan's house. Naomi's flight was a bit more erratic as it became immediately apparent that cars weren't the only vehicles that Naomi had difficulty operating.

"Okay, I'll see ya over there!" Papa Doc yelled out as he placed his crutches in the side car of his bright yellow 1958 Harley Davidson, put on his vintage black leather helmet, and started the engine. The roar of the bike followed the streaking witches around the street corner. As did Papa Doc's exuberant exclamation of "Wheeeee!"

"Damn, that's fun!" Papa Doc stated out as he parked his bike in the Cabot's driveway. Victoria descended until her black boots gently settled upon the front lawn. "Now where the hell is Naomi?" she asked aloud as she scanned the night sky. There was a sudden black streak that crashed into a nearby tree. Small branches and brown leaves tumbled out of the majestic maple. As did the remnants of a once-charming birdhouse. "I'm okay!" Naomi yelled out as she tossed her broom to the ground and began climbing down the sturdy limbs. "Wow. That's a really stupid place to put a tree. I could have been killed! But man, was that fun! I've never flown before! I was supposed to one time on a plane, but we were stuck at the gate for a really long time, like, for two hours or something, and this lady who was sitting next to me suggested that maybe I should ask about taking another flight. Or rent a car. Or do anything except be on this flight. So, I did! I totally got my money back too! The flight attendant said it would be no problem at all! And everybody was so happy for me that they applauded as I was leaving the plane! So, I rented a car and drove to New York instead of flying. Oh, it was such a nice drive. The weather was perfect and…"

"Oooooh, this is bad, bad, bad!" Sophia was yelling out as she frantically paced in the living room. Gabriel's black furry head followed her movement back and forth, anxiously awaiting the moment that someone might throw a ball. Or a stick. Or anything to get him off the couch for some much needed exercise. "I know how you feel about Connor, Lori, and I like him too, but we need to deal with him. I don't know how. I've never dealt with this before. Plus, we have to figure out what the hell Naomi can do! She can obviously read the book! But what is she? Maybe Voodoo Priestess, coming from Haiti and everything. Is that racist? Oh, who cares? As long as she doesn't turn out to be a goddamned witch! I will not have my granddaughter involved with…"

Sophia's rant was interrupted by an urgent pounding. She ran to the front door and cautiously cracked it open. "Well, speak of the goddamned devil!" she yelled as she flung the door open. She looked upon the faces of Papa Doc, Naomi, and Victoria. "Okay," Sophia said. "I think I know why this rogue's gallery is all here. Fine. Papa Doc and Naomi, come on in. This other bitch can park her broom up her ass someplace else. *Anyplace* else. Just not in *my* home and not on *my* lawn. Now get to steppin' bitch."

"Oh, you old *hag*!" Victoria screamed out. "If it wasn't for me and my sisters your precious granddaughter would be the one feeding that tree and not those little snots. So, just get off your high horse, bitch!"

"Who are you calling bitch, *bitch*?" Sophia roared back followed by Victoria's well thought out response. "I'm calling *you* a bitch, *bitch*!" This enlightened exchange carried on for far too long before they were silenced by the demonically booming voice of Papa Doc that rattled through the home. "That will be *enough* you two! That will be enough from *all* of you! Now get in this house and let's get down to business! I haven't much time left for this. I just *know* the coven has used too much onion in the gumbo. I just *know* it and I need to get back to check on it before it's too late. So, all of you will listen to me. I am a healer, and it is beyond time that we heal this silly little rift between witches and mediums."

"*Mediums* and *witches*," Sophia stated smugly. She could feel Papa Doc's scathing stare and decided to end her contributions for the moment. "Sophia, my dear," Papa Doc continued. "It is most ironic that is *you* and *Victoria* who seem to have the deepest of ill feelings toward one another. Yes, quite ironic indeed. To witness two blood relatives carry on this way is quite ridiculous. And beneath your last names."

"*Blood relatives?*" Sophia and Victoria yelled out in unison. "Yes, I *thought* that might get your attention," Papa Doc replied through a slight chuckle. "Yes, several centuries ago, there was a Cabot woman who was hunted and burned at the stake. She would have been Sophia's great, great, great, um, oh who cares? It was a distant descendant, alright? Anyway, she had two daughters. Twins, in fact. One was a medium, like her mother. But the *other*. The *other* was a *witch* like her daddy, who happened to be a warlock. The medium girl was placed with a sympathetic family, and she went on to have a daughter and so on. This then was the lineage of Sophia's family. This was the origin of the ladies Cabot. The *other* little girl was taken away by her father and *she* is the origin of Victoria's family. Now, Victoria, just what do you think that her father's last name was? Cat got your stubborn little tongue? Well, if you guessed 'Colombo,' you would be correct. Gee, where have I heard *that* name before? Oh, right. That is *your* last name Victoria, and *that* little girl was the beginning of a long line of witches that thus far has ended with you. So, we have Victoria *Colombo*, and we have Sophia *Cabot*. Anyone know what those two names might have in common? Anyone? No? They both mean 'explorer.' Which is exactly what the two of you are. Explorers. Explorers for new incantations to summon new spirits. Explorers for new spells and concoctions to connect with nature. The two of you are descendants from the offspring of the same mother and father. You are cousins. You are blood. So, knock this bickering shit off, shake hands and let's get to work. We have a common threat to address. Well? What are you waiting for? I said shake hands!"

The grey headed, blue eyed Sophia looked awkwardly into the suddenly familiar blue eyes of her blonde, thirty-year-old adversary. Victoria mirrored the uncomfortable gaze as she shuffled her black boots on the carpet. They each let out a deep sigh before breaking down in tears and embracing while saying, "I'm sooooo sorry!"

"Ahhh shit," Papa Doc muttered under his breath. "This is going to take a while. And in the meantime, my gumbo is being ruined. Sometimes, I wish I wasn't such a good healer."

A half-hour later, Papa Doc tried to reestablish his control over the group. "Okay, this has all been very nice, but in case you have all forgotten, we still have the little matter of Connor O'Sullivan knowing something is up. And, more importantly, my dance party is supposed to begin soon. So, are we all out of questions? Shall we recap? Yes, Morgan and Naomi are best friends, and one is a medium and one is a witch. Yes, great. How Shakespearian. Sophia and Victoria have swapped their life stories. Lovely. Just lovely. And Lori has fed the dog which makes me feel a bit safer. Great. Now, can we get down to business? I've done my part. All I could do was help Naomi find her true nature. And that was done *hours ago*! Now, it's *your* turn. Mediums and witches working together. Or we can just let Connor do his thing and let the vampires and werewolves get to him. Y'know. Once they figure this out. It could be a while. Neither of them are terribly bright."

"Noooooo!" the entire group yelled out in response. "No, that won't be necessary," Sophia stated. "We are ready. What shall we do?"

"I think that I know," Victory answered cautiously. "I mean, if I might be able to make a suggestion." "But of course, cousin, please do," Sophia politely responded. "Any suggestion that you might have is quite welcome at the moment. Why I'm just sure that it's…"

"Okay, okay, okay," Papa Doc interjected. "Enough with the

damned mutual admiration society. Victoria, dear, what is your thought?"

"Okay, thank you Papa Doc," Victoria began. "And thank *you* Cousin Sophia for your kind words. I believe we need to do two things. We need a spell to allow Connor to open his heart. The key to this, I believe, is the feelings he has for Lori. Naomi and I can cast a spell allowing him to fully open his heart to the love he has for Lori. Then, my Cabot cousins can use an incantation to summon a spirit to take Connor on a guided tour of all the ill deeds that their victims have committed. Once he comes out of it, he will be filled with love for Lori and understand the justification for their actions. He will never say a word about this. In fact, this might just turn out to be a good thing. We'll have someone on the police force to run interference for us. Y'know, If we ever need it."

"At this rate, we're *definitely* going to need it," Sophia chortled. "And Victoria, that is a *wonderful* idea. And I know just the spirit to summon. She just *loves* to torment people with their bad deeds. Only *this* time, her power won't be used to torment. It will be used to enlighten. Okay ladies Cabot, Colombo, and O'Sullivan. Let's hold hands. Cousin Victoria and Naomi will go first. Then Morgan, Lori, and I will summon our spirit. And Lori. In order to summon her, you must let your emotions flow. The spirit must understand just how much you love Connor. The time for inhibitions is passed, my dear. Let the spirit know how you feel. Let *Connor* know how you feel."

Connor picked up then immediately placed the phone receiver back on its holder for the seventh time. He got up from his desk and began pacing. "But who in the hell am I going to call?" He said aloud to himself. "Who would believe this? That my kinda girlfriend casts spells or something to kill people? That she does it through emojis? I'll be locked up in the nut house! But I know that it's true! I know that all three of them have some sort of power and that they use that power to injure or kill others. But what can *I* do about it? I mean, there are laws against murder, sure, but who has jurisdiction over ghosts, or spirits or, hell, maybe they're angels! And maybe, just *maybe* those people had it coming? But no! It's still wrong. Nobody gets to be judge, jury, and executioner. Nobody. No, I *have* to do something about this. Don't I?"

As his final conflicted sentence trailed off, his eyes were drawn to the picture of Lori that was placed prominently on his desk. He looked upon her bright smile on her beautiful face that was framed by flowing strands of golden hair. His heart swelled with the love that he had for her. The feeling was so intense that he began weeping uncontrollably at the mere thought of not being with her. It was an anguish so great that his mind could no longer imagine any possible scenario where he could not be by her side. He fell to his knees just as he felt Lori's love for him rush into his soul. It was as though their hearts were now connected in a destined finality.

His mind was then assailed by images of horrid deeds that had been performed by each of the victims of the ladies Cabot. One by one he was shown just how dreadful each of those individuals were. One by one he was shown the depths of their depravity and cruelty. And one by one, he witnessed each of their violent deaths. He then felt one final thing. He felt the relief that everybody that was associated with the victims experienced following the deaths of their tormentors. He felt the relief of spouses, children, co-workers, neighbors, and others. He felt their relief from not having to endure the abuse, ridicule, disparagement, harassment, belittlement, or threats any longer. He felt their relief and he understood. He now understood three things. He understood the love that he had for his Lori and that she had for him. He understood the freedom, safety, and dignity that hundreds of people now rightfully experienced because of the actions of the ladies Cabot. And he understood the action that *he* needed to now take.

"Oh my God, that was exhausting," Lori stated as she and her sweaty collaborators collapsed on the couch and chairs. "Now what?"

"Now, we wait," Sophia answered while holding the drenched palm of her beloved daughter. "We wait and we shall see. We shall see whether this man truly loves you. And we will see just what type of man that he is. We shall see if he is capable of truly understanding the meaning of the word 'justice.'"

A PING came from Lori's laptop. She looked at the notifications and noticed that she had an email. It was from one Detective Connor O'Sullivan. "Well, here goes nothing," she said as she opened the brief email.

Lori- I know. I know what you are. I know what you have done. And I know what you can do. I am a sworn officer of the law. But it seems to me that what you are able to do is beyond my jurisdiction. So, I know. And I do not care. All that I care about is that I love you and I want to spend the rest of my life with you. Regardless of what happens to us in the future, your family secret is safe with me. So, you wanna grab a burger or what?

Lori flashed a devious little smile as her cursor hovered over all the possible emojis that she could respond with. Her mind was telling her to be reasonable. Slow down. No, don't use that one. *Oh, screw off,* she thought to her rational self as her heart was exploding with unbridled joy. She finally made her choice and pressed the button on her mouse. Her only response to Detective Connor O'Sullivan was the 'Heart' emoji.

CHAPTER 21

ODD BEDFELLOWS

A swooning Lori answered the front door and flung herself into Connor's unsuspecting arms. She kissed him passionately, looked lovingly into his eyes, and smiled. "So," an equally swooning Connor stated. "I guess I'm out of the doghouse then?" He then heard growling coming from beneath him. He looked down and saw the snarling Gabriel. Saliva was dripping from his exposed fangs as he glared at Connor's jugular. "Um, and speaking of dogs, is that…"

"Uh, yeah," Lori hesitantly replied. "Gabriel! Go to your spot. This is Connor and he's my, um, friend." Gabriel began wagging his tail, jumped up on Connor and began licking his face in a warm, moist greeting. "Okay, okay," a laughing Connor stated as he pushed his new friend down. "Good boy, Gabriel. Well, it seems as though this is yet *another* little detail that I'm going to have to leave out of my report. Listen Lori, and weird old bent over guy, and blonde that I've never seen before, and Naomi and…Naomi! What are *you* doing here?"

"Hiya, Uncle Connor!" an exuberant Naomi said. "I'm a witch!" "You're a *what?*" Connor exclaimed as his once settled mind began whirling once again. "Yep, witches are *real*, and I *am* one!" Naomi continued. "And this is Victoria, and she's a witch too and she's teaching me how to drive a broom. I'm not very good at it yet, but I'll get better. They just plant trees in stupid places in this town. And this is Papa Doc and he's a Voodoo Priest! He's like a healer or something. Cool, right? And you've met Gabriel. He's really a sweetheart once you get to know him. And you might be thinking that Morgan, Lori, and Sophia are witches too! You are, aren't you, Uncle Connor? Well guess *what?* You'd be *wrong* about that! They're mediums that can summon spirits to take care of bad people. And they really do take care of bad people, Uncle Connor. It's really not Morgan's fault what the spirit does. All she does is give them a little ringy-dingy and the spirits take care of the rest. It's the spirits that determine the punishment. So, please don't be mad at her or her family. Now, me and Victoria are witches, and we can cast spells and stuff that controls forces of nature. Like, make me light as a feather and control wind currents so that I can fly on a broom! I'm not very good at it yet, but I'll get better. I just need to avoid the trees. I wonder if there's a speed limit on flying. That wasn't on the driver's test.

"Anyway, you know how I've always been good at combining ingredients to make the perfect dish? Well, now I know why! It's because I'm a witch and witches are *really good* with combining stuff from nature. Like how Victoria was able to control that huge tree in the cemetery and have those bullies that beat up Morgan dragged into the earth to become part of its root system. So, that mystery's solved, I guess. You can go ahead and write that one up, Uncle Connor."

"Um, no, I think I'd better not," Connor muttered before Naomi's barrage of words continued. "So, you see Uncle Connor, witches and mediums and Voodoo Priests are real! And so are vampires and werewolves, I guess. But I haven't met any of them. They sound nasty. Are you going to tell my parents, Uncle Connor? *Please* don't tell them. I don't think they'd understand. *Please* can we keep this hush-hush like my speeding tickets. And accidents. And curfew violations. Oh, and that time I spaced off and drove away without paying for my gas. And remember that time I..."

Connor smiled at his niece and warmly embraced her. He whispered into her ear, "No, Naomi. No, I won't tell your parents." He then released her from his loving embrace and looked at each anticipatory face as tears welled up in his eyes. "In fact, I won't tell *anybody* about *any* of this. Yes, I am an officer of the law. I am an officer of *human* law. I really don't think that I have any jurisdiction over the laws of nature. And it seems to *me* that *that* is what you folks are ruled by. The laws of nature. I'm not sure what I'm going to say in my report, but..."

His statement was interrupted by a police cruiser pulling into the drive and parking behind Papa Doc's motorcycle. Deputy Holloway approached the open front door, peered in, and looked suspiciously at the motley crew that was assembled. "Um, hey Detective," she began. "I know that you told me I could take off, but the captain wanted to get this stuff back to the Cabots as soon as possible. I have everything that we took in the trunk. You wanna maybe help me get it?"

"Um, sure," Connor answered tentatively. As the pair were retrieving the various items from the cruiser, Deputy Hollway asked, "So, what's the deal here, Detective? Are you conducting interviews? I thought that *I* was running point on that. You know. To avoid any conflict of interest."

"Um, yeah, you are," Connor immediately replied as sweat began pouring from his forehead. "I was just, um, well, I was just... I heard a report about that missing dog being here, so I wanted to check it out. Similar dog, sure, but its not the one that killed the principal."

"I see," the deputy replied. "So, since they're all here, um, and *then* some, would it be okay if I interviewed them a bit? You know. See what connection there might be to Lori's husband's death and some follow-up on those missing girls? That okay with you?"

"Uh, sure," Connor answered while looking down at his shuffling feet. "Let me just make sure they're willing to voluntarily speak with you, okay?" Connor picked up a large tote of belongings and placed it inside the living room. He then turned to Sophia and said, "Hey. You know of any spirits that can connect you guys with my thoughts? The deputy wants to interrogate you folks and I think it would be better if I could tell you what to say. But I can't say it aloud." He then reached into the tote and retrieved the ancient book. "Here it is. Is there something that you can do?"

Sophia fondly took the book and began turning the pages. She looked into Connor's pleading eyes and said, "Are you frightened?" "I've never been so frightened in all my life," Connor replied in a trembling voice. "Lori could be in trouble. Real trouble. And that scares the hell out of me." "Good," Sophia said. "Hold onto that. I know just who to call." Sophia placed her hand over a seemingly blank page in the book. "Now, place your hand upon mine. Let me in. Let me feel your fear. Timor meus giude meus erit. Timor meus alios ducet. Timor meus giude meus erit. Timor meus alios ducet. Timor meus giude meus erit. Timor meus alios ducet."

"Wh-what did you just say?" Connor whispered. "I said," Sophia answered. "My fear shall be my guide. My fear shall guide others. Now, we are ready."

"Whoa! Man, did the wind pick up!" Deputy Holloway stated as she rushed inside the house with another tote. She fought against the sudden gusts and finally closed the door. "Whew. Didn't know it was supposed to be windy tonight. Okay, so is it alright if I ask a few questions? Y'know, just to tie up some loose ends?" The entire group silently nodded as Connor took a seat in the corner of the living room and closed his eyes. "Okay, thanks. This should go easy. Just a few questions. But first, Lori and Morgan, I was so sorry to hear about your recent loss."

"We're not," Morgan immediately answered. "We're not sorry at all. My dad was an asshole. We're not even going to the funeral. He's nothing to us." "Alrightythen," a somewhat dismayed deputy replied. "So, Lori, we noticed that you were one of the last people to have contact with him. You must have been pretty pissed after what he wrote to you."

Lori's mind began searching for the appropriate response until she heard the voice of her love in her head. She smiled slightly then repeated the words that she was being instructed to say. "Yes, I *was* quite upset. That's why I responded with the 'Angry' emoji. I just wanted to let him know that he had made me angry, but I didn't want to do or say anything that might complicate my upcoming custody hearing. So, I just did that. Just left a harmless emoji. I certainly didn't wish him harm, but I must admit, my life got a lot less complicated once I heard the news of his passing. And what a weird way to go. I heard that he, I don't know, slobbered to death? Is that even a thing? Maybe he was doing some messed up drugs or something. I guess the medical professionals are going to have a head scratcher there."

"Uh, huh," the deputy replied as she furiously scribbled notes in her pad. She then looked over at the book that Sophia was holding. "That sure is a weird book. When I first open it, I can see words. They look like Latin. But then they just disappear. Except for Naomi. *She* can read it, but Detective O'Sullivan and I couldn't. What's up with *that?*"

"Oh, not just me!" Naomi yelled out the words that were being fed to her. "Lots of people in this room can read it. You see, we all practice the black arts and only people who practice the black arts can read this stuff. I mean, it's not a big deal. We just go around calling spirits or casting spells or putting together potions and stuff. It's really nothing to worry about, deputy." Naomi then looked around the room at the amused faces of her co-conspirators. The entire group burst out into laughter on Connor's cue.

"Oh, Naomi," Sophia stated as she let out a deep sigh. "What will we *ever* do with you? Black arts, indeed. Here, my dear. There really isn't much to this book. Just a trick ink that disappears in light. But, if you tip it just so and shield it a bit from the light, then *anybody* can read it. Here, let me show you." Sophia got up from her seat and sat next to the deputy. She opened the book, tilted it slightly and brushed her hand up against that of the deputy so that they both had a connection to the open page. "You can read it, can't you? As can I.

As could anybody in this room if it is tilted like this. So, when Naomi was looking at it, it must have been slightly shielded from the light. Or maybe it was the black arts. Which one makes more sense, deputy?"

Deputy Holloway began chuckling and said, "See Detective? There's always an explanation. Man, you had me going at the station earlier. Okay, now Morgan, I just want to ask you one more time about the night of your assault. Is there anything else that you remember?"

Connor's voice crept into Morgan's consciousness. She opened her mouth and said, "Yes. Actually, I was going to call you, but I was still pretty pissed about you invading my room and everything. I'm over it now. I understand why you did what you did, and I want you to find those girls. I mean, I could care less if they're okay or not. Hell, it would be alright by me if they'd been swallowed up by the earth or something. But if they *are* okay, then I want you to find them. I want you to find them so that I can press charges and you can bring them to justice. So, I did remember one more thing. I was laying there and pretty beat up. They had just branded me. I was kinda drifting in and out, y'know? One of the girls picked up a large rock and said they should finish me off with it. Then, another girl asked about Naomi. The first girl said that they should do her too. The other two girls then kicked the shit out of the first girl and said that they weren't going down for murder. The girl that was being beaten begged them to stop. She said she wouldn't kill us and that she had a cousin or friend or something in Mexico that could help them hide out. Then, they left. I just assume that they went to Mexico. Or maybe they've been murdered by someone on the road. I kinda hope so. But if that *did* happen, I want to find out about it."

"Okay, well, I guess that gives me everything I need at the moment," Deputy Holloway stated as she closed her notebook and started toward the front door. She briefly thought about continuing her inquiry, then discarded the notion. She still had questions. She just didn't know *what* questions. "Sorry to bother you folks again. Detective, are you coming?"

"Um, no," a relieved Connor answered. "No, Deputy, I'm going to stay right here. While you write up that report, I 'm going to have a long overdue date night with my girlfriend."

"Okay, Detective, okay," Deputy Holloway replied with a hint of uncertainty. As the deputy shut the door behind her, Victoria whispered to her newfound cousin and ally, "She's going to be trouble." Sophia silently nodded in response.

Connor wiped the sweat from his forehead with his shirt sleeve and said, "Jesus, I need a drink." "Drink, you say?" the suddenly animated Papa Doc exclaimed. "Well, I know the perfect place! And it's just now midnight! The witching hour! Come on, bitches! Let's boogie!"

Morgan's Tempest roared to life and whisked its way around the winding roads on the outskirts of Plymouth as it followed a delighted elderly man riding his motorcycle. Sophia looked up into the sky and chuckled as she saw Victoria flying in a perfectly straight line while Naomi followed in an erratic zig-zag pattern, narrowly missing the tops of the surrounding trees. The entire group arrived at the large shack behind the cranberry bog. Brilliant lights were flashing through the filthy windows and a thunderous beat was pounding into the night air.

"No, no, no!" Papa Doc yelled out as he retrieved his crutches from his side car and began shuffling rapidly toward his door. "They *know* that they aren't to touch the stereo! I have *told* them time and again! They *never* put things away right and they blow out my speakers! And this isn't Seventies disco! This is Nineties alternative! Oh, never trust a witch to do the voodoo that only I can do."

There was a loud crashing sound, followed by a scream, followed by a huge plume of soot that encased the makeshift dance hall. Sitting inside the large fireplace was Naomi O'Sullivan, covered in black ashes. "Well, *that* was a stupid place to put a chimney!" she yelled out to uproarious laughter. "Oh, cool!" Papa Doc exclaimed as he watched the beams of disco lights flash through the dense shroud of soot. "I've never thought of this before! Turn up the music ladies! We have ourselves a fog machine!"

"So, what do you think of my friends?" Lori asked her beau as she mixed him another whiskey sour. "I don't know *what* to think, Lori," he replied as his amazed eyes darted around the room at the somewhat organized mayhem. "But it looks like Naomi has finally found a group who will accept her for who she is. She's such a sweet girl, but has always been the object of ridicule, because, well, you know. She's just a bit overactive. But look at the fun she's having with her um, coven? Jeez, this is so weird. I just hope she doesn't start dressing like them. Her parents will never let her go out of the house looking like that."

"Sooooo, you noticed how the witches are dressed, huh?" Lori asked in a slightly jealous tone. "You know what?" Connor immediately countered. "I'm not going to play this game with you. I think that I've proven my loyalty and commitment to you just a little bit tonight, alright? Plus, a *dead* man could notice how they're dressed. So, sue me." Lori began giggling at her immature reaction and hugged him. "Okay, sorry. So, what else do you think?"

"I think that the ladies Cabot are very strong and formidable. I think that the ladies Cabot have natural justice on their side. And I think that I, nor any kind-hearted soul, have *anything* to fear from the ladies Cabot. Well, except for causing an old schlep like me to completely fall for one of them, that is. I don't think that I've been so frightened in all my life, Lori."

"Just take my hand," Lori whispered. "Follow me. Let's go into one of the back bedrooms and I'll show you that you have absolutely *nothing* to fear from me or anything ever again." Connor looked into Lori's intense blue eyes, gulped, and said, "yeah, that doesn't help much. I'm still really scared. But let's go into the back bedroom anyway. Maybe you can calm my nerves. But I doubt it. Maybe I just want to feel this type of fear for the rest of my life."

As the tittering pair were leaving the room arm in arm, they could hear Papa Doc lamenting, "I *knew* it! I just *knew* it! Too much onion! This entire dish is ruined! And I thought witches could follow a recipe!"

On the other side of town, another tittering pair had found their way to a bedroom. They stared at each other intensely. One wore a devilish smile. The other, an ugly grimace. They had forged their alliance. An alliance with only one purpose. To destroy Morgan Cabot.

CHAPTER 22

THIS IS SO WRONG

"Morgan!" Lori yelled out as her daughter was flying around the house on this mid-December morning. "Put a coat on! It's too cold for just that jacket! And don't forget you have to help me prep for my catering gig tomorrow and Connor's coming over to decorate the Christmas tree tonight, so don't be late!" "Sorry, Mom!" Morgan yelled back. "Can't hear you! In a hurry! Gotta pick up Naomi and get to school! Last day before winter break and I don't want to be late!"

Morgan put her sunglasses on over her blue eyes and looked at herself in the full-length living room mirror. *Yeah, this looks cool,* she thought to herself. *White T. Black leather jacket. Designer blue jeans. Cool canvas shoes. And now, the sunglasses. If you got a bitchin' car, you gotta look the part. Plus, now that all the mean girls are gone, me and Naomi have finally found some peace. Hell, we're downright popular. Who woulda thought? Me, a popular kid. Well, my subjects should get a kick out of this cool new jacket. Yeah, I'm lookin' hot.*

The front door slammed, and Lori could only shake her head. "Dammit," she said to her mother. "She'd better not expect me to wait on her hand and foot if she gets a bad cold." "Oh, dear," Sophia replied. "I remember you at that age. You hardly ever wore a coat. Too bulky, you said. You always wanted to show off your cute little figure for a certain basketball player, now didn't you?"

"Well, yeah, kinda," Lori chuckled. "It's so weird how stuff works out. We had a crush on each other since our sophomore year, but never could quite put it together. He was super popular and almost always had some brain-dead cheerleader on his arm. And I hung out with the shop kids, goths, punks, and brains. We lived in two separate worlds within the same building. We did go out on that one date, but that was it. Then, I went to college and got married. I'll never regret that, though. That marriage, as messed up as it was, produced my Morgan. And he went on to serve in the National Guard then onto the police force and a marriage of his own. But now, it's like our destiny is finally being fulfilled. I've never been happier in all my life. My catering business is booming. I'm in love with a wonderful man who adores me. My daughter is finally happy and can be who she is without the fear of being bullied. Hell, I don't even mind living under the same roof as my bitch mother."

"Oh, shut the hell up, you ungrateful little snot," Sophia retorted through her laughter. "Plus, don't forget that you now wield the power to exact revenge upon anybody that tries to harm you. Or any of us. It's been quite peaceful these last several weeks, since all the hullabaloo around Halloween. Perhaps people in this town have finally figured out not to mess with the ladies Cabot!"

"Okay, Naomi. Just get in the car," Naomi's mother was encouraging. "Morgan's here. Just get in the car. We can talk about this tonight, dear. Naomi, would you *please* just go to school?"

"Sure, Mom, Bye!" Naomi squealed as she pranced down the driveway and pounced onto the Tempest's red vinyl seat. "Hiya bestie! Ready for the last day before break? Oh man, I'm gonna have so much fun! You're going with me and the coven next week to Salem, aren'tcha? You know, to celebrate the winter solstice? It's usually a trip for just us witches, but since Victoria and Sophia have made peace, now mediums are welcome too! Please say you'll come.

I told my parents we were going on a trip together and I can't lie to them. Plus, I still don't know my coven all that well yet, and then there's going to be all these other witches from all over the world there. I'm going to be so nervous that I'll be positively speechless!"

"Yeah, I somehow don't think that's going to be a problem," Morgan replied as she navigated the Tempest's majestic black frame through the town's streets. "Oh, have you heard the news?" Naomi excitedly began once again. "The parents of the missing girls are really pissed at the cops for not finding their kids. They hired a Private Investigator to look for them. He's down in Mexico right now but hasn't come up with anything. Oh, and I heard that Jasmine and Hermes aren't returning to school at all! Like, never! Their parents are allowing them to homeschool together cause they're too afraid something bad might happen to them. Plus, Hermes is so erratic. You never know when he's gonna pop off. Yep, I guess they've been doing home study together since around Halloween. Whatever. Works for me. They're really not very nice. Oh! And I heard that Hermes has to sit in a big plastic bubble or something so that he doesn't attack Jasmine and that she wears a boxing helmet, just in case. Can you believe it? The two most popular kids in school are like, banished!"

"Well, not so much banished as dethroned," Morgan replied as the shining Tempest growled its way into a parking spot at the high school. "And somebody must fill the power vacuum. Come on. Let's go greet our loyal subjects."

Naomi and Morgan flung the heavy doors open and strutted their way through the metal detector then waited as their designer book bags were searched. Morgan turned her black-dyed head to look down the hall. From behind her sunglasses her confused blue eyes widened. Every student was pointing at her. And laughing. Morgan's face turned beet red as Naomi said, "Um, what's going on Morgan?"

"I have no idea," a bewildered Morgan replied. "What in the hell are they laughing at? Is my hair okay? It can't be the jacket or the jeans. I look cool, right? And they're all looking at their phones. What in the hell is so funny? Why are they all laughing at me?"

At that moment, the new principal grabbed Morgan firmly by the arm and said, "Come with me, young lady." Morgan slumped into the large chair in front of the principal's desk. He turned his computer screen around and sternly said, "Just what is the meaning of *this*, young lady? And take off those sunglasses!" Morgan removed her shades revealing her anxious blue eyes that began welling up into tears as she looked upon the images on the screen. "Wha-what *is* this?" she meekly asked. There was image after obscene image of Morgan. A nude Morgan lying on a bed in a provocative pose. A nude Morgan defecating on the American flag. A nude Morgan doing something unnatural to a tree. And those were the tame ones. She finally screamed out "Turn it off!" when she looked upon her ecstatic face with a horse.

"I didn't do this! *Any* of this!" she cried out. "My God, that body has a tattoo on her ass! I don't *have* any tattoos! This is some sort of computer AI shit! I swear, I would *never* pose for these pictures or do anything that is *in* those pictures! That's not me! That's my face over some other perv bodies!"

"I see," the principal replied as he tried to calm himself. "Perhaps these *are* doctored photos. But Morgan, these were posted from *your* social media account. Even if you didn't pose for these, why would you post them?" Morgan stared at the account on the original post and said, "Yeah, that's mine. But that's an old account! I haven't used that for like, two years or something! I swear! I've been hacked!"

"Alright, Morgan. Alright," the principal replied as his anger turned to empathy. "Yes, it would seem as though you may be the victim of a joke. A very, very *cruel* joke. I've seen some bullying before, but this is beyond the pale. This is downright grotesque and deplorable. I will contact the authorities to look into this, but they usually have a hard time tracking this stuff down. Why don't you just go home for the day. I promise you that we'll handle the student body as well. I will call an assembly for this very afternoon. I will make a presentation about cyber bullying, and I will make it clear that anybody caught engaging in this, including distributing these awful pictures, will be severely punished. I don't care what the school board says. And I sure as hell don't care what their parents say.

"It's their fault anyway. If the parents hadn't raised some of these kids to be spoiled, self-entitled, cruel little heathens, then we wouldn't be in this place. But they did. Always making excuses for them. Always insisting that their kid is the best at everything they do, even when they suck. Not every kid is going to be the football star or the rock star or the award-winning actress. But they are raised to believe that they will be. They are raised to believe that they are the most special little snot nosed thing on the planet and that they are entitled to anything that they want whenever they want. And they learn that there are no consequences for their cruel actions. Which leads to things like this. Or worse. I'm sorry that this has happened to you, Morgan. And I'm sorry that I was cross with you. I don't know why I just immediately jumped to the conclusion that you had done this. What sane young lady would do such a thing? You have been nothing but the model of civility in the short time that I have been here, and I'm truly sorry that I doubted you. Okay?"

Morgan wiped the tears from her eyes and for the first time in her young life was able to sincerely smile back at an authority figure from outside of her family. She felt the respect that this man held for her, and she felt the same toward him. He was one of the few people who had genuinely earned the respect of Morgan Cabot. "Thank you. Thank you for believing me. Is it okay if Naomi gets the day off too? I really need my friend right now."

"I'm shutting it all down!" Morgan roared as she and Naomi entered her home. "Every single account! I'm going off the grid! I don't need this shit! If people have something to say to me, they can say it to my face! But they won't, because they're pussies! They'll just hide out in mommy's basement and throw their bullshit out into the world without any regard for its impact. Besides, I don't need all the stupid insipid memes and bullshit arguments and ignorant posts from people who have no idea what they're talking about. I mean, we all carry the world in the palm of our hand, and people just keep getting dumber! It's like all they care about is their selfies or stupid games. And if I see *one more post* about what somebody had for dinner, I'm gonna scream! Who in the hell cares about your goddam enchiladas? Nobody, that's who!

"So, they spend all their time entertaining themselves and feeding their tender egos by making themselves into some self-appointed online superstar. But they don't know anything! Nothing! They have no idea what is happening in our country or in our world! All they know is that stupid gas prices are too high. All they know is what is right in front of their nose, and they lack the intellect to try to learn about why things are what they are. Nope, why should I bother actually being informed when I can post yet another stupid meme about high gas prices. Idiots. So, I don't need this shit anymore. Any of it. I'm deleting it all! Starting with my email!"

Naomi sat in uncharacteristic silence as Morgan took out her phone and opened her emails. "You assholes," Morgan said softly as she read a pair of emails from two unknown sources. The first was from someone that called themselves 'Stinkbomb.'

*Hey there, you little dyke bitch. Have fun at school today? I know you did. I've heard from my troops. And just so you know, this is just the beginning. Go ahead and call the cops. They'll never track us down and you'll never be completely sure of who we are. Oh sure, you'll have suspicions. But you'll never truly know now, will you? But we know who you truly are. And after we're done with you, you'll never be able to step outside of your home again, you piece of...*The sentence ended with a 'Poo' emoji.

Morgan's anger was rushing through her psyche as she read the second email from someone called 'Babbles.'

Oh, and since your reputation is going to be ruined forever and you'll never get laid, why don't you give me a try? Come on, baby. I know you're into chicks because you're a devil worshipping heathen, but let me try to convert you. Believe me, I've got everything that you need to never want to be with a girl ever again. Now, just bend over and let Babbles in, heh, heh, heh. The post ended with an 'Eggplant' emoji.

An infuriated Morgan intensely glared at the posts as Naomi somberly looked down at the floor. Her trance was broken when she heard the front door slam and her mother's voice. "Morgan? Are you home? Why are you here? Why aren't you at school?"

"Yeah, I'm home alright!" Morgan yelled out. "Hey Mom! Could you bring me the book and show me the incantation that you used to kill dad? I have a little score to settle!" Fifteen minutes later, a heartbroken Lori pointed to the incantation in the book and quietly left the room. Morgan placed her hand over the open page. She could feel her rage flowing from her tingling fingers into the fleshy paper. She wore a wicked little smile as she closed her eyes and said, "Contra eos qui suis vocibus alios opprimunt, habebunt locutions. Contra eos qui suis vocibus alios opprimunt, habebunt locutions. Contra eos qui suis vocibus alios opprimunt, habebunt locutions." Morgan opened her eyes and gleefully posted an 'Angry' emoji next to both malicious emails. She heard a voice within her soul say, "Well hello Morgan. Thanks for calling. I've had so much fun with your mother, and I've been so hoping that I could have fun with you too. Now just relax and enjoy the show, heh, heh, heh."

"Skylark cream cheese calculator douche douche douche treeline skateboard!" Hermes was yelling out in excitement. What he had intended to say was, "Oh my God! We are going to destroy her! And she's going to be so pissed!" "Yeah, she is, and I'm glad you like what I wrote for you," Jasmine responded through her wired jaw and sparring helmet. For the past six weeks, Jasmine and Hermes had been homeschooling together. Hermes remained in a plastic bubble to protect against an unintended violent outburst. Jasmine wore protective gear just in case. Over the past few weeks, they had learned many things. They had not learned anything about history, or civics, or science. But they *had* learned how to communicate with one another.

Jasmine had learned that Hermes would do the exact opposite of what it was that he was feeling. If she asked if he wanted spaghetti and he laughed and clapped that meant that he did not want that. If he frowned and tried to punch her in the face, then spaghetti it is. They had also become quite proficient in mastering AI generated images, including placing Morgan's face over repulsively embarrassing images. And they had learned how to hack into others' social media accounts.

Hermes was angrily kicking into the air to communicate his pleasure at their first salvo of the destruction of their sworn enemy. He was thrilled at the thought of crushing the life of the young woman that had stripped him of his ability to communicate with others. He spit in the direction of the regally dressed Jasmine to communicate his appreciation for her. Jasmine's cast-covered ankles dangled down the front of her wheelchair. She smiled broadly when she looked at her phone and saw Morgan's response. "She's read it, my friend. Now the games will *really* begin," she said with an eerie calm.

The overjoyed Hermes yelled out, "Helicopter anal probe beer bong saturated sheets!" Then, a miracle occurred. For the first time in several months, Hermes was able to communicate what he was truly feeling. He began wailing in anguish as his penis began expanding in his pants. The pain and pressure were so great that he was forced to pull his pants down. Jasmine sat in shock as she stared at his growing, engorged eggplant. His uncontrolled screaming continued as she yelled out, "Oh my God! Put that away! I can smell it through the bubble!" She then began echoing his screams as flies poured out of her mouth, ears, nose, and other less exposed orifices. "What is happening? What is that smell?" she cried out, harmonizing with her friend's wails. "Oh my God! There are flies *everywhere*! All over me! What is happening? Oh my God! Gross! Is that smell coming from…me?"

"Jasmine, dear," her father said from outside of her door. "What are you doing in there? What is all this screaming? And what is that atrocious smell?" Her father opened the door to find the pained face of Hermes helplessly looking down at his throbbing eggplant. He began gagging when he saw flies swarming all over his daughter's body. He began vomiting when he got a good smell of her.

Morgan was laughing hysterically as she was transported to the hospital along with Jasmine and Hermes. Her mind was a split screen as her soul rode with Hermes in one ambulance and with Jasmine in another. She was nearly wetting herself from laughter as she watched paramedics vomiting all over Jasmine's once-perfect face as a reaction to her potent stench. Her gleeful squeals increased as she heard one of Hermes's paramedics say, "Oh my God!! I think it's going to blow!"

Hermes's eggplant exploded, covering the entire back of the ambulance, including the paramedics, in gallons of eggplant pulp and other less savory sticky substances. Morgan did not have to worry about Hermes trying to "convert" her ever again, because Hermes would never again possess the necessary equipment for such an endeavor. And although Morgan would have to live through an embarrassing few weeks at school, it would pass in time. Morgan most certainly would be able to step outside of her door. The same could not be said for Jasmine who would be forced to live in an airtight chamber by herself for the rest of her life to protect society from her never-ending and putrid stench. Or, she could be constantly covered in another person's vomit. It was her choice.

Naomi was rolling on the floor in unbridled laughter as Morgan recounted what she had seen. Sophia and Lori just stood in amazement and mouthed "Wow" to one another every few minutes. Following her story, Morgan said, "Thanks for being with me today, Naomi. And thank you for being my friend. You are kind and genuine and it is my honor to be your best friend. Why dontcha go home now, okay? I feel like getting some writing done."

Following Naomi's thirty-five-minute good-bye, Morgan laid on her bed and opened her notebook. "Hmmmm," Morgan said aloud to herself. "Which character do I want to write about tonight? Happy go lucky Larry, or..." Her thought trailed off for a moment before she answered her own question. "Naw. Sorry Larry, but I feel like having Maddy kill someone tonight. Hello, old friend, heh, heh, heh."

CHAPTER 23

———

FROM MY HEART AND FROM MY HANDS

"Morgan! Would you please get my phone?" Lori yelled out from the kitchen where she was mixing a fresh batch of Christmas cookies. "Who in the hell is calling you on Christmas Eve?" an irritated Sophia said. "I dunno," Lori answered. "Probably another damned telemarketer or scammer. They don't take holidays off."

"Mom, it's your attorney, Anne Bulanschaser," Morgan said as she handed her mother the phone then proceeded to stick her unwashed finger into the cookie dough. "Would you stay out of that?" Sophia growled as she slapped Morgan's hand.

"Yeah, hey Anne, good news about the dickhead's estate?" the attentive Morgan and Sophia heard Lori say from the living room. "Well, of course they're fighting it. They don't want Morgan and I to get anything. No money, no house, no nothing. Yes, I understand it wasn't the best look to skip the funeral, but we can't stand him and didn't want to be hypocrites, so…So what recourse do I have? Wouldn't Morgan at least be his rightful heir? Oh, he did, did he? And this new will has just now conveniently come to light? Hidden away in his safe in his office they say? Yeah, I bet it's a forgery, but you know what? It's okay. We really don't care. We never got anything from him when he was alive, and we sure as hell don't need anything from him now. And that goes for his asshole family, too. Let them have it all and choke on it." Sophia could not help but smirk when she heard her daughter use that particular phrase.

"It would have been nice, though. Would have paid for Morgan's college and been a nice little nest-egg for me. But that's okay. We have a roof over our heads and my business is going really well. So, just like pretty much every other woman in this world, I'll work twice as hard as the men, and I'll kick their ass. And I'll do it *my* way without being under the thumb of some asshole with a penis. Thanks Anne, for your help. If you see any way around this, let me know. Otherwise, I'll just finally be done with that entire family. And, you know what? The peace of mind is kinda worth it. Have a nice holiday, if you're into this sort of thing."

"No money, huh?" a disinterested Morgan asked as she discreetly licked cookie dough from her fingers. "Not surprising. You said that he'd find a way to screw us over one more time, and there it is. But you know what? I really don't care. Taking money from his estate would almost be like taking blood money or something. We don't need it. And we sure as hell don't need to be involved with my grandparents and the rest of those dicks. Besides, we got the last laugh. The only reason why they even *have* that inheritance is because their son is a shriveled prune lying in a grave somewhere. So, screw them. I'm going upstairs for a bit. Let me know when the cookies are ready."

Sophia and Lori were laughing as Morgan made her way up the stairs, grabbed her notebook, and flopped onto the bed. "Okay, Larry, let's try this again," Morgan said to her illustration of the bubbly 'Larry the Leopard.' "Hmmmm, how about this one? Ex corde meo et ex manibus meis nunc intelliget populus meus." Morgan looked around the room and waited for something to happen. "No? Nothing?" Morgan said to the universe. "I mean, I love this character. Hell, I love *all* my characters. And I'm channeling my feelings when I'm saying the incantation. How come gramma could invent all these incantations and summon spirits to do *her* bidding and I can't? I guess I just haven't stumbled onto the right words yet.

Screw it. It's Christmas. I need to do something to get me into the holiday mood. I think I'll just have Maddy kill someone. That should cheer me up. How about a corrupt insurance executive, heh, heh, heh."

"Whoa, I musta really zonked out," a drowsy Morgan said as she wiped the sleep from her eyes. "And Mom musta covered me up. Why is it so cold in here? Why did Mom open my window?" Morgan went over and closed the window then heard clattering coming from downstairs. "Oh, wow! It's 7:30! It's Christmas morning!" She excitedly ran down the stairs to find her mother, grandmother, and Connor drinking coffee in the kitchen. "Merry Christmas, dear!" Sophia exclaimed as she embraced her granddaughter. "Would you like some breakfast?"

"Nope, presents," an anxious Morgan replied as she was bouncing on the balls of her feet in excitement. "How about some coffee?" her mother asked. "Nope, presents," Morgan again replied. "Well, shouldn't we put on a little Christmas music to get in the mood first?" Connor contributed. "Nope, presents," Morgan eagerly answered.

"All right," Lori conceded through a chuckle. "I guess we've made you suffer enough. But enjoy this one. Once you turn eighteen, you'll be an adult, so if you want to *receive* presents, you'll have to *give* presents just like the rest of the adults. Got it?"

"Yeah, whatever, presents," the entranced Morgan answered as Connor handed her a brightly colored package. Twelve minutes later, the group was encased in discarded bows, wrapping paper, and boxes as Bing Crosby played quietly from the stereo. Morgan was excitedly holding her new clothes up to herself in the mirror. Lori was nearly in tears as she stared in wonderment at her sapphire necklace. "I've always *wanted* to try this myself!" Sophia exclaimed as she opened her home brew kit. And Connor silently smiled while fixated on his new Bruins jersey and tickets to an upcoming game. "This was just the most wonderful Christmas, ever!" Morgan exclaimed. "Oh! I wonder if Naomi is up yet? I think I'll go call her!"

Morgan began bounding up the stairs with an armful of her new treasures. Just as she hit the third step, she looked down at the living room and noticed a large, gold wrapped box hiding behind the tree. "Hey! Who is *that* present for?" Morgan asked as she came back down the stairs. She went to the back of the tree and began pulling it out. "Uh! This is really heavy!" She said as she pushed the box into the middle of the living room, bulldozing the shredded wrapping paper in its wake. "Hey! It has my name on it! Yay! But who's it from?"

She looked up into three pairs of confused eyes. "Never seen it before," Sophia stated. "No, me either," added Lori. "Well, don't look at me. I got her that pile of records," Connor said. "Maybe it's the cop in me, but I don't like mystery packages. Plus, it's not like you folks haven't made a few enemies. Let me just inspect it. I mean, I'm sure it's not a bomb, but…" At that moment the box exploded, and a bright yellow and black streak started bounding around the room.

"Well, hello everybody! So nice ta meetcha! I'm so happy to finally get to greetcha!" the bouncing blur said in an animated voice. "What the hell is *this* thing?" Sophia yelled out. "It's, it's, a Christmas miracle!" Morgan stammered. "It's Larry! Larry the Leopard!" The cartoonish, black-spotted, and garishly yellow "cat" pounced in the middle of the holiday carnage and said, "Yep, you got that right, it certainly is me! I wanted to surprise you, so I hid under the Christmas tree!"

"Larry!" Morgan squealed out as she lovingly embraced her now-living creation. "Okay, what the hell is going on?" Sophia asked. "Well," a joyful Morgan began explaining. "You see, this is Larry the Leopard and he's my creation. He's the star of the children's book that I'm writing. He's super sweet and works to bring people together. Anyway, I just love him so much that I wanted to see if I could come up with an incantation to summon a spirit to make him come to life. And well, here he is! It worked!"

"It sure did, worked right as rain, now put the saying in the book so that we'll never be apart again!" Larry shouted out as he bounced over to the bookshelf, grabbed the ancient book and handed it to Morgan. "In your blood, it must be written. Here let me help you with the claw of a kitten!" Larry yelled out. He took Morgan's hand, and gently pierced the skin of her index finger with his claw. "Now repeat the saying as you write it, and then I'll be around for more than a bit!" Morgan began writing the Latin words in the fleshy page as she said, "Ex corde meo et ex manibus meis nunc intelliget populus meus." The words glowed for a moment, then became absorbed in the morbidly whitish paper.

"And just what in the hell does *that* mean?" Sophia roared as a confused Gabriel hid behind her legs. "Um," Morgan began to answer. "It means, 'From my heart and from my hands people will now understand my creations.'" "Yes, that's right, that's what it means and now I'm here where I can be seen!" Larry enthusiastically agreed.

"Um, dear?" Lori began asking. "Um, well, I have a few questions. Like, does he need a cat box or something? I mean, do cartoons poo?" Larry immediately responded. "No need to worry about whether I poo, that is something that I wasn't written to do!"

"Isn't that the *least* of our problems?" a bewildered Connor asked. "It sure as hell is!" an agitated Sophia answered. "The *main* problem is that everything that he says is a rhyme and *that's* going to get damned annoying!" The delighted Larry once again responded. "Well, it may be true, Sophia, that I constantly rhyme, but I'm sure you'll come to love it, if you give it time!"

"Is it too early to drink?" Connor asked as he fell back onto the couch. "Nope, I'll fix ya right up," Sophia answered. Larry sniffed the glasses of bourbon, sneezed and said, "Well, I suppose a holiday is like a vacation. Just be sure to enjoy your spirits with moderation!" "Oh, shut up, Larry!" the unified voices of Lori, Sophia, and Connor stated just before taking another slug.

"My, oh my, that's not very nice! I will teach you how to be warm to others and not cold as ice!" Larry said before licking the faces of the dismayed trio. Larry then went over to the cowering Gabriel. "Well, hello there pup, so nice to see you. You will see that you and I will be the best of friends too!" Gabriel let out a slight whimper and proceeded to retreat down the basement stairs with his tail tucked between his legs.

The entire group jumped as Connor's phone suddenly began ringing. "Ah, shit, that's the office's ringtone. I'm sorry. Just a second." He went into the kitchen and answered. "Yeah, this is O'Sullivan. This better be good. You've found a *what*? And you think it's *who*? And *where* is it at? Ah, shit, okay. I'll be right there."

Connor re-entered the room. His sickened face was pale as he said solemnly, "Wow. This is going to be a really great Christmas for *that* family. I'm sorry, but I've got to go. They just found a body, um, well, what's *left* of a body hanging at the construction site over by the mall. Actually, it's just the torso that's hanging. The arms and legs have been sawed off and the head has been pulverized. They found a sledgehammer next to it, so they assume that's what was used. I guess it's an absolute bloodbath. Whoever did this is filled with rage and is *really, really* dangerous. Please tell me that none of you had anything to do with this."

"No, we swear, right?" Lori answered as she looked into the eyes of her daughter and mother with trepidation. "No, Mom!" Morgan exclaimed. "I swear! I didn't do *anything* except bring Larry to life. And he's as harmless as can be!" "Nope, not me either," Sophia replied. "I haven't done anybody in since that food critic. I think you've just got a real, run of the mill lunatic on your hands."

"Okay, that's good, I guess," Connor stated as he was putting on his grey overcoat. "Well, enjoy the rest of your holiday. I'll be back if I can. I'm really sorry about this." "No need to apologize," Lori said softly as she hugged her beau. "Just find that killer, okay? I mean, I know I've been involved in some, um, well, this just sounds down-right gruesome."

"Morgan!" Sophia yelled out later that evening. "Would you and Larry stop jumping on the bed? It sounds like the ceiling is about to crash in!" "Sorry Gramma!" Morgan replied followed by Larry. "Yes, we will stop causing such a commotion. Maybe we'll just look out the window quietly and stare at the ocean!" The tittering pair went over to the window and gazed at the majestic snowfall that glistened on the nearby branches and ground. Morgan had her arm around Larry's soft shoulders and was resting her head against his. She had never felt so safe, warm, and happy in her life. Her abusive father was gone. No one was bullying her. She had the love of a best friend and the love and security of her family. And now, she had her animated companion of her own creation. She shed a single tear of happiness as she stared at the tranquil landscape. Morgan was finally home.

Suddenly there was another pair of piercing eyes staring back at her from outside the window. The red-headed, green-eyed young woman that was sitting on the roof scowled at her and yelled out, "Hey! Are ya gonna open this fuckin' window or *what*? It's *cold* out here! Why didja think that I kept it open, anyway? Oh whatevs. I'll just do it myself." The young woman lifted the unlocked window open and crawled into Morgan's bedroom. She was dressed in black and covered from head to toe in blood. "Wh-who are *you*?" Morgan stuttered.

"Who am *I*?" the young woman roared back. "Well, isn't *this* just a fine how-do-ya-do? To not even be recognized by your own creator. That hurts, Morgan. It really hurts." "M-M-*Maddy*?" Morgan stammered. "Uh, yeah. Hi kid. Sorry about the mess, but that douchebag was *quite* a bleeder. And man, are my arms sore! All that sawing then bashing his stupid head in. It kinda takes a toll, y'know? Hey, you got a shower that I could use? And maybe a set of jammies?"

"Maddy!" Morgan yelled out. "What are you *doing* here? You aren't *real*!" "Oh!" Maddy bellowed. "But *this* come-to-life-cartoon *is*? Listen, kid. You really should be more careful with your incantations. You never know what you might bring into this world by being willy-nilly with that shit. Now, where are we at with the whole shower and jammies situation? Chop-chop, sister! I'm getting blood all over your floor."

"Whose blood *is* that?" a shocked Morgan asked as she looked at Maddy's spattered face and saturated black hoodie. "Well, you should know," Maddy responded. "You wrote it. Right after you said the incantation. You wanted me to find a corrupt insurance executive. You know, the type of dickhead that denies people critical care then laughs all the way to the bank when they die. And it was so easy! I found one leaving a local bar last night. All I had to do was flirt with him a little bit, then have him drive to that construction site. Oh man, was *he* surprised when I unzipped my hoodie. He thought that I was gonna show him my, um, well you know. But instead, I pulled out a big knife and slashed his throat! Then, as he was clutching his throat trying to stop the bleeding, I dragged him out of the car. He was still alive when I sawed off his right arm. And he was still kinda kickin', well, not exactly *kickin'*, heh, when I sawed off his left leg. He was dead by the time I took off his head and smashed it with a sledgehammer. Man did *that* feel good! I guess I have some repressed anger or somethin'. Maybe I should see somebody about that. Nah. I'm fine. Anywhoo, I kinda got lost coming back to the house. I've never been in this town before and it's not like you wrote much of a description. So, how's about that shower and jammies. And maybe a little ice cream, hmmmm?"

"Um, um, um," was all Morgan could manage to say as she heard her mother's footsteps coming up the stairs. Maddy placed her hand on Morgan's shoulder, looked at her with her glimmering emerald eyes and said, "Listen roomie. Whether you like it or not, you're stuck with me. You called me here. You wrote the incantation in the book. So, *you're* here and *I'm* here. And Morgan…we're gonna have a *lot* of fun together, heh, heh, heh."

THE END...or... TO BE CONTINUED. IT'S UP TO MORGAN